TERROR
WITHIN

TERROR
WITHIN

BY
ROGER W. MARSHALL

iUniverse, Inc.
New York   Bloomington

FOR PERMISSION, CONTACT:
Roger W. Marshall
2050 Hunting Ridge Drive,
Owings Mills, Maryland 21117
Roger.marshall2007@gmail.com

Cover design is by Roger Marshall.
Author's photograph is by Kathryn Davis.

iUniverse books may be ordered through booksellers or by contacting:

iUniverse
1663 Liberty Drive
Bloomington, IN 47403
www.iuniverse.com
1-800-Authors (1-800-288-4677)

ISBN: 978-1-4401-2356-6 (sc)
ISBN: 978-1-4401-2355-9 (ebook)

Printed in the United States of America

iUniverse rev. date:02/17/2009

This book is dedicated to the wonderful people trying to save our environment, and those protecting the rights of this planet's inhabitants, including its people, animals, and even habitats. May all those who support peace and respect nature fall under this dedication.

Special thanks

FIRST, I WANT TO THANK MY PARENTS, Janet and Wayne Marshall. My Dad taught me at an early age how marvelous our natural world is. Family vacations in the State Parks of New York were truly inspiring. My Mom taught me that we all can make a difference if we try. Second, I thank all the environmentalists I have read about who have inspired me, including Julia Butterfly Hill, my fondest inspiration.

I also give a special thanks to Jessica Marshall, who helped me when I started this journey. She typed the crude original drafts and offered countless comments, never once suggesting that I surrender my dream.

My "ghost writer," Daniel R. Vovak, also deserves great thanks, since he was much more than merely a "ghost." I am not the easiest person to work for, but he tirelessly put up with me, helping me to turn a exceptionally rough draft into this inspiring book.

My test readers also were wonderful: Kathryn Davis, Veronica Marshall, Cathy Newman, Dennis Glorioso, Ashley Lininger, and Ryan Passudetti. They caught many mistakes and plot holes from seemingly developed drafts. However, I want to give special thanks to one of the test readers who stood out from the others. She dedicated endless hours of discussion with me without ever complaining. She added much to the current story, rooted in her dedication to eliminating ALS (Lou Gehrig's Disease), she has been a truly inspiring and motivating factor. Thanks, Kathryn. And last, but not least, I want to thank John Pew and John McKibben. Each—in his own way—showed me how fragile and precious life is.

Peace to All,

Roger W. Marshall

CONTENTS

PRELUDE

"QUICK, HIDE HERE," shouted Shaka as he and Devi hid in a near-hidden pocket inside a ledge of overhanging rocks. Seconds later, a massive (and unprecedented) explosion rocked the small island on which they lived. Soon a mushroom cloud rose high in the South Pacific above their once-peaceful island within the Marshall Islands. The billowing cloud looked beautiful to them, one of 66 they would see from 1946 to 1958.

"That's the biggest one yet," said Devi, unknowingly referring to "Castle Bravo," the largest nuclear test ever conducted by the United States military. Indeed, the sudden unleashing of energy was a sight few people had ever seen. Then, along with other villagers, Shaka and Devi rummaged through the rubble of their village, searching for survivors.

Later, members of the United States military were ordered to "completely clear" that particular island, herding the inhabitants onto boats and sailing off with them, never to be seen again. The only inhabitants who remained were Shaka and Devi, who had learned where to hide when danger appeared.

Their lonely world consisted of a barren island, a hidden pocket of rocks, and a small spring of water that bubbled from below, forming a small pond with clear, blue water. Shaka and Devi caught fish and ate seaweed, drinking from that spring.

As the years passed, Shaka and Devi changed, developing webbing between their toes and fingers. It was the result of actual radioactive fallout caused by man's quest to push technology to its limits during the Cold War. Soon gills developed, allowing them to stay underwater for long periods while hunting for seafood. True to their beliefs, they thanked their god for bringing the changes to their bodies necessary for their survival.

Later, Devi gave birth to four children, all with long but graceful necks. Interestingly, their children also developed webbed feet, mutating further and developing long tails and fins. Unlike their parents, they lived almost exclusively in the sea. However, sometimes they would sun themselves on small rock islands, witnessed only by sailors who occasionally passed on small ships. Scared, they would gracefully dive into the sea, hiding from mankind.

GABE & MARTI

CHAPTER ONE

ANNAPOLIS MARYLAND—With faded yellow glass and a distinctive lip protruding from its circular top, the jar at the end of the bar contained clues that could expose one of the most classified operations of the United States military. However, to a civilian in September 2010, it was merely a harmless container for business cards, carelessly tossed inside for a free chance to win a dinner for two at the elegant Santa Maria Restaurant inside the Marina Hotel. Surely retired reporter Gabe Channing was oblivious to their potential. Nowadays, Gabe was more interested in his Jim Beam and Coca-Cola than in being a good journalist.

Gabe placed both his elbows on the mahogany bar as he sat and held his near-empty glass. In the background was Jasmine, the new piano player, who played a soulful rendition of "What a Wonderful World" by Louis

Armstrong. Remembering his younger days in the Navy, Gabe was only beginning to feel the effect of the alcohol, systematically swirling the ice to savor what remained in the glass before he ordered his third drink of a long evening. It was all part of his nightly routine with the same bourbon, chewing on the same peanuts, in the same bar, on the same stool for the past forty years.

For his entire career after leaving the Navy, Gabe worked for the *Annapolis Triangle*, a prominent weekly newspaper covering Anne Arundel County. He became the senior reporter, but that only took five years to achieve, at age 30. Countless times he had declined prestigious job offers for Washington, D.C. publications. Gabe didn't want to drive an hour to the big city and work for a daily newspaper, which involved actual work, deadlines, and traffic. Besides, he had not driven a car for over twenty years. One too many D.U.I's convinced him the world was safer without him behind the wheel.

Retired from journalism for six months, he was bored, but not much more bored than he was before. The difference was that now he was not part of *any* action, even though the activity of running a small-town weekly too excited in the first place. On the flip side, Gabe had a reputation for producing heartfelt and intellectual stories, even as he was pressed against merciless newspaper deadlines.

"That drink of yours is just slush," said Marti, a bartender with long red hair and a smile that could melt an iceberg.

Marti liked Gabe, and often tried to make him smile or laugh, a difficult task, considering his rough demeanor. Sitting alone on the far end of the bar, Gabe continued to swirl his ice. At the tables in the hotel bar sat visitors from out of town, munching on hors d'oeuvres. Gabe asked, "Marti, have you made any retirement plans?"

"Of course," she replied. "I throw the last customer out by 2:15 a.m., do a little cleaning and then head home to *retire* in bed by four."

"Cute," said Gabe, scratching his head. "Real cute."

Nate Baschard, a man in his twenties wearing a pinstripe suit, threw a business card into the jar and approached the bar, then glanced at an orange flier he was holding. "Excuse me, ma'am, where is Conference Room 'C'? I'm trying to find the meeting for Ethics and Biotechnology. I don't want to miss the opening comments by Admiral Nelson Owens."

Marti wiped the bar with a white washcloth. "Just walk between those two large ferns by the door on the other side of the room."

"Thanks," he replied, and headed for the ferns.

Marti scribbled a mark on a cocktail napkin. "That's number twenty-one."

"Damn," said Gabe, a twenty dollar bill on the bar next to him. "I never thought *that many* people would attend."

"I win again, so the next round's on you," said Marti, winking at him from behind her thin gold-speckled glasses. That's just how many people *asked* for directions to that room. I bet there's seventy people back there in all. It's a hell of a lot more than twenty."

Just then, a young woman walked up and asked for directions to the same conference room. "It's over there," said Gabe, pointing to the room on the left.

"Thanks," she said, heading that direction.

Gabe was eager to change the topic. "I've been thinking about writing a magazine story about retirement plans."

"Magazine story? When did *you* decide to start working again? You haven't done anything for months."

Gabe straightened his wide red tie with thick black stripes. "My point is that lately I've had plenty of time to think about my retirement package."

Marti cleaned a glass in a small sink. "You should have been thinking about your retirement plans when you turned down all those job offers decades ago."

"That's my point," said Gabe, putting a handful of peanuts into his mouth. "I have *plenty* of contacts. I'm sure several magazines would run a story with my byline. It would pay well, too. Plus, a little freelance work on the side will do me some good, especially a story on retirement."

"Retirement?" questioned Carley Polowski, 31, an exceptionally attentive waitress. "Why not write about something interesting?"

"Like what?" asked Gabe, washing down some peanuts with his drink.

Carley looked at Gabe, tilting her head. "I don't know, ah, like a story on stem cells . . . or global warming . . . or even civil liberties."

"That involves a lot of research," said Gabe, firing back.

"What do you know about retirement planning, anyway?" Carley retorted. "You didn't do *any* planning based on what I've seen."

"Never mind, then," he said, shifting in his chair.

"With all this crazy stuff going on with stem cell research, gene splicing, and global warming, the last thing on peoples' minds right now is retirement," said Carley, her shoulders shrugging. "I'm not sure I'll even live long enough to retire."

"That's exactly my point," said Gabe, nodding. "When I was your age, the Cold War made me think I wasn't going to live after an atomic bomb dropped. But I did, so that's why I should aim the story at people your age who don't plan for their retirements because they think they're going to drop dead because of all the hysteria hyped by the media."

"Whatever," said Carley, rolling her eyes as she headed to a different table to take a cocktail order.

Jasmine, motioned to Carley. "Hey, Carley, is something *big* happening?" she asked as she bent down to adjust her sound equipment.

"Yeah, some speech on biotechnology," Carley whispered in her ear.

"Oh," Jasmine responded. "Maybe some of these suits might come over and say 'hi.'"

Carley winked, knowingly.

As Gabe sat up in his stool and reached for a pen in his sports jacket, he absentmindedly scribbled some notes on a cocktail napkin, now mostly talking to himself. "Most people begin putting money into a retirement fund or into social security by age twenty-five. By the time they're sixty-five, inflation cuts into their earnings, along with taxes and other stuff."

Marti rolled her eyes. "Another drink, big thinker?"

Gabe nodded, then gulped what remained of his drink. "I've decided to write a story on this, a big feature story. Magazines will jump all over it."

"Sounds boring to me," said Marti, wrinkling her lips. "Who cares about it except someone who's retired?"

"I'm telling you, with my writing skills—"

"Writing skills? Where did *you* learn how to write? I've read every article of yours for decades. This whole town knows you made up half that crap you wrote," Marti teased.

"Oh, come on, Marti," Gabe cut in.

Now Marti was having fun, two old salts talking at the top of their games. "Remember when you quoted the mayor after that big fire in ninety-nine? The freaking fire station burns down and you wrote the mayor was 'perplexed and saddened' by the event. A whole bunch of quotes from him even. Thank God you were the *only* reporter who quoted him in this whole damn town. Not even a single television reporter could find him, and they had every crew out that night from Baltimore to Washington. Regardless, you rambled for most of your story about how bad the mayor felt to lose an Annapolis historic building."

"That story won an award," said Gabe, snickering.

Carley glanced at Marti and Gabe, then scurried into the kitchen, quietly singing to herself. "Ashes, ashes, they all fall down."

"They did that just to make fun of you. 'Best reporting story of ninety-nine.' Absurd!"

"I was on the phone with the mayor for hours that night," said Gabe, taking a drink.

Marti looked from side-to-side to make sure no one was listening. "That story *saved his ass and mine!* Our mayor owes you his career."

"I know."

Marti was eager to change the topic. What's your angle on this new story? Retirement stories are done all the time."

"I know people—real interesting people—who would *love* to have their name in print."

Marti laughed.

Gabe continued, "I'll make you another bet."

"Go ahead."

"I'll write a top-notch story with top-notch sources in it and get it published in one of those top-notch magazines."

"Yeah, or what?"

Gabe stalled for time, straightening his tie. "I'll get that story published or I'll-l-l-l. . . . Hell, I don't know. I'm just telling you I'll make it happen."

Marti smirked. "See, you can't even decide on a bet, let alone make good on it."

Six out-of-town businessmen entered the bar, drawing Marti's immediate attention.

Silently, Gabe sipped his drink and glanced around. It was almost midnight, and the bar was pretty empty. On the other end of the room were two men, setting their sight on two women for whom they had bought an evening's worth of vodka and shots. At a table were four lobbyists deep into a conversation about genetic engineering, and weakly enforced policies by the National Institute of Health. Then his attention drifted to the yellow jar on the bar next to him. He looked at the many napkins he had carelessly scribbled on, creating an outline for his ambitious story on retirement, rare proof of him finally becoming absorbed in his writing—a shimmer of the enthusiasm from his youth erupting.

Still staring at the yellow jar, Gabe finished his fifth Jim Beam and put thirty dollars on the bar top, his usual fare for drinks and a sandwich. He again glanced at all the other customers and—convinced nobody was watching him—quickly placed his hand inside the jar as he stood, retrieving a large handful of business cards. Smoothly, he placed them into his sports coat pocket and quietly walked home.

THREE DAYS LATER, Gabe sat in his office at an old IBM computer, discouraged by a bad case of writers' block. His eyes moved from one towering stack of papers to another throughout his office. Never one for organization, Gabe's thoughts drifted to cleaning his office—anything to spare him the pain of crafting a meaningful paragraph.

After a six-month break from writing, his life-long profession had somehow lost its comfort zone. At first, he repositioned his chair to all seven settings. Then he dusted the tables around him, which caused more clutter with the stacks of paperwork. The shades were not adjusted properly. The temperature was too cold, then too hot. Then he became thirsty, then hungry. Preparing his food became more of a joy than a chore. Of course, that caused him to go to the bathroom more. Whatever problem he encountered always led to the same result: delaying his writing.

Gabe was perturbed. At sixty-five years old, was he too old to write a stellar magazine feature story? Hell, was he even too old to *begin* a stellar magazine feature story? Frustrated indefinitely, Gabe gave up his writing—for the third consecutive night—and decided to watch some television coverage on the Iraq War.

Bombs were falling out of the sky. People were running, screaming, and weeping. Pieces of buildings were falling everywhere. One woman shouted at her friend to hide under a shelter of rock. The footage then showed the village flattened by the bombs. Dead people were everywhere.

The television coverage reminded Gabe of when he was twenty years old and heading to Vietnam. Back then, you really didn't have a choice when your number was picked. You either went to war, went to jail, or fled. He wondered if the volunteer force of today was a better way. Did it allow people to avoid their civic duty? He had never seen the Vietnam War Memorial in Washington, D.C., because it evoked too many memories of friends once known. He wondered if anything was actually accomplished in Vietnam. He thought again about how history seemed to be repeating itself by what was being done in Iraq. Then the bourbon took over and he drifted to sleep.

TELEVISION CAN BE A GREAT ESCAPE for writer's block. Initial starvation of the creative process soon transforms into unknown worlds of bravery, chivalry, love, and even science fiction. Throughout his career, television had helped Gabe to develop his imagination.

He began watching an old movie on the Science Fiction Channel about aliens landing on earth to abduct a young man to perform tests on him on the mother ship. The sequence was one of frequent repetition in the 1960s, when the television era substantially developed in the United Sates. People were already worried sick over being drafted, unemployment, nuclear attacks, Russia, Cuba, and assassinations. Why not add a possible abduction by aliens to the list?

The television scene was graphic: aliens experimenting on a helpless human, resulting in a series of scary looking human-like creatures. In this particular flick, they were blending plant and animal DNA. The goal: to develop a food source that included all the vitamins, minerals, fiber, and protein they needed to maintain themselves. The human component focused on adaptability. Humans were the only species on the planet capable of adapting to the environment rather than waiting millennia for evolutionary adaptation to occur.

GABE BEGAN HIS DAY at nine o'clock, with shaving and a long shower. He would then dress and have oatmeal, orange juice and coffee for breakfast. Every morning, he made six cups of coffee, each with half and half and two tablespoons of sugar. Other than a good story, little else can keep a writer awake sitting in front of a keyboard.

In spite of being retired, Gabe decided to begin his work day as he usually did, at ten o'clock in the morning. He checked his printer, booted his old computer, did a little dusting around his work space, cleaned up the previous day's coffee cup and peanut shells from around his desk, and drank his first mug of coffee while he read the morning newspapers. By eleven o'clock he would begin work.

Gabe may have been lazy, but he was definitely not sluggish about reading. Being a news junkie, he was an avid reader of public policy, sports, technology, and science. Aside from Navy football, his love of sports was limited to the analytical sport of national politics, with its back-room wrangling and arm twisting. Thus, he developed a heightened ability to read between the lines of any article, spending as much time pondering the motivation of what spawned a story as what actually appeared in black and white.

Gabe stared at the eighteen business cards heaped together on a pine-wood credenza in his office. Stolen from the jar at the Marina Hotel, the cards originated from people who attended the speech about Ethics and Biotechnology. Not being at the top of his game, Gabe never considered the narrow audience the cards represented. After all, who was qualified to enforce ethics within the field of biotechnology? And what qualified his old friend, Admiral Nelson Owens, to be the keynote speaker other than his many decorations of valor and loyalty?

ADMIRAL OWENS SAT ON A BENCH in the no-salute area inside the Pentagon. A career military man, he wore his well-decorated uniform along with a perfect butch haircut and facial expressions that consistently commanded the respect of anyone in whatever room he was in. He began to peel an orange, making an effort to peel it into one long strip.

Sitting next to him was Special Agent Zack McHenry, the go-to man in Homeland Security. Mechanically-minded but cynically spirited, Zack had slowly built his stature to a point where it was greater than his title. Dressed in khakis and a polo shirt, he liked the fact that he could hide his rebelliousness even as he always verbally towed the party line.

"The threat of bio-terrorism was rarely considered pre 9/11," said Zack, chewing on a sandwich. "Now it is our foremost worry. There's only a handful of true experts in the world. Differentiating between the experts and the BS-ers has become difficult for us because the information is so technical that we don't know which people are telling the truth."

"I know," said Owens, still peeling his orange.

Zack swallowed hard, knowing Owens was not in the mood to talk much. "The rules of bio-terrorism are different than in other forms of terrorism. For us, *the many* are more important than *the one*. With bio-terrorism, all it takes is one error, and society changes. Let me restate that: all it takes is one error, and society *permanently* changes. Until 9/11, the United States government only prepared troops on the battlefield against bio-terrorism, and never against everyday citizens."

"You're not telling me anything I haven't already learned from my days in the Marshall Islands," said Owens.

"I'm only warning you because Jamie is really concerned and wants to know if any of those attendees from the speech the other night became testy during the Q and A section," Zack pressed.

"So far everything is calm," said Owens, finally finishing the perfect peeling of his orange. "I know Jamie's inflexible order: any resistance will be stopped, even at the threat of public outrage. Just because she's the one who does the real work for the director, doesn't mean I don't have to still put up with his crap."

IN MARCH 2011, Gabe swirled his Jim Beam and Coca-cola as Marti spoke with a new customer at the bar. Carley, wearing a short, black cocktail dress trimmed with lace, held a tray with six empty cocktail glasses on it. "That last table was asking about you," said Carley. "They say City Hall's not the same since you left."

"Really," said Gabe as he stared at his slushy drink. "At least I'm enjoying my retirement."

Carley rolled her eyes at the comment. "They asked me what you've been doing in your, ah, retirement, and I didn't know what to say, though it's not like you're listening to me talk or anything."

"Yeah, whatever," said Gabe as he read a newspaper. "Hey Marti, I'll have another."

Marti and Carley exchanged looks while Marti nodded as Gabe continued to speak about sports with her other customers.

Gabe looked at Carley. "What did you tell them?"

Carley readjusted the glasses on her tray, careful to balance them properly. "I told them you were working on a big retirement story. You know, the same one you've been working on for the past six months."

Marti smirked as Carley headed to the kitchen. "What a smart ass," Marti muttered.

"What does she know about writing anyway?" Gabe answered.

Marti walked over to Gabe and handed him his third drink of the evening. "You know," Marti began. "She's right. You either need to write that story or start talking a new game. . . . Have you at least interviewed anyone yet, I mean for quotes and all?"

"Damn, Marti, all I've done is sit at my keyboard and tap a key here and there. It's not the same as having a real deadline and all. I could wait another year to write that story and no one would care."

"Well, maybe it's time to just give up the writing thing altogether. Give it a rest and all. Why don't you take up gardening or Tai Chi?"

Gabe took the last bite of his sandwich and talked to Marti with his mouth full. "What the hell am I going to do with a whole bunch of tomatoes and green peppers? I don't ever cook, and I'm not about to start now. Besides, I'd much rather watch Navy football than do weeding."

"How about buying some season tickets then?" asked Marti, silently sympathizing with Gabe, her long-time friend.

"I already have season tickets," said Gabe.

Marti said, "Buy a second seat so you can take a friend."

Carley exited the kitchen and walked over to Gabe, leaning against the bar. "Did I just hear something about season tickets?" she asked. "Now that sounds like your style, instead of some dumb old story about retirement."

"You could even start betting again," said Marti as she cleaned a glass in the sink.

"No, I gave up betting on that Navy team decades ago," said Gabe as he flipped the page of the *Baltimore Sun* to a half-page color advertisement for a Apple laptop computer.

Marti looked at the ad and grinned. "How about a bet, like a real bet, but a clean one?"

"Oh, I really shouldn't be betting," said Gabe, sarcastically. "You know I can't stand to lose, and then, well, you know what I had to go through before."

Gabe thought back to the years just after the Navy, when he drank too much, gambled too much, and ended up losing his right to drive and almost everything he owned. The only thing of value he managed to keep was his boat and that was because the courts didn't know he had one.

"I know all your old war stories," said Marti, flashing a smile at him. "But this bet will be a win-win bet."

"Like what?" asked Gabe.

"How about that?" asked Marti, pointing to the computer advertisement.

"An Apple?" blurted Gabe, perplexed.

"How about you bet your season tickets, the second seat, for the Naval Academy football games against that new Apple computer?"

"Who wants a Mac anyway?" asked Carley as she darted to a new table of customers.

"That's exactly my point," said Marti. "I don't need those season tickets, and you don't need a Mac."

Gabe said, "Hell, all I do now is give those tickets away, and most of the time they go unused. I don't want to give up my reliable IBM anyway. But if a bet gives me a push to get my story published then I'll think about it."

Marti grinned. "And if you, God forbid, publish that story, then I'll buy you that computer." She stares at the price. "What do your tickets cost?"

"They're a little more than that price."

"Is it a bet then?" Marti asked.

Gabe paused, to consider the six months of writer's block that had brought his career to a complete standstill. He never wanted to leave the *Annapolis Triangle* in the first place, but the buyout package was just too good to pass. Since then, most days he had wasted away watching the History Channel and the Discovery Channel, something that had become somewhat of an obsession. It was embarrassing, though, to do nothing with his life. Maybe a little spice would be good for him, he deduced. "But you don't even like college football," he said.

"Don't worry about that," said Marti. "You buy the tickets and I'll buy the Mac. If I lose, then I'll give you the Mac. And if you lose, you give me the second seat of your season tickets. . . . Is it a bet or not?"

"Yeah, you're on," said Gabe, twirling his watch.

Marti fixed her eyes on Gabe, carelessly playing with her red hair to try to soften her otherwise hard words. "It's about time you get your butt out there in the real world instead of just pining away in here. Gabe, you need to get a life."

LATER THAT NIGHT, Gabe sat in front of the television watching the History Channel as he pondered Marti's bet. An old friend, Marti had Gabe's best interest in mind when she placed the bet. And though Gabe never officially shook on the deal, it was an understood bet, known as a gentleman's bet. It was a fair bet, too, in that Gabe really had no more need for a second set of Navy season tickets than he did for a new computer. Moreover, Carley was correct in that some change in his life—no matter how small—would probably be good for him.

Tonight's History Channel episode was about the Marshall Islands. A narrator spoke as visual images were shown on the screen: "Although they were settled by Micronesians in the 2nd millennium BC, little is known of the early history of the Marshall Islands. In 1526, Spanish explorer Alonso de Salazar was the first European to sight the islands, but they remained virtually unvisited by Europeans for several more centuries. Eventually, British captain John Marshall visited the islands in 1788, a visit to which the islands owe their current name. Then, in 1885, a German trading company settled the islands, making them part of the protectorate of German New Guinea some years later.

"Japan conquered the islands in World War I, and administered them under a League of Nations mandate. Then, in World War II, the United States occupied the islands in 1944, and they were added to the Trust Territory of the Pacific Islands, including several more island groups in the South Sea.

"Between 1946 and 1958, the U.S. reported testing 66 nuclear weapons in the Marshall Islands, including the largest nuclear test the U.S. ever conducted, Castle Bravo. Nuclear damage claims between the United States and the Marshall Islands are ongoing, and health effects still linger from these tests.

"After the nuclear tests, the U.S. government shifted the category of much of the territory into an "off-limits" classification, prohibiting entry to anyone without a top clearance. After the extensive "testing," rumors from passing ships of strange sightings of mermaids in that area occasionally appeared in the press. But with an orchestrated campaign, the U.S. government was able to debunk most of those stories. Hence, most people viewed the rumors as the byproduct of sailors hitting the rum a bit too hard."

ABOUT ELEVEN O'CLOCK, Gabe sat at his computer, a habit he had developed when he worked at the *Annapolis Triangle*. Unsure what to type—and grumbling to himself—he looked around his office. Making a bet was not a good idea, bringing up memories of a bad habit long stopped. Yet losing a bet was a problem, too. Marti knew his weaknesses, and being a long-term friend, Marti would not steer him wrong.

Gabe's office contained an array of photographs with him with every President, going back to Kennedy, one of the perks of being a top reporter in a suburb of Washington, D.C. The Kennedy shot was from a college visit Kennedy made to American University when he was still a senator. In his early days, Gabe aspired to be a great journalist, in the fields of science and technology, which were growing fields at the time. Then reality set in and he realized that the research behind it was exhaustive. Maybe finding a wife would have helped iron out his rough edges, but work deadlines ruined any opportunity for actual love. There was little time for play when deadlines pressed and each weekly newspaper needed to be put to bed at an obscure hour late Tuesday night.

In time, he learned enough about history to help him float through the paragraphs of difficult stories. And, although history and science did not work themselves into most of his journalism experiences, he liked to think that he had peripheral knowledge that he could draw upon during pressurized situations. Over the years, his avid reading led to him earning numerous awards in Anne Arundel County, including the coveted award from the Washington Press Club for the 1999 story about the fire at the fire station.

Marti was correct in pressing the point about the truthfulness behind the fire station story. Mayor Jake Malone did indeed owe him his career, and not just for the concocted story either. Gabe always supported the mayor because the mayor always showed kindness to him. Democrats to the core, they understood each other, developing a friendship over several decades. As Gabe did his best to peck away at the same keyboard that had given him a simple home in prestigious northern Annapolis, he could not help but become somewhat emotional about all the people who had helped make his career, all names that had been spelled by the same IBM keyboard that Marti now wanted him to ditch for some stupid Macintosh.

How would he ever learn all the technology needed for the modern computer world? Of course, he had to admit the leading reason the *Triangle* management wanted him to leave was because his stories had to be retyped rather than simply reconfigured through a downloaded email attachment. Gabe didn't even have an email account. Gabe felt comfortable at the same desk he had sat at for decades, with the same clunky computer, at the same time of day, and with the same determination for him to complete his story. He thought about his boat docked at a small private dock on the Severn River. "Mistress" earned its name because it was Gabe's way of secretly taunting the woman (and the Mayor) for their tryst—a secret only the three of them knew. He seldom used it except for rare opportunities when he needed a change of scenery, a distinctive break from his monotonous day-to-day existence seemed like today was a day for memories.

Gabe made a mental note to stock The Mistress for a long voyage. He thought he deserved a nice vacation once he finished his story, heading to the Caribbean.

He refocused on his keyboard, realizing the big problem was that he was truly not prepared to write an exhaustive magazine story on retirement. He hadn't even started the data accumulation. Then he looked at the eighteen business cards still heaped together on his credenza. Clumsily playing with them, it dawned on him that he actually had to call all those people to get some fresh quotes. Such a creative approach was not appropriate for a national story, which usually followed a pre-approved outline format. Dismayed, he stood, clicked off the lights, and went to bed. The story could wait yet another day.

ON FRIDAY MORNING AT 10:01 A.M., Gabe sipped his coffee as he made his first phone call to the top card on his list: Nate Baschard, Research Analyst with First Global Investments.

"Yes, hello, is this First Global Investments?" asked Gabe.

"Yes it is," said a woman on the other line.

"I'm looking for a Nate Baschard. Is he available?" Gabe asked.

"Whom can I tell him is calling?" asked the woman.

"Ah, this is Gabe Channing," he answered. "Tell him Gabe's on the line."

"Okay, and the purpose of your call?" she questioned.

Gabe hadn't anticipated needing to answer a lot of questions since his business was only as old as this phone call, and had certainly not developed to the point where he had considered naming it. He had to think fast. "I'm with the Anna—, ah—. . . . I'm with The Channing Group. I'm writing a story on retirement planning and I thought Mr. Baschard would appreciate being interviewed for a magazine feature story."

"Let me see if he's available," she said. "Please hold."

It was Gabe's introductory phone call with his young business. Thus far, he was at least earning a passing grade. He waited for two minutes until the woman returned to the phone.

"I paged him, and he is not responding. May I leave a message?"

"Sure," he said. "Tell him Gabe Channing called from The Channing Group. I'm writing a major story about retirement options and thought he would appreciate the exposure and that he could add to the story." Gabe then gave her his number.

"Thank you, sir. I'll leave him the message," she added before hanging up the phone.

AS THE DAY PROGRESSED, Gabe called all eighteen names among the business cards on his credenza, making careful notes on each card. In the end, it was merely a two-hour project, and that was with adding as much procrastination as possible, with frequent coffee stops and bathroom breaks. By one o'clock, Gabe had accomplished his goal. It wasn't so bad after all, a veteran reporter calling names from a simple stack of business cards. He laid down for a nap until his rotary phone rang loudly, awakening him, and causing him to run into his office to answer the phone—a relic from an era he rebelliously didn't want to let go.

"Hello," said Gabe, still in a daze.

A woman's voice was on the other line. "I'm, I'm sorry. Is this The Channing Group?"

"Ah-h-h. Ah yes. Who is this?"

"I received a call from a Gabe Channing. Is this Gabe?" the woman asked.

"Yes, ma'am. This is he. Can I, ah, ask you some questions about your retirement planning?" Gabe asked.

"I don't have a lot of time, but I wanted to return your call. About how long will this take?" she asked.

"The, ah, the interview will only take about five minutes. Who's calling, please?" asked Gabe.

"I'm Rita Perez, Senior Researcher with GenXY, a Rockville biotech."

Gabe frantically scribbled notes, responding nervously. "This is a rather simple interview. How, ah, have you made any retirement decisions?" He was off to a rough start, but that was about to change, he hoped.

"Excuse me, sir, but how did you get my name?" Rita asked.

Her initial question panicked him. Gabe wasn't about to tell the truth, saying he had stolen her business card from a yellow jar at the Santa Maria Restaurant. He was forced to think quickly. "My computer randomly selects phone numbers and you—along with several others—were called."

"Okay," she said, still in the listening mode.

Somewhat more relaxed, he continued. "As I said, ma'am, the interview will not last long. Because my questions are all rather preliminary, they're easy to answer. The whole interview will take just five minutes, and we've already used about one minute. . . . The first question is: have you made any retirement decisions?"

Rita said, "Yes, I've actually thought a lot about my retirement."

"Are you invested into stocks, bonds, a 401-K, or into precious metals?"

Rita answered, "Well, ah, stocks. . . . I, ah, I've invested in biotechs, which makes sense because I work for a biotech firm."

"And approximately what percentage of your overall retirement funds would you say is invested in biotechs?" asked Gabe.

"One hundred percent," Rita Perez replied.

"I see. That's a rather high percentage for one industry, don't you think?" Gabe asked.

"Not really," she said, curtly.

"Aside from you working within the same industry, why have you picked that industry for your investment?" continued Gabe.

She paused, thinking of how she wanted her words to appear in print someday. "I believe the future is bright for biotechs, and significant developments are being made in the field of biotechnology. Biotech stocks hold great promise, with revenues that should pay high dividends by the time I am ready to retire."

After a few more generic questions about age, expectations, and goals, Gabe continued. "I've called people across several industries, so I'm trying to convey a broad perspective for magazine readers. Are you willing to share the name of any of your favorite biotech companies to our readers?"

"Lately there have been many inside developments that could substantially trigger the biotech industry. It's . . . it's just a wise investment. From how I see it, the biotech industry is developing so rapidly that some of the work could dramatically change mankind. The biotech market is enormous, so I think a diversified portfolio of biotechs is the way to go."

Gabe smiled, knowing the interview had gone successfully. "Thank you, ma'am. May I call you again if I have further questions?"

"Well, I guess so. For what magazine is this?" asked Rita.

"I'm a freelancer," said Gabe. "I worked for forty years at the *Annapolis Triangle* before I retired, and I just recently began freelancing, but the story is shaping itself into one that should find it's way into a national magazine."

"Okay, that's fine," said Rita.

"Thank you," said Gabe, hanging up. Twelve months into his retirement, he had finally re-found his groove.

NATE, HARLAND, RITA, SANDRA
CHAPTER TWO

IN APRIL 2011, the research department at First Global Investments gathered for their weekly strategy session in their conference room on the 50th floor overlooking Central Park. In attendance were all the senior members, who decided which companies they would list as a buy, a sell, or a hold. Also in attendance were the junior analysts, presenting their latest research findings. These ratings would be disseminated to millions of investors and the mass media. Today, Nate Baschard, 25, was on the schedule to talk about the biotech sector he was following. Nate stood at the podium, unnerved by a series of intense questions from David Spelling, chairman of the research committee and the firm's most powerful executive. With the use of his power as research chairman, he could add or subtract tens of millions of market capitalization on a company. Companies researched by First Global knew that David Spelling needed to be satisfied.

David had tried to refute Nate, but was unsuccessful. As always, Nate was well prepared. Nate tugged on his cuffs beneath his navy pinstripe suit. "The book value of some of these biotech firms is growing too fast compared to their revenues and visible funding sources."

"That's true," said David. "But there can be many explanations for this nearly off-the-chart growth. For instance, the early internet frenzy had similar results until the market realized the balloon was destined to bust."

But where are those firms now?" David asked, rhetorically. "They're dead and buried. All this fancy chart shows to me is a pale comparison to what many of us veterans have seen throughout our long careers."

Nate remained calm as David continued to attack his judgment, confident of his intricate knowledge since he had tracked the biotech industry beginning as a high school senior. Later he earned a fine scholarship to Cornell, when he began cross-comparing the biotech sector against other high-flying sectors. His tenacity and research made him the youngest expert in his field, though at the expense of a social life.

"With all due respect to your many years of experience," Nate began, "the hula-hoop industry, or any other, over the past fifty years doesn't compare. Some of these biotech firms cannot be explained based on available information. It's not merely a trend limited to domestic firms. Portugal, Korea, South Africa, and Peru all show certain biotech companies with similar growth. Considering the vast differences in those diversified economies and wholeheartedly different approaches to the biotech field, it is, dare I say, obvious, that unprecedented financial profit is occurring."

David saw his opening and pounced. "I agree that it's unexplainable, so let's table it and move on."

Nate coughed. "What? . . . Table this?"

David glared at Nate over his thin wire-trimmed glasses. "Yes, table it."

Nate decided to assert whatever clout he had gained over the past few years, always scoring in the upper third of company-wide investors for picking the highest-yielding firms. "All I'm asking is that you explain yourself a little better."

"I advise you to spend your efforts on industries with long-term profits that are easier to explain. I can't imagine a single one of our wealthy clients wanting to buy into these high-risk biotechs with all their unexplained valuations. They'll all implode under their own weight eventually, just like the dot-coms."

Nate knew it was time to refute David, even at the expense of losing whatever respect he may have previously had for him. "Let me put this opportunity into terms someone from any generation can understand, and using terms our clients will appreciate. I have tracked these biotech companies directly or indirectly since I was seventeen years old. Someone at your age should be quite familiar with the careers of: John D. Rockefeller, Henry Ford, Andrew Carnegie, Walt Disney, and, just for fun, let's throw in Babe Ruth—all men who once dominated their industries."

A soft chuckle went through the room when Babe Ruth's name was added as an "industry," revealing that everyone in the room was completely captivated with

Nate's tact against Spelling. Two rams butting heads always made the meeting more enjoyable. And watching a youngster like Nate debate with an old pro like David was a prime-time bout.

"We need some popcorn down here," someone chimed in. David was starting to get angry with Nate's refusal to back down.

His presentation lasted a passionate fifteen minutes. With another five minutes remaining of his allocated time, he distributed a thick research report full of charts, all showing significant growth in a particular biotech sub-sector, a complex sector dealing with gene splicing that few Wall Street analysts followed.

Nate said, "I understand your concern about value, and that's why I have included eleven pages in my packet about other bubbles that have burst, and others that have sustained. I have also included quotations from prior leading Wall Street experts, like yourself, about Rockefeller, Ford, Carnegie, Disney and, yes, even Babe Ruth."

The sound of rustling papers filled the room as several analysts flipped through the packet.

"And what is your point?" asked David, crossing his arms.

"This sector may be the strongest engine of growth for the next twenty years. It is an industry in which I have invested most of my time and money. And all my investments into it have already paid off. I mean, how many twenty-three year olds have already made over half a million dollars in three years, beginning with just a $10,000 reallocation of a student loan?"

"Is that true, Nate?" asked Larry Williamson, 59, a senior member of the committee."

"Yes, it is," said Nate. "In the past quarter alone, these firms have returned over 50%."

"Which parameters did you find most useful in spotting these future high flyers?" asked Larry.

Nate grinned. "I'm not going to reveal all my secrets, but I will tell you that it's ironic that watching the History Channel can be quite useful in evaluating future trends."

Nate said, "My point is that something dramatic is occurring in this sector, and some of us will stand to make a significant amount of money on it, myself included. But getting back to my projections, Ford, Carnegie, and Disney had their greater earnings realized by industries that splintered out of their original investments, not necessarily on their original investment. Money, indeed, leads to money, something all of us can appreciate. I mean, who would have imagined that Rockefeller's original money came from kerosene, not oil?"

David's position was unmoved. "I can't see a long-term profit coming from those biotechs, and I believe that there are a dozen industries where there is a better investment for our clients. This DNA thing is good for science fiction writers, but it's not going to make our clients, or us, wealthy. They are just too risky, too speculative and not the type of investment our firm endorses."

From Nate's observation, it seemed that David was the only person in the room unconvinced by the data and his analysis. Nate said, "I remind you, sir, even the company that owned the hula-hoop knew it was a fad, but their goal was to make as much money on it as possible. They then turned their attention to the Frisbee. My point is that, similarly, in these firms, one profitable discovery evolves into another profitable discovery. Babe Ruth set several records, not just home runs. There's something unprecedented happening in this sector, and I think it should be studied further because exponential growth like this is unprecedented."

"Tabled," said David, glaring at Nate. "Next up is energy."

AS THE MEETING ROOM EMPTIED, David Spelling lingered. David slowly picked up his cell phone and dialed a stored number.

Expecting David's call, the voice on the other end answered immediately. "Yes, David. What is it?"

"I just got out of that meeting with that Nate kid," David said.

"And?" Zack asked, breathing heavily.

"He may be a real problem," replied David.

"How so?" Zack asked.

"First, it's not going to be easy to move him away from those investments you and I talked about earlier . . ."

"Damn."

". . . and second, he's connecting the dots."

"*Which* dots?" Zack asked.

"He's already linked his research to something he saw on the History Channel."

"How did he do that?"

I don't know," said Spelling. "And I think—"

"Wait a sec," said Zack, pausing as someone whispered into his ear. "I'm back. Here's the deal. Either you have to stop him or we will. Understand?"

"I understand," said Spelling.

"Keep us posted," said Zack.

"I shall."

"You haven't much time."

THE PENTAGON—In a basement office of the Pentagon, in an office rarely visited and with information rarely discussed, sat Harland Parker, an employee of the Department of Defense. He was quietly reviewing complaints by various military personnel. His office, the Office of Ethical Weapons, was created by a senate ethics committee following WWII complaints filed by soldiers regarding exposure to non-conventional weapons. Harland's department was severely understaffed and underfunded. The department's existence allowed the military to claim it had an ethical weapons division—an oxymoron if ever there was one—to monitor soldiers' complaints.

Several rooms contained piles of paperwork, all under 24-hour guard by armed personnel. Harland was the only line employee in the department though a staff of fifteen was technically on the books. In truth, the department was only composed of Harland, and a part-time secretary, creating a huge delay—by design—so that by the time any findings were reviewed, most of the complainants were dead or retired.

Since no complaint was allowed to go unexamined, and since the unit was operating at below 10% of allocation, the complaints currently backlogged to the 1980s. That meant that Harland was hopelessly behind on his paperwork. In spite of his gloomy situation, Harland would still diligently spend eight to ten hours each day researching complaints, following in his father's footsteps as a "good soldier."

On that particular day, Harland was reviewing paperwork from an officer stationed in the Marshall Islands who complained about being attacked by an almost six-foot long animal that looked half human. The bite marks appeared to be human, too. However, because so much damage was done, the soldier believed he was going to die within days. Harland scoffed at the claim, initially.

However, as a matter of proper diligence, Harland adjusted his thick glasses and read the complaint:

July 29, 1983

Dear Sir in the Office of Ethical Weapons:

I have honorably served in our military for fifteen years, and will proudly retire from the Navy, the Good Lord willing. During my time, I have participated in thousands of drills and been responsible for hundreds of sailors. It has always been my greatest duty to loyally serve our President, especially during these troubled times of war."

During my long, distinguished career, I have literally been to every country in the world that can be serviced by a Navy Destroyer. This information is not shared in this report as a bragging matter, but as a serious statement of the credibility by which I make this report. The last territory which I visited was the Marshall Islands, and it is from these islands that I sit on the Wilson Destroyer in the infirmary and write this report.

It is customary within our military that, sadly, reports filed are often exaggerated, though before I came to this island, the exaggerations were usually within a certain understood tolerance. However, the reports from various officers in the Marshall Islands can't be explained away as stretched ethics.

To explain my claim, I must state that at least ten other sailors witnessed the attack. As I was standing at the stern of our landing craft, dispatched from the Wilson, a fish-type creature approached. I bent down to get a closer look and that was when two arm-like appendages grabbed my leg. I say "arm-like" because they were clearly not arms, yet they also were not fins. Or, perhaps they were fins with webbed arms.

Before I could pull my leg away, the creature— about six feet long—pulled itself up and bit my leg. I fought back and—in the process—sustained several more deep bites to my legs and arms.

The doctor on the Wilson tells me that everything will be fine, but I think he is lying to me. Captain Owens asked me whom he should contact. I said, "my wife," and he nodded, then walked out. Oh, and one last observation, the bite marks on me look human.

Truly yours,

Ensign Sterling Parker

Harland nearly fell off his chair when he saw his father's signature. Normally, a report of that nature would be shredded the next day, along with most of the other complaints reviewed. However, with this report Harland made an exception. He made a quick copy and then shredded the original after he filed his report: "complainant deceased."

Harland knew his father had sometimes discussed the Marshall Islands with him, a location where atomic bombs were tested extensively by the United States military following WWII. Harland pondered how his father was killed in action in the Marshall Islands. Since there was no real action there during his Father's last tour of duty.

ROCKVILLE, MARYLAND—Rita Perez, 31 and a geneticist for GenXY, was working alone in her office on a quiet Sunday morning, her favorite day to conduct research because of its long periods of quiet, aside from a noisy heating and air conditioning system that occasionally tried her patience. A citizen of Argentina, Rita was driven to excel, pushing research technology to its pinnacle throughout her limited, though distinguished, career. She arrived in the United States at age 19, attending one of the best schools her family of vineyard owners could afford, the Johns Hopkins University in Baltimore, Maryland. Originally, she planned to become an M.D., but while in medical school, she switched to research after reading a book titled "Arrowsmith," by Sinclair Lewis and became a top scholar within the field of genetics.

Rita's love for genetics evolved out of her family's wine-making business. As a teenager, she would drink the wine from grapes her grandparents had perfected. Over the years, she learned the value of family heritage along with the value of a good tasting grape. Any variation in the soil, even something as seemingly simplistic as a couple inches variation of rainfall would make one year's wine significantly different from the previous year.

She loved her family, though she could not be with them but a couple times a year. But such was the life of the researcher. At least in her spare time on Sunday, she would study grapes, which was a derivative of her research. Hence, Sundays remained a family day for her, though it was a family day rooted in developing superior wines in one of America's most advanced genetics laboratories. Rita would spend her Sundays studying the genetics of grapes under one microscope and researching gene splicing with the other.

Over the past five years, since earning her Ph.D. in genetic research, she was involved in a highly classified experiment of amphibian DNA. Considered to be an absurd project by the other scientists in her department, Rita accepted the project with gusto. Her goal was to push the limits of science, believing no knowledge was unethical and dangerous.

Today, on Sunday, Rita had conducted her own idea of Holy Communion by drinking a glass of red wine from her parent's vineyard with her lunch, consisting of bread, cheese, and fruit. The Malbec tasted warm and smooth as it slid down her throat. The aged cheese, combined with the warm bread, created a sensation of peace and comfort. The ripened fruit awakened her mouth with bursts of cool sweetness. Rita felt like her life was going wonderfully at times like this.

DUPONT CIRCLE, WASHINGTON, D.C.—In a small home office, Sandra O'Callahan, 24, a vegetarian with waist-length blond hair and a lawyer with a bias against business and politicians, sat reviewing pending legislation. She had ousted politicians and stopped trees from being forested, and now she was in a small bedroom office in a row house just off the Circle, surfing the net between sips of organic white tea. As the clock struck 7 p.m., she began getting ready to head out for the evening. Newly hired as a legal analyst for a high-profile ethics group, Sandra had attained her dream job and was searching for a project to lead to her first magazine cover story.

At Berkeley, Sandra had led demonstrations against the Iraq War and was proud to have been arrested on two occasions, each time using her prowess as a budding lawyer to later have the charges dismissed. Although her father was a senior partner at a top Boston law firm, Sandra maintained the naive belief that her current job was the result of her legal savvy, and never the result of her elitist background.

Sandra flagged a cab and headed to a cocktail party at the home of Jacob Btok, the ambassador for the Solomon Islands. Wearing a sleek black dress, she had hoped it would give her a subtle edge with her next target, Jonathan Summers, young, single and successful, and the ambassador to the Marshall Islands.

"A glass of wine for you, miss?" asked the bartender, impressed.

"Yes, thank you." I'll have a glass of that Argentinean Malbec," Sandra answered.

"Excellent choice, if I may say so myself," said the bartender.

Sandra took the wine and headed out to the terrace, looking for Ambassador Summers. When she got outside, she saw him standing alone, with his eyes closed, deep in thought.

Sandra cleared her throat, causing Summers to open his eyes. Then his eyes blinked, and focused directly on her.

Sandra reached out her hand.

As the ambassador was still trying to collect his thoughts, he only heard a few of her many jumbled words, focusing his attention instead on her short black dress.

"I'm Sandra O'Callahan with the . . . please to finally meet you. I've heard . . . Marshall Islands. . . . nuclear tests. . . . I couldn't believe it. What do you think?"

"Whoa, you're talking faster than I am hearing," the ambassador replied.

"I'm sorry."

"That's okay. Let's just sit down and slow all this down a bit." His glass was almost empty. He pointed to a bench. Sandra was feeling quite confident.

"I'll be right back. I need to get my drink freshened. Can I get you anything?" the ambassador asked.

Sandra shook her head, her long blond hair gently swaying as she spoke.

"Please hold my seat there next to you," said Ambassador Summers. "I'll be right back."

Obviously, Mr. Summers was going to be easy to milk for information. Amazing, she thought, what a little cleavage and a large slit up the side of a dress could do to so many men.

When the ambassador returned, Sandra had her questions ready regarding the Marshall Islands. Mixing them subtly in with small talk, big smiles, and flirty innuendos was easy. After an hour or two, she had gotten enough of what she needed to know. The magazine article was almost in the bag.

As Sandra was riding back to her apartment she thought about her career and what she was trying to accomplish. All her efforts fell into a "pro-environmentally anti-war" categorization. She wondered if this was a form of rebelling against her father for his work defending polluters and companies that were destroying the environment. Was she his counter-balance? Was she trying to undo some of the harm he had defended?

THE LOOKOUT STARTED SHOUTING. "On the rocks, port, look!"

On deck, all the sailors rushed to the port side to look. "Hey, we don't have binoculars. What is it you're seeing?" said one of the sailors.

"You're not going to believe this," he said. "Here, look for yourself."

He handed another sailor the binoculars.

"Holy crap. It's a damn mermaid," he shouted. "A mermaid! It's a mermaid! I can't believe it!"

The other sailors started grabbing for the binoculars.

"Let me see," said one with a tattoo of a mermaid on his arm.

"You're full of it," said another sailor.

By the time the binoculars made it to the fourth viewer, their shouting and hollering was so loud the creatures on the rocks became startled and dove into the ocean.

The sailors tried to get the captain to turn the ship around so they could try to track down the mermaids. Thinking they were pulling a fast one to try to get some R&R, he ignored their pleas.

When the ship finally docked in New Zealand, the sailors hit the pubs with stories of real, live mermaids. But nobody believed them except for Hugo Charlemagne, a young busboy, listening intently to their every word as they described the mermaids in great detail. Hugo decided then that when he was old enough to afford a boat, he would sail to the Marshall Islands and try to find his own mermaid.

Lying in bed that night, Hugo swore an oath to himself that he would be the first person to actually capture a live mermaid. To him, they sounded like the most beautiful creatures in the world.

REACTION

CHAPTER THREE

WATCHING FOUR LARGE HIGH DEFINITION MONITORS simultaneously as cells mutated was Rita's dream job, though she would never have let her dreams be limited by her position. She had believed science was a frontier—still largely unexplored—and she was determined to discover something great, something previously not considered or imagined. Every work day she watched her monitors for proof, believing she could accomplish more work looking at several screens than merely looking through a single microscope.

Rita had aided in the development of the technology to monitor cellular-level change through computer-enhanced digital images. It was not a major development, as developments go, but it did make it possible for her to watch multiple images of cells without being physically present at the microscopes, and have the 3D-view digitally enhanced and rotateable.

It was a clever technology: four high-definition screens, each thirty-inch flat screens. All the screens followed the movements of the cell's structure, movements difficult to track under a traditional single angle microscope. The computer generated a trail for each cell, created in multi-colors and blurs of light, each spawned in their uniqueness. In essence, it was a fingerprint for each cell's development, beginning with the embryonic state as a stem cell. The program was written by Rita's brother, Pedro Perez, and later programmed into her laptop. The program linked the data output to a computer algorithm which projected extrapolated changes after maturation of the genetic modification being tested.

On this particular night, Rita was in the laboratory, watching her four monitors. The day had been long, and the evening was dragging, so she pulled the cork on a bottle of Merlot and poured herself a glass. She usually had a glass around eight o'clock at night, after getting home, but now it was pushing ten and she was still at her desk.

After fourteen hours at work, the cells on the monitors began to blur together. She was definitely not drunk, but she was totally exhausted. Sometimes working hard late into the night has the effect of producing amazing results, even unexpected results, and such was to be the case this special evening.

Rita clicked on yet another file, one of about three hundred still-unviewed files on her laptop, connected to the four large monitors in her office. She kept staring, and that is when she saw it.

"It's different," she said to herself, jumping up. "It's changed."

Then she repeated herself. "Oh, yes, yes I've seen something almost identical before."

Rita was referring to something that neither she, nor anyone she knew of, had ever observed before. These cells, on this particular file were much different. They appeared to be human, but they couldn't be, she thought, because she was working with amphibious DNA. After studying literally thousands of cells, she was convinced she was right. And she was, sort of.

RITA WAS PERSISTENT AS SHE STARED AT HENDERSON.

"These cells are not animal," she said. "We've been experimenting with human cells."

Henderson had no patience for her today. As her immediate supervisor, and the man who reported directly to senior management, he was nearly irate at her insistence on being correct.

"You know I respect your work," Henderson began, "but those cells are not human. They are *definitely* from animals. I checked the file—again. They originate in the Marshall Islands. In fact, the file says that island didn't have any humans allowed on it for decades. The U.S. Navy patrolled the specific island where they were found for 15 years, enforcing the policy. Why do you *think* they're human?"

Rita sighed. "I've studied these cells for months on end, maybe even years, if you count some of the peripheral work I've done. I've conducted numerous tests on these animal cells, well, cells I thought were animal for the longest time. Embryonic research is a serious ethical violation for me, you know. I realized today from this latest batch of computer synchronizing techniques that these cells follow human sequences. I'm telling you, they're human.

"That's impossible," said Henderson, testing her. "How can you be completely sure. Do they match *one hundred percent* with human DNA?"

"They're *definitely* human," said Rita, curling her report in her hands. "I've studied these DNA sequences, and some of them are distinctively human. Some of the details in particular are peculiar though. For instance, I studied these cells, duplicated my research several times, comparing their genetic sequences with other sequencing from various animals in the lab. I have concluded they don't match with human DNA."

"So they're not human," said Henderson, spotting a weakness to her conclusion.

"Henderson, nothing is this close to being human. Obviously, apes are similar to humans but not human. These cells, I'm telling you, are human, well, at a minimum, they're *more human* than anything else on this planet, excluding humans."

Henderson backed down, sitting at his desk, another long evening for the both of them. "It's been a late night, for both of us. I promise I'll call management and tell them what you have revealed to me. Maybe, and I'm saying maybe only because I have immense respect for you as a scientist, maybe there is something wrong with the cells we've been testing. We just get these batches of cells from management and they all tend to look the same after a while."

"It's the research that concerns me," said Rita. "I refuse to kill people."

Henderson sighed. "I'm not going to argue with you, especially since I respect your religious beliefs. But cells are not people."

Rita smiled. "You also know I respect your opinion, and I'm thinking these cells may not be human. What we have in those specific cells is mostly human, but not entirely human. Anyway, I would appreciate your looking into this for me. It's really starting to creep me out a bit."

"I'm glad you understand it then," said Henderson, slurping his coffee. "Let me read your report and I'll review what you've told me with management."

"Okay," said Rita, relieved. "It's their similarity to humans, though, that worries me. I'm telling you, Henderson, something is wrong in those Marshall Islands, and I'm guessing we're not the only group out there who suspects that."

AS RITA EXITED HENDERSON'S OFFICE, he reached for his cell phone.

The voice on the other end of the line sounded annoyed. "Do you know what time it is?" asked Zack, looking at his watch while laying in bed. "This had better be important."

"Of course it is," said Henderson.

Impulsively, Zack sat up in his bed and reached for his laptop, opening the screen. "Alright, what's the matter?"

"It's about Rita Perez. Do you still have her file near you?"

"Give me a second. . . . Okay, I have her on the screen. Go ahead," said Zack, thinking to himself that Rita was actually quite attractive.

Henderson sighed. "Rita has figured out that the research she is doing is on cells that are almost human. She also knows they come from the Marshall Islands. . . ."

As Henderson continued to speak, Zack clicked on the internal link with all her pictures on it. He kept thinking about how attractive she was. Should he make a surprise visit to GenXY and meet with her anonymously under the guise of a routine government visit? "I heard you," he said, finally cutting Henderson off. "What do you recommend? Reassigning her?"

"No, not yet," said Henderson. "She's way too good a scientist to take her off of Project M.I.X. I'll try BS-ing her first, maybe even mixing some of her cell samples. If that fails, we can send her to Alaska, or somewhere else to isolate her."

"I understand," said Zack.

"Good," said Henderson.

"Besides, it's a much better option than the alternative," said Zack, smugly.

HARLAND STARED AT A PICTURE OF HIS FATHER, Ensign Sterling Parker, which had sat on his desk for twelve years, since the day he had been given his position. His dad had an ear-to-ear grin and was half-hugging Jennings with his right arm as Jennings half-hugged Harland's dad with his left arm. Usually, he hated to be photographed, avoiding the camera even at Christmas gatherings and especially at church, which is why the photo had such a dear place to Harland. His dad was so happy about being on a fishing boat, surrounded by fish of all types and colors.

Not only was it the last photograph of Sterling, it was the only photograph of his father over the past five years of his life. Thus, it was a constant reminder of the contacts his father had made for him, helping to establish Harland as an esteemed military man.

The picture was from Sterling's last vacation, at least that was what he was told. It was a picture taken with Admiral Tommy Jennings, Sterling's closest friend in the Navy. Admiral Jennings had been on a vacation with his father at the Marshall Islands, back in 1983. It was a working vacation, one where the goal was to be pleasurable more than to do actual work.

Later, they had been scuba diving when Sterling was attacked by a shark. Because his leg had been severely mangled, they pulled him to the closest island, where he unfortunately bled to death before help could be obtained. Admiral Jennings never much spoke much about it, except to say it was one of the freakiest accidents he had ever seen from one really big, and weird looking shark that attacked out of nowhere. His explanation never made much sense, but Harland never pressed the military brass for answers about how his dad had died. Instead, he kept his memories of him rooted in his father's joyous life instead of in his tragic death.

After Sterling's death, Admiral Jennings had used his credentials to force the Navy to switch Harland to an office job and—though Harland didn't know that the Admiral was behind it—he actually welcomed it despite his original plan of becoming a Navy Seal. Eventually, he decided that he did not want to travel the world, as being a military brat had been rough on him. His goal instead became to find a wife and settle down. Having local roots was important, so he believed living in the District was the perfect place to live. It minimized any commuting time and guaranteed him a future, as long as he would accept any job at the Pentagon.

As a favor, Admiral Jennings got Harland the office job in the Pentagon basement, a thankless one no one else wanted because it had no stature and no opportunity for promotion. Regardless, in Harland's eyes that meant he had job security and would easily be rooted again in Washington, D.C., fitting his basic needs to survive.

Now all that he knew—or thought he knew—about his father's death was probably some military cover-up. How else could he explain the report he was now carrying, the one his father signed? He didn't die of some freak accident, at least not the way he was led to believe. But why the lies? Why the big deal? Something definitely didn't make sense and Harland felt he had to try and learn the truth of his dad's death.

Harland snapped back to the present when he heard his son calling from his bedroom. Young Sterling, it seems, was busy having a nightmare about sea monsters. Harland chuckled and gently rocked him back to sleep.

He missed his dad, in addition to missing his wife. ALS was what got her, a fast and ruthless end to her life. It finished her off before he really even understood what was happening to her. Harland felt tears welling up in his eyes. He then turned off his light and tried to get some sleep.

WATCHDOG GROUP'S WASHINGTON LOBBYIST had scheduled a meeting with Sandra to discuss an upcoming green project in the Amazon rainforest in Brazil. It was the most prestigious job at the firm, and was Sandra's foremost task of business in her new position. Watchdog Group was to find the ideal candidate to lead the five-person project in the Amazon.

The project was fully funded for a three year time period, with the small group being given a generous stipend covering all expenses in Brazil, as long as they would maintain a specific schedule. In truth, it was a three-year vacation, as the itinerary required only eight days of research in the Amazon each month, intermingled with eight days of analysis and administration in Rio de Janeiro. Eight days were allocated to travel between Rio de Janeiro and the Amazon river basin, with the remaining six to seven days allocated as personal time. With wiggle room, it was understood that actual work amounted to about a week per month, with three weeks of time given to tequilas in Rio.

MADELINE HASTINGS WAS A BOARD MEMBER of Watchdog Group, dealing with the highest level of environmental research. In her mid-thirties, she was homely and self-righteous. Never married and without children, she was consistently ranked as one of Washington's most eligible bachelorettes, but the ironic classification was done just to help keep the list well-balanced.

Democratic Senator Bob Dugan from North Dakota—a divorced and glib man in his fifties—included Madeline Hastings in his list of "Top Ten reasons global warming exists." However, insiders knew Senator Dugan had a long-term crush on Madeline, and his comment was the equivalent, he thought, of saying she was real hot.

Madeline entered Sandra's office, wearing a long, vegetable dyed, hand-painted cotton dress with canvass sandals, of course. Not one to fret over protocol, Madeline wasn't one to like to shake hands with other women, so when she entered Sandra's office at 2 p.m. on a Thursday, she cut right to the chase.

"Capital Hill is disappointed no one has been given the top job yet on the Brazil Project," said Madeline, looking at herself in a mirror and basically avoiding eye contact with Sandra. "They want someone to head down there right away. There's been more clear-cutting lately, which is hurting the water flow. We need to fill this position immediately!"

Sandra was dismayed, her eyes widening. She pointed to a one-foot stack of resumes on a credenza next to her desk. "That's how many people applied for the position."

"That's less than we thought," said Madeline, smoothing a wrinkle in her dress.

"Those are the resumes from last week alone," said Sandra, trying not to raise her eyebrows at Madeline's vanity. "And that doesn't count emails. It's pointless to keep going through them."

"That's the same feeling on Capital Hill," said Madeline, reaching into her French sac and removing a container of Burt's Bee hand cream. "I've consulted with the board, and we want to offer the position to you."

"What?" said Sandra, an earnest reaction of shock. "Are you serious?"

"Of course," said Madeline, massaging her hands with the cream. "You don't really think you're supposed to go through all those piles of resumes, do you?"

"Well, that's been what I've been doing until eight at night, most nights for the past two weeks. I was told when they hired me I was not being considered for the position."

"They lied," said Madeline, thoroughly rubbing the cream into her hands. "You're the one they always wanted, though we had to keep interviewing just to make it look like we were actually being fair about the process."

"Believe me, I'm flattered, but I thought with my resume, I would never get my current job, let alone that one."

"What do you mean? You're perfect!"

Sandra was aghast. "I'm bad luck, and I thought everyone knew it, including you."

"That's ridiculous," said Madeline, putting the hand cream container back into her sac. "Like I told you when I hired you, you're life-long quest to preserve the environment proves that you are sincere and driven."

"Oh," said Sandra, glancing again at the pile of resumes.

"There isn't a single person out there more dedicated to this cause other than, well, myself."

"With all due respect, I was hit by lightning in a redwood tree, for God's sake," said Sandra, still trying to cope with reality. "I never even got to meet Julia Butterfly Hill during that whole tree sitting episode in California. You know, the book *Legacy of Luna*?"

"So what," said Madeline, checking her email on her new Apple I-Pod.

"When a group of us rented a boat and motored over to Portland to save those beached whales, we had to stay away because our boat was leaking gas," continued Sandra.

"Happens all the time," said Madeline. "At least it wasn't leaking oil like the Exxon Valdez."

"I was involved with that, too, as a kid. Remember those ducks they spent $80,000 to save and release back into the ocean? Well, I saw them get eaten by a whale."

Madeline stood and finally stared directly into Sandra's beautiful green eyes. "None of that is bad, it just shows your dedication to the environment, which is why we're offering you the position in Brazil. The expedition has just been moved up, to July, instead of December. The job is yours, so stop fretting over all these resumes and start preparing me a budget and interviewing four helpers to go down there with you."

Sandra wanted to go but didn't want to stop what she was doing. "What about the article I'm working on, about the Marshall Islands? I just met with the ambassador. I think this could be big!"

Madeline was impatient. "We will assign someone to work on it here under you."

"But under whose byline?" asked Sandra.

"Yours, of course." Madeline then turned and left, gently closing the door behind her. Alone, Sandra cried out her emotions. Finally—finally—she had been given a break!

AS MADELINE HASTINGS LEFT SANDRA'S OFFICE, she reached into her purse to retrieve her cell phone. "Mission accomplished," she said. "Sandra is under our control again. The diversion worked."

"Great," said Zack, drinking a cup of coffee. "She was asking too many questions. In Brazil she can play all the environmental games she wants. Let's just hope the margaritas will convince her to chill out and finally enjoy life."

"Be careful," said Madeline. "I'm calling you from my cell phone, you know?"

"Of course I know that," said Zack. "I'm the one who monitors the people who monitor everyone else."

AT 8:35 A.M. AT HIS MIDTOWN OFFICE in New York City, Nate sipped his coffee. He had already scanned the *Wall Street Journal* and read the entire *New York Times,* except the business section, which was a change from his daily routine. An avid news junkie, Nate always tried to weigh how various market conditions would affect biotechs, always looking for the whiff of a problem that could send the industry tumbling or a breakthrough that could send it soaring. Heavily correlated to the political climate, biotech was a sensitive sector influenced by conditions outside the industry. His research had proven repeatedly that it was also a growing sector, one that with government cash could make an already soaring industry explode with profit.

Today was the day Nate's biotech research was to be printed in the *Times* weekly First Global article, an advertising section First Global Investments bought every week, which read more like a newspaper column than an ad. Finally, Nate found the First Global article, believing his report would cover half a page. But to his surprise, he found himself reading a article about textiles by David Spelling. Distraught over his first professional failure, Nate sunk his head into his hands. Why would Spelling kill his article? Nate was certain the facts in his article would make him a rising star on Wall Street. It was the big break that he thought would propel him into an upwardly mobile career with leading interviews in business magazines, and hopefully even his own byline in the *Journal,* or the *Times*.

Although unusual for his generation, he was more comfortable with reading a physical newspaper than online versions, believing a broadsheet newspaper was more efficient for his limited time schedule than endless clicking on the internet, Nate knew electronic copy was more environmentally sound. For correspondence, the internet was ideal. How else was he going to reach so many key people in the biotechs he covered, and how else could they efficiently communicate with him? But, for him and his habit of highlighting, underlining, and marking questions and ideas in the margins, hard copy still best suited him.

After his newspaper reading, he turned on his monitor and read his email. Today, like every day, Nate hoped for an email from a director of equity research who recognized his potential and would offer him a huge step-up in the industry. When his email was properly logged on, he noticed one from a senior vice president who certainly trashed his opportunity: David Spelling.

He clicked on the email and angrily read it, wanting to throw his coffee at the monitor. "Nate, what's your schedule like for lunch today? If you're free, please join me at Angellino's at noon. I want to bounce some ideas off you. After further thought, I've been reconsidering some of your points from your biotech presentation last month. Please reply by 10 a.m."

Although his laptop computer was equipped with excellent speakers and great graphics, there was no bullshit buzzer on it, which would certainly have been ringing really loudly right now.

"What the hell does he want?" Nate muttered to himself. "And Angellino's? Why does he want me to meet him there? He killed my story and now he's going to fire me. I hate that bastard."

ANGELLINO'S WAS A POSH ITALIAN RESTAURANT in Midtown New York, a restaurant long regarded as a neighborhood staple, one that survived off of daily $100 bottles of wine. When David ordered a

Rothschild Bordeaux, a $1200 bottle of wine over lunch, Nate nearly dropped his water glass, but managed to keep a poker face. Nate knew the value of the wine from reading ads in the *Times* about the family-owned business that had deep New York roots and a first-rate wine cellar.

The waiter poured the last of the wine into Nate's glass, which capped off an hour of conversation about every topic under the sun—except biotechs. That's when David finally exposed his true colors. David began condescendingly. "When I was a young smart ass like you, I had prepared a presentation for J.P. Morgan—and I'm not talking about the company, either, but J.P. Morgan, the grandson, himself. He didn't do much with the business either, just living off the inheritance, but boy was he interested in my presentation. He interrupted a skiing trip to Vail, Colorado just to show up to listen to me. I had spent months preparing myself, and I knew about every factor and condition of the sector for which I was responsible—textiles. Nate, do you know anything about textiles?"

"Just a little," said Nate. "It's a bull sector rooted in Asia, with limited growth. But go ahead with your story."

"When I started here, textiles were hot—a real hot—sector. Let me give you a little background. The old man who started this company, Rudy, always gave me a lot of hell, especially for the first two years after I started. Personally, I thought he hated me. In time, I began to think that the only reason he kept me around was because he believed in the money I could make him more than he believed in me. You get my point?"

Nate politely nodded as David sipped from his second glass of wine. Nate kept wondering if he was going to get fired. Why was he talking about all this gibberish?

David continued. "I had spent years on textiles, traveling throughout Asia with the company, even going to goat and sheep farms and watching them make silk with bamboo in the urban areas. Well, let me get back to my J.P. Morgan point. I gave a presentation to thirty people, telling them how I believed the textile market was going to open up in Taiwan and Japan—a point that has become completely true by the way. The whole room was completely captivated when I ended my presentation. Then I asked if anyone had any questions, and Morgan was the only person who raised his hand."

Finally, Nate was engaged with David's story, a striking similarity with his own budding career. "What did he ask?" Nate asked, leaning forward in his posh chair.

"He sat there, and—with a cunning look in his eyes—he asked me, 'What color of silk is the Japanese Emperor's favorite?'" David stared at a marble statue of Plato and chuckled, repeating the question. "'What color of silk is the Japanese emperor's favorite?' I mean, I have never heard a more difficult question in any meeting in my entire life. How would *you* have answered that question?"

"I don't know," said Nate, shaking his head.

"You'd want to save face; wouldn't you?"

"Well, ah, yeah." Nate answered.

"Knowing you goddamn well don't know the answer, right?"

Nate blinked, pausing. "Right. . . . What did you say?"

"That's when I just simply said, 'I don't know.' J.P. stood up to leave and said to me, 'You need to know your facts before we invest further.' Then he left. He actually left that room, taking those six ultra high net worth investors with him and making me look like a horse's ass."

"That's embarrassing," said Nate. "What happened next?"

"Nothing. Berringer tabled the topic and then everyone else left the room within minutes, leaving me alone with a bunch of slick poster boards and charts. I was numb. In fact, I thought I was going to be fired because I didn't know the Japanese emperor's favorite color of silk." David chuckled.

"Why did he ask that question?" Nate asked, sipping the last of his wine. "I mean, who cares about such a simple question?"

"That's exactly what I was thinking," said David. "It seems like the most stupid question in the world, but it mattered to J.P. The next day I called all over Japan until I found out the answer. The next week I was given a promotion, and they moved me into the automotive sector. Quite a raise they gave me, too."

"That doesn't make any sense either," said Nate, wiping his forehead with a handkerchief. "They *hated* your report but gave you a promotion *and* a raise?"

"I tried for a solid week, five times a day, to get through to J.P. with the correct answer. A couple of days later, I received a handwritten note from J.P. All it said was congratulations on your promotion."

"And?" Nate asked, still wondering if he was going to be fired.

"I know you put a lot of work into that biotech presentation you gave the other day. It was one of the finest I've ever heard."

Nate gritted his teeth. "I put six weeks of work into that presentation, and I thought everyone was happy with it, until it didn't show up in the First Global article in the *Times* today."

"I've got good news for you," said David, his eyes blinking. "Larry and I had a meeting and we're giving you a raise for all the hard work you did with that article you wrote."

"What?!" said Nate, moving forward in his chair.

"Don't worry about anything," said David, grinning. "There'll be other articles you can write in the future. Larry said he'd make you a vice president in charge of the alternative energy sector. You'd be the youngest V.P. we've ever had, and it's a better sector, too, especially with the boom in energy consumption occurring in China and India. I can help you with the other details."

"Don't think I'm not thrilled about getting the raise and promotion, but I just don't understand it. I thought you were going to fire me today."

David leaned back in his chair, grinning. "That's the same thing I thought when this happened to me forty years ago, when Barrington sat with me at this same table and shared a personal story with me. Then he pointed to that picture over there." David pointed at an exquisite medieval painting with its peculiar golden flare that featured a centurion with a whip standing above a man tied with a thick rope. Beautifully painted, the rope was accented with intense gold shading under the sun's hot rays. "Do you know the name of that painting?" David asked.

Nate delayed his response. "No."

"It's true name is the Golden Rope, but Barrington called it the Golden Handcuffs. I'll give you a week to accept the promotion and conditions, or you need to resign." Spelling then signed the check for the lunch, got up, and walked away, leaving Nate sitting alone, thinking.

BEGINNING IN THE 1970s, villagers began returning to Enewetak Island, many experiencing severe health problems. Consequently, on May 15, 1977, the U.S. government directed Admiral Nelson Owens to decontaminate the Marshall Islands with an extensive cleanup project costing hundreds of millions of U.S. dollars.

The cleanup required the mixing of contaminated soil and debris from the various islands with Portland cement, burying everything inside a blast crater at the northern end of Runit Island on the eastern side of an atoll. Eventually, the crater grew to a spherical 25-foot-high mound covered with an unprecedented 18-inch concrete cap.

The government contractor in charge of clean-up certified that all the containments were neutralized. Despite the certification, the U.S. government kept the area off-limits, maintaining a perimeter. Navy ships maintained a 24/7 quarantine, with no one allowed in, and no one allowed out. Soon plants of never previously identified species began growing, adding further distrust of the safety in the island. Rumors continued to circulate that not all villagers were evacuated prior to the detonation of the nuclear bombs.

SURVEILLANCE
CHAPTER FOUR

IN AN UNDERGROUND FACILITY in Fairfax County, Virginia, a computer printer spit out four sheets of paper with heavy text. A Homeland Security agent with a badge that read "Brad Cho" looked at the sheets as Zack McHenry and Erin Blaine watched him.

"We've got another hit with the same guy," said Brad as he looked at his watch noting the time as 12:11 p.m. "He's called five people on our Red List, nine on the Orange list, and two on the Yellow List, all within a two hour period."

"How many calls did he make in all?" asked Erin.

"Twenty," answered Brad. "Two of the calls we are working on, people who are either Code White—so we don't have to worry about them—or people who have not yet triggered our system with suspicious activity."

"What about the other two calls?" asked Zack, chewing on a bite-sized doughnut.

Brad answered, "One was to an Apple Store—"

"Oh-h-h, he could be a pro," said Erin, looking at a mood ring she wore every day.

"The other call was to a hardware store," said Brad. "We don't have his house wired yet, so we're not sure why he called them."

"Get someone assigned to that right away," said Zack, scribbling on a hand-held computer pad. "Let's meet back at 1600 hours tomorrow and I'll want answers." Then Zack left the room, sipping his coffee as he walked.

"The hardware store call confuses me," said Erin, struggling to use her intuitive mind, a skill that was her expertise within the department. "I wish I knew more about him."

Brad nodded. "I've assigned Tasks Control Management to analyze his activity for next week. There's no telling what he's building, or even if he's building anything at all. All we know thus far is no one calls that many people on our hot lists unless something is in the fire."

"It's odd that his number has never been a match before," said Erin. "He may be an isolated wolf, like Timothy McVeigh. What do we know for sure about him?"

Brad pecked away at his keyboard. "It's not much, because he's not on any of our suspected terrorist lists. His phone number is not a hit, neither is his address. About all we know is his name: Gabriel Channing, a long-time local writer in Annapolis. His friends call him 'Gabe.'"

Erin shook her head. "Maybe he's snapped. All writers have a crazy streak. What else do you have?"

"Anyone who'd buy an Apple toy should go right on the Red List," said Brad, causing Erin to chuckle briefly. "Gabe's longest call was to Rita Perez, Senior Researcher with GenXY, a Rockville biotech."

"Whoa!" said Erin. "She is definitely on the hot list."

Brad fiddled with a ring displaying a skull and crossbones on his right hand. "I know that name. She's the top researcher working on Project M.I.X., and she's never been fully briefed on it, either. The lab on the Marshall Islands that provides her those cells is one of the highest classified zones we have. Top-level clearance is required to go anywhere near M.I.X. Only a couple of scientists and four-star generals are allowed in there."

"I still don't think we should be sending those cells halfway across the world," said Erin.

"I agree," said Brad. "We've discussed that specific issue several times in clearance meetings and it remains tabled, so I'm not ruffling any feathers upstairs, if you know what I mean."

"Pfft. 'Feathers.' That's a good one."

Brad remained serious. "Seriously, on a scale of 1 to 10, what do you—"

Erin hackled. "Scales?! Boy, you're in a weird mood today."

Mechanically minded, Brad had no sense of humor. "You know the labs on those islands are only so big, and finding scientists to live out there is nearly impossible. The radiation problem doesn't help matters either. Just remember, this guy's a reporter, and he may be about to break that story."

Erin nodded. "The fact that he went to a hardware store makes me wonder if it's really a story he was working on, or something else. We need to watch him. He lives too close to the hub to ignore. Annapolis is only thirty miles from the White House and the Pentagon. With all those hits in two hours, he could be onto something confidential."

"So they're not buying the retirement story upstairs?" asked Brad, reaching for another doughnut.

"You saw what McHenry did? When was the last time you saw him move that fast?"

Both of them chuckled, then answered in unison. "September 12, 2001."

Erin continued. "He was the first person in line that next morning for accolades after that fourth plane went down."

"And he deserved them, too," said Brad.

"That's for sure."

GABE SAT AT HIS KITCHEN TABLE AT 12:30 P.M., eating a fried egg sandwich and drinking leftover coffee from the morning. The coffee tasted burnt and the eggs were really over-done. Even the toast got burnt, crumbling as he bit into it.

Making all those calls certainly was not fun for him. Some were quick calls, other seemed to be endless, waiting on hold sometimes for ten minutes or more. Most of the people had secretaries, too, with only a few having a direct number. Even the cell numbers were sometimes forwarded to secretaries' voicemails. It was enough to make him want to take a nap. He began to doze, after finishing his sandwich, a habit that had lasted his whole career at the *Triangle*, though that was tolerable because deadlines could keep him awake some nights until two in the morning. Indeed, he was a creature whose habits resulted from his work environment.

The phone rang, jolting Gabe awake, and causing him to accidentally spill his half-full cup of coffee as he reached for the phone. Thinking more about cleaning the spill than about his telephone survey for the magazine article, he answered the phone.

"Yeah," he said into the black rotary receiver. He sounded like he was still sleeping, too, which only made his professionalism drop further.

"Is this Gabe Channing?" asked a woman.

"Yes, what can I do for you?" he answered, realizing she may have been someone he called earlier. It was too late to change his previous demeanor.

"This is Sandra O'Callahan, legal analyst for Watchdog Group, returning your call."

"Can I put you on hold while I finish my last call?" asked Gabe.

Sandra wrinkled her nose, her intrigue as an investigator piqued. "Ah-h-h, sure."

Gabe clumsily laid down the receiver, then scurried into his office where he picked up the extension and carefully laid it on the table. Then he hurried back to the kitchen again and picked up the receiver once again.

"I'll just be another minute," he said. Then he hung up the kitchen phone and returned to his office.

"I'm sorry about the delay, but my secretary isn't in, complicating things around here."

"This isn't being tape-recorded, is it?" Sandra asked.

Gabe was surprised by her question. "Definitely not. I do take notes, though. You don't have any qualms with that, do you?"

"Notes are fine," said Sandra, relieved. "I just thought I heard some clicking on the line after you picked up. I did some internet research on you and I see the Washington Press Club awarded you, in 1999, the best journalism story. You must be legit."

"I'm just a hardworking reporter," said Gabe. "Been at this for forty years."

"Did you uncover any corruption down there, in the Annapolis area and all? Anything tying in to D.C.?"

" I was always writing about some form of corruption," Gabe answered as he looked at her card in the mix. Recalling that she worked with Watchdog Group, he added, "I oversaw my local government mostly, kept it clean. You probably know how clean Annapolis is."

"Sure," she answered. "Clean government is only a response to good investigation, so maybe I'm thinking you're probably a good reporter. It's just the law of predictable mass that good journalists find the corruption, whereas bad journalists—too indoctrinated into the system—turn the other cheek to it. For what story did you win your award?"

"Oh, it was nothing," said Gabe, sidestepping her question. "The retirement story is something I'm doing now that I'm retired—"

"That makes sense," she chuckled.

"It's actually a pretty interesting story, as well as timely."

"And how did you get my number?"

"It was randomly dialed."

"From a rotary phone?"

"Huh?"

Sandra's investigator skills were active. "I deal with people every day, people, that is, who lie every day. And I can usually tell a lie when I hear one. The old rotary phone swap is the oldest phone sounds in the book. My grandparents used to have a rotary phone. The sound is distinctive. You *definitely* have a rotary phone. There's not a doubt in my mind. I bet you don't have a secretary either, not with the tired way you answered the phone. Home office. Definitely a home office. Let me know when I'm wrong. Seriously. I make a living at this and you're as simple as they come." She waited for a response but one was not forthcoming. She added, "The hard part, though, is finding out how you found my name. Automatic dial? I think not. Give me a break. Who do you work for?"

Gabe was dismayed. "Myself. I'm retired, just doing a little freelance work."

"How many calls did you make this morning?"

"Maybe fifteen, twenty perhaps," said Gabe.

"How is someone supposed to get a hold of you when you don't even have call waiting. I mean, the only time I hear a busy signal is when I call Senator Burns' office. Talk about rotary phones. They operate with carrier pigeons down there." Sandra chuckled. "You get it?"

Gabe felt like hanging up, but decided to ask one last time. "Are you going to let me ask any questions, or is this interview all yours?"

"I'm sorry. I just like people being up front about everything. How did you get my name?"

Gabe was quiet. "I called about your retirement planning. What decisions have you made for retirement?"

"I'm certainly not planning on social security helping me—"

"Then what's your plan?"

Sandra paused. "Look, I'm twenty-four years old. Retirement is the furthest thing from my mind. When I'm thirty, I'll make some decisions on it. I have other— are you playing with your phone again?"

"What?"

"There it goes again."

Gabe nodded silently to himself. "I think I heard something that time, too. Yeah, there it is again."

"I gotta' go," said Sandra. "I don't need you recording my phone calls, especially for such a dumb story." Then Sandra hung up.

Gabe stared in dismay at his receiver, wondering if the noise was from her line, or his. After a couple more phone calls, he realized there was indeed something wrong with his line. Was his phone bugged, he thought?

Meanwhile, Sandra called one of her girlfriends about meeting for lunch. As she was talking, she noticed the same interference on her line again. She thought, who would want to record the line of an environmentalist?

She decided that the reporter deserved an apology, making a mental note to herself to do.

CONVINCING DENNY, the previous mailman, to take a long vacation was one of Zack's more difficult jobs at Homeland Security. Historically, the government went through people's mail, opening the contents and resealing them. The trouble nowadays was that much of the mail would pass through, unannounced. There was still a segment of the population, to which Gabe belonged, that did absolutely nothing online, making it difficult for Homeland Security to effectively monitor him without installing special surveillance tools. In addition, Gabe's bank was local, with only two branches, both in Annapolis. His checks were handwritten and because he paid nothing on the internet or by credit card, his purchasing patterns were impossible to track without alerting the local bank.

Another problem was if there was any delay in the mail, people quickly became suspicious, leading to additional problems. Sometimes the letter carriers would become suspicious, especially if unusual patterns of mail delivery began with long-time residents.

Just as Denny knew the types of mail Gabe received, Gabe knew Denny's patterns, so when Denny was 75 minutes late with his mail, Gabe was curious. When a man with a freshly shaved bald head slid his mail into a slot in the front door, Gabe was suspicious.

"What happened to Denny?" Gabe asked.

"He's ta- taking some ti- time off," said the tall man, stuttering.

"Taking time off? He never told me he was taking time off, and we talk almost every day."

The new mailman said nothing, nodding.

"What's your name?" asked Gabe.

He muttered something under his breath then he turned and left.

AS 7:00 P.M. ROLLED AROUND, Gabe turned off his computer, put on his sports coat and headed down the street. He was running a little late for his 7:30 appointment with his seat at the Marina Bar. He loved the ten minute walk to the bar. The sounds of boats and the sea birds flying overhead made him happy.

DRESSED ALL IN BLACK, the driver parked in front of Gabe's brick house in an equally black Chevy Suburban. He then walked to the back door and easily entered, as Gabe was prone to be trusting. In the forty years he lived there, there hadn't been a single break-in on the entire block.

Inside the house, he activated a powerful night vision system on his cap and walked confidently to Gabe's circuit breaker box. Because he had memorized the blueprints of Gabe's house over the past week, he quickly turned off the proper circuit.

Directed by his night vision system, he then headed to the office and saw Gabe's keyboard sitting on a cluttered desk. He shone his light on the recessed lighting fixture in the ceiling directly above the desk.

"Perfect," he muttered to himself.

With his hands unencumbered, he carefully climbed onto Gabe's desk after moving some papers carefully out of the way, sliding the fixture downward, which stopped comfortably on a metal coil on both sides of the latches. He easily remembered the latch mechanism from the training course he had taken, just as he knew the latches would stop without causing the light to fall.

He made some minor adjustments then placed some fast-setting putty to hold everything in place. He mounted a pen-sized camera containing a miniature microphone, aiming it so that it could monitor Gabe's keyboard, screen, and phone in the putty. Then he slid the light fixture back into place and climbed down.

He removed an I-Pod video box, activating it. Instantly, the I-Pod revealed the top of Gabe's desk. He then made some more adjustments, wiggling the camera until it also included the monitor. That way they could see what Gabe saw, hear what he heard, and see what he was typing. He hated these assignments where the target was so low tech. Life was much easier when there was high quality electronics to tap into.

He moved the papers back to where they had been and headed out the door. Then he checked his watch, seeing that two minutes time had elapsed.

HENDERSON WAS EDGY as he sat in his chair. His phone conversation was an unplanned call to the Homeland Security Department, something frowned upon by that department, as it was their policy to do the calling more so than being called.

"We'll take care of it," said Henderson. "I'm doing my best to calm Miss Perez down. Her suspicions are increasing, more than we had anticipated."

"What do you mean?" asked Zack.

"I know it's not in your interest to discuss politics, but she is avidly pro-life, something I didn't know until she discovered these results. We're not allowed to screen employees for political or religious viewpoints, you know."

"Why is that a problem?" asked Zack.

"She thinks she's looking at human cells now."

"They're *not* human," said Zack.

"*I* know they're not human, and *you* know they're not human, but *she* doesn't know that they're not human. The more she researches them, the more she's questioning whether or not they are human. She's not completely certain if they are, or if they're not. There is a scientific component to her research that is—"

"It's not the concerns of our office about the science, remember?"

"Hell, I know that, but my next call has to go into Senator Weinthrop, and believe me, his *only* concern is the science."

"What is she doing that caused you to call me today? I don't have time for this crap. What is the specific problem?"

"She's confused by the way the cells' DNA nearly perfectly matches human DNA. When they arrived, they correlated 88% with amphibian DNA, which is an industry standard. And amphibian DNA is quite different from human DNA."

"Yeah, so?" said Zack.

"But after she reprograms part of the D.N.A using her methodology, they move to the highest correlation with humans, which is too close to humans to suggest it's just a coincidence."

"So."

"I know you don't care about the science, but she does. She is a *scientist*, you know."

"And?" Zack was clearly irritated.

"She's our best scientist, and not just the best in terms of knowledge, she has the best work ethic, too. I think she can take it to 100%."

"That's her job, to take it to 100%. We *need* that 100%."

Henderson sighed. "The problem is that if she brings it to 100%, in essence, if she converts the amphibian DNA into human DNA, then she will believe— according to her religious beliefs—that she is working on human cells."

"That's your opinion. So what. They're not human."

"They will be human if she gets it to 100%," said Henderson. "That means she will think she has been working on human cells for years."

"But she hasn't killed anything. This is getting absurd. I gotta' go."

"I'm warning you, and I know you record all these calls. I'm warning you that it's going to cause a problem for all of us, if she thinks she's been killing human embryonic cells for the past few years. What you and I call 'finding the 100% match,' she will call genocide. And I mean, *genocide* that she *believes* she is conducting."

"Paraphrase this nonsense!" blurted Zack.

Henderson paused. "The same moment she could find the cure—the 100% match—something no one else has even come close to doing—is the same moment her ethical buttons will go nuts, because in her religious mind, finding that match proves she has been working on humans. The truth is in only the last DNA—the 100% one—the chain is human, and that's one she will never destroy. But the problem is she doesn't know she's been working with human cells. Holding back information from her about the nature of these cells hurts her ability to achieve the scientific discovery we need."

"You know, she can *never* be told what's classified about those cells," said Zack.

"I know. I know. But when she discovers the path to 100% correlation, she'll automatically discover the truth about them. It's inevitable."

As Zack hung up, he made a mental note to someday question Rita directly. (And hopefully someday soon!) He also realized that too much crap was piling up, leading him to privately fear that the whole project was going to implode.

SATELLITE "ARCHIE" WATCHED THE HOMES of suspected-terrorists in the mid-Atlantic region from its fixed orbit. Using the most advanced cameras and microphones that the agency had developed, ARCHIE was capable of monitoring hundreds of simultaneous targets within a two-hundred mile radius. It's technology was the most sophisticated ever developed, making it the military's most prized and confidential possession. No wonder it's focal point—the center of its territory—was 1600 Pennsylvania Avenue.

The only trouble with having ARCHIE add a suspected terrorist to its watch list was having to bump another suspected terrorist off the list. Watching someone was not the problem, nor was recording and comparing months (or even years) of notes. The trouble was making the programming changes to the confidential security surveillance procedures on a timely basis.

The terrorist list of 800 was more dangerous to national security than was the information collected from the 800. Realistically, going through years and years of data was a perennial budget battle. Just consider how many negative statements the average American household makes against the government in a year's time—taxes, spending, the War, pro- this and anti- that. Now, compare that to people already on the list of 800 targets, multiplied across tens of thousands of short conversations, most of which were in complicated languages, needing interpretations beyond what a computer satellite could quickly provide.

Considering all the red tape, even Zack—in spite of all his connections—had a difficult time bumping the bottom five targets: two Iranians, a former Russian ambassador, a Chinese scientist and a hooker with ties to a senator, off the terrorist list, just to add the likes of Gabe, Nate, Rita, Harland, and Sandra. To avoid further scrutiny—and to push the process more quickly—he added all their names to a high risk classification, which included those involved with Weapons of Mass Destruction, such as bio-terrorism, which required Code 24 clearance, something only a handful of people in the government had.

Code 24 clearance was even higher than the clearance level of a U.S. President, which meant no U.S. senators could see it, except for the chairman on the Senate Intelligence Committee. And since, the chairman knew the 800 names were frequently shuffled, he did not usually view the changes. In essence, the higher the clearance, the more difficult it was to challenge the date's credibility.

It was a sneaky strategy, but one that usually worked. Ironically, the information from the four innocent civilians (plus Harland) was collectively dangerous enough to change the course of genetic science and Project M.I.X. Although the government was capable enough to divide the information so no one person had all the components to properly fit together the puzzle, if those five people shared their knowledge as a group, spending hours of time deciphering what they knew—and when they knew what they knew—they could permanently change the direction of the project.

Although it was not likely that Gabe, Nate, Rita, Harland, and Sandra would meet and have ample time to decipher their knowledge and data, it was nevertheless a strong enough possibility that it could not be ignored. Fortunately, if even one person in the group didn't join the others, then the margin of error was great enough that national security would not be breached. However, if the five *did* get together, they could ruin twelve years of top-secret work—rooted again in the Marshall Islands—and force all the current genetic research to stop. Sure, the project could be shut down and restarted with different players, but to develop it to where they had them now would take years—longer than anyone had patience for.

AT 1600 HOURS, Zack, Brad, and Erin started their weekly meeting.

"So, what have we accomplished and learned in the last 24 hours?" asked Zack, adding sugar to his coffee.

Brad was quick to respond. "Gabe Channing's house is fully wired and completely operational. Plus, the mail is now delayed for just one additional hour, so it can be fully analyzed before delivery. The surveillance is now operational and we've got devices planted on Miss Perez, Mr. Parker, Nate Baschard, and that Sandra O'Callahan quack."

"What about the terrorist list?" asked Zack, stirring his coffee. "Do you think anyone will suspect Project M.I.X. may be leaked?"

"I'm not sure," said Erin. "The situation needs to develop more before I can analyze it properly."

Brad's computer monitor popped up an instant message. "N.S.A. just approved the next step. They should all be neutralized in no more than a month."

DEAR DIARY, May 5, 1982.
Tonight I am leaving on Hugo new boat, named after me—*Ellen's Adventure*. In all there will be four of us: myself, Hugo, Jason and Amy. Although we're planning to vacation for about a month, I've made a promise to myself that I'm going to continue to write in this diary on a daily basis. In spite of this being the longest vacation of my life and the most technology-free one to date, I don't want to stop my habit of writing in my diary, which I have been doing every day since June 2, 1974, my sixteenth birthday. I'm a little annoyed that I forgot to bring a camera. I'll try to sketch a little if I see anything really worth the effort, though.

We're planning on hopping through the Loyalty Islands, then to Fiji, Vanuatu, Tuvalu, through the Gilbert Islands, then to the Marshall Islands, the Caroline Islands, past Papua New Guinea, then onto the Solomon Islands, to New Caledonia and then finally back to North Cape, New Zealand. It's an ambitious schedule, but Hugo thinks he can do it in one month, and I believe him. Jason has his doubts, though.

Amy plans on writing poetry during the trip. I guess we'll be doing our writing as the men talk sports over games of chess.

One thing, though, that seems to keep popping into my thoughts is that Hugo has some ulterior motive for this trip. Why did he insist we sail this route anyways? Why the Marshall Islands? Plus, all that new gear he just purchased makes me think he's hoping to capture something strange, something really big, something that lives in the sea and needs an aquatic habitat to survive. I think he wants to capture something alive and bring it back home.

Every time I question him, he says he doesn't know what I'm talking about, then changes the subject.

And Jason. He either knows and isn't saying anything or Hugo has him in the dark, too.

BUILD-UP TO A MEETING
CHAPTER FIVE

AFTER A MONTH AND A HALF of barely working on his article, Gabe, dressed in a sports-coat and tie, walked into the busy Santa Maria Restaurant at 5:05 p.m. on a Friday and sat on his usual bar stool, next to an empty one.

"Did someone die?" asked Jasmine as she began playing a blues piece.

Gabe smirked at her comment, then adjusted his tie as he pulled out a business card and put it on the bar, waiting for Marti to greet him.

Marti poured a Jim Beam and Coke and slid it over to Gabe. "Hey old man, Carley said someone you know died."

Carley grinned as she put some ketchup and mustard next to Gabe. "Jasmine gets credit for that one," said Carley. "But you sure do look like someone died."

"Can't a man wear a sport-coat without someone wise-cracking a joke? Believe it or not, I actually have an appointment here at 5:30."

Marti noticed Gabe's business card "Well, what is this? The Channing Group?"

"I bet I'm the first person you gave one to," said Marti, who then headed off to help a new customer who just walked in.

Dressed in a dark suit and wearing dark glasses, the new customer sat at a stool next to Gabe and quietly leafed through a menu.

Gabe looked at his watch: 5:12 p.m. He took a long first gulp of his drink. When he put the glass down, he noticed a handsome young man in a blue pinstripe suit walk into the bar as he talked on a mobile phone. Gabe stood to greet him. "You must be Nate Baschard, with First Global Investments?"

Nate smiled. "Gabe Channing?"

"In the flesh. This is as close as I get to an office, so I hope you don't mind meeting me here."

As Gabe greeted Nate, the stranger placed a small eyeglass case on the bar and—positioning it just right—gently pressed it once.

Secretly, Jasmine glanced over at the stranger and adjusted a microphone so that the end of it was pointing straight towards Nate.

"I like this place," said Nate as he adjusted his high-tech phone to vibrate mode and put it on the bar in front of him. "It's an even better place since it went smokeless."

"I gave up smoking after they made all those stupid laws against it. Back in my day, I did cigars, but nothing more. . . . I'm so glad you drove all this way from New York City to meet me. And you're even early."

Nate sighed. "New York is a long trip, but not too long. I had a meeting at two around the corner from here. I frequently meet with biotech firms, so meeting you was not a big problem, aside from having trouble finding a parking space."

"Yeah, parking can be a real bear out here," said Gabe as he opened a cluttered briefcase. "Fridays are the worst. I don't even have elbow room here at the bar." He then reached down to grab his briefcase, opening it atop the bar, with all its contents clearly visible to Nate. Gabe rummaged for his yellow notepad and a pen, removing various items. First, he removed a pile of notes, then bills, and then a small stack of business cards, bound together with a rubber band.

"Where is my pen? I thought I put one in here just before I left the house."

The spectacle gave Nate time to take in the contents of the briefcase, and to read them. Eventually, Gabe found the right file sitting on top of a thin, well-worn phone book and put it in front of both of them.

"Alright," Gabe began, still looking for his pen. "Let's begin."

"Hey Marti," Gabe called out to Marti. "Do you have a pen I can borrow? I can't seem to find mine."

Marti, who was talking with another customer, turned to face him. "*Borrow* a pen? I can't remember the last time you returned one."

"Oh come on, Marti," said Gabe. "I just need a freakin' pen. Can I have one for God's sake?"

"Let me see if I can find one."

"Thanks," said Gabe.

Marti walked towards the cash register while Gabe's eyes casually followed her, giving Nate a brief opportunity to glance at the stack of business cards and the open file. He recognized his own business card on the top, which made him wonder where Gabe got it, because he knew he had never given it to him. The notes were confusing, too. It seemed everyone he called was listed with a note that marked the person as busy or not available.

Marti walked back over to Gabe, tossing him a pen, heavily chewed on the end. "Here," said Marti, smugly. "You left this here the other day. It has your name all over it. And God knows no one else will use it."

"Thanks, Marti, you always say the nicest things," Gabe said as he shot daggers at her with his eyes.

"Yeah whatever," she said as another customer called her attention.

Gabe smirked. "I've been coming to this joint for forty years, and you'd think they'd give me just a little respect."

"Forty years?" asked Nate, scratching his head. "I can't fathom forty years in one location. I've never lived in one place for more than five."

"Yeah, forty years. Let me see. I started at the *Triangle* in 1967, when I was twenty-five. Now, that would be, ah, *forty*-some years. Marti's been here for the last twenty We go way-y-y back." Gabe grinned as he scribbled the date on his notepad, while Nate sat back and shook his head, in amazement.

"I can only imagine," said Nate as he stared at the cards and Gabe's notes. "Looks like you've been busy making calls about this story."

Gabe gazed at his notes, only then realizing they were directly in front of Nate. "Yeah, I've been up to my eyeballs with this story. People aren't too eager to talk about their retirement plans."

"Why are you writing the story then?" asked Nate.

Gabe stared into thin air for a moment, then said, "Well, it's just the right thing to do, kid. It's just the right thing to do." Gabe maneuvered out of his chair. "Hey Nate, you don't mind if I hit the john do you?"

"No, go right ahead," said Nate.

"Can you watch my stuff while I'm gone?"

"Sure."

Gabe headed out of the bar, leaving Nate alone with the open file and stack of business cards in front of him.

The bar was loud as people laughed as they drank, typical of what would be expected during a Friday happy hour. Nate reached for his phone to check his messages. The high-tech phone was able to receive emails and take color photographs. With its games and electronic writing pad, it was a perfect tool to use on the road.

Nate fiddled with his phone, twirling it in a playful way as he began to read Gabe's notes. Then he picked up the bundle of business cards and tapped them against the marble bar top. Nate looked around the bar to see if anyone was watching, particularly Marti, because Gabe was obviously a long-time friend of hers. Then he quickly unraveled the rubber band and placed the cards on the bar. Impulsively, he took a quick photograph of the business cards, slyly positioning his phone near his right ear, as if he was lazily leaning his arm on the bar. Quickly, he then gathered the cards together and spread out the notes, four sheets at a time in the small space in front of him. He took several photographs before he started to worry about Gabe returning. He restacked the papers just as the door opened and Gabe reentered the room.

Brad looked over at Erin. Nate taking pictures of materials from Gabe's briefcase was an unexpected twist. Who was using whom? And why? Brad shrugged while he talked into a walkie-talkie, "Try to get a close up on that."

The ordeal—which only lasted about a minute—provided Nate with vital information, a trick he used frequently throughout his young career. Just as teens steal merchandise from stores, Nate stole data, thriving on it. Reading seemingly useless data was fun for him. Gabe's openness caught his fancy. How did Gabe get his business card? And why would he so openly show him all the notes in his briefcase? *No* reporter was *that* sloppy. As he waited for Gabe to retake his seat, his suspicions of the old man grew steadily. He deduced that there was more to Gabe Channing than his pursuit of a simple retirement story.

IN A HOTEL IN WASHINGTON, D.C., Nate uploaded his photographs of Gabe Channing's business cards into his laptop, using the WiFi link between it and his handheld P.D.A. He then zoomed in on the photographs, reading each one.

In all, there were eighteen business cards. Eight were in the biotech sector, four were journalists, three were in the military, and another three were in watchdog groups. (His was the only card in business, which he lumped together with the biotechs, because that was the sector he covered.) Interestingly, only his card was from an area outside of the Mid-Atlantic region.

It was a mix of contacts that seemed to have nothing that logically bound them together, or at least nothing that Nate could quickly conceive. Fourteen in the group were men, and four women, typical numbers for people in powerful positions. However, it was their influential positions that intrigued him the most. All were in mid-level or upper-level management with titles indicating college degrees and multiple advanced degrees.

The question, though, that puzzled him the most was how his own business card was in the mix. Nothing about it was logical, either. When he had asked Gabe about why he was contacted, Gabe would always stick with his explanation that he was randomly contacted through a computer-generated list. Although he wanted to confront Gabe over the card, he did not believe it was an effective maneuver, because Gabe would then confront him about how he knew about all the cards in the first place. And, since Nate frequently resorted to photographing data with his high-tech phone, he refrained from hurting his professional career in the process.

Furthermore, there was a business name which Nate had distinctively recognized: GenXY, a Rockville biotech, the business card belonging to Rita Perez, whose title was "Senior Researcher." He had recognized the name because he owned thousands of shares in GenXY and followed it in his research. It stood out because its stock price was appreciating faster, percentage-wise, than all other companies in his portfolio.

GenXY's exponential growth was illogical, and Nate realized that what David Spelling was saying made perfect sense. Nate had added the company to his portfolio initially on a lark, long before he became a professional stock analyst. Originally, to remain neutral with the companies in his portfolio, he used the old dart-throwing technique for half of his holdings and then each quarter the underperformers were expelled while replacement companies were added using the same throw-the-dart method. Although the method was not scientific (and perhaps not even good business), it was fun. Since it was random, it provided him with the names of companies he might never have otherwise considered. Having used random selection over several years, he trusted his methodology. It provided him with a bedrock of business philosophy: keep initial qualifier variables simple. (The other half of his holdings were divided among companies he followed professionally.)

After further investigation, Gabe's notes revealed he had only interviewed four people: himself, Harland Parker (Major with the Department of Defense), Sandra O'Callahan (Legal analyst with Watchdog Group), and Rita Perez (Senior Researcher with GenXY). Out of pure curiosity, Nate decided to contact each person, beginning with Rita.

THE REPORT WAS IN AN ORANGE BINDER, tied with a single, black elastic band, similar to those that women used to tie their hair. Brad was even more serious than normal, tone deaf to humor of any sort. "I've got the report on Gabriel Channing," said Brad. "Here's his file."

Erin nodded. "He's not exactly the type to be toying with government agencies."

"Isn't that the preliminary report?" asked Zack.

Brad was expressionless. "No. That's the whole thing."

Zack reached for it, removing its black band and silently flipping through the papers.

"Come on, Brad," said Zack, prodding. "I've been here long enough to say that no report has *ever* been this sparse."

Brad paused before he answered. "Just because most people trigger 200-page reports, doesn't mean we can't find someone sometimes with only thirty pages."

Zack flipped to the last page. "Correction, twenty-nine pages."

"I was including the index," said Zack.

"Let me see that again," said Erin, reaching for the report and quickly flipping to one of the pages. "From what I've read in here, there's *nothing* about him that would alarm *anyone*."

Brad shook his head. "It's the story he could be writing that's the problem, not him. This agency doesn't want that story coming out. Ever. . . . Under any circumstance whatsoever. It's got to be killed."

Zack stared at Brad. "You mean the story, right?"

Brad was silent for a moment. "Let me ask this one question: why has he contacted so many people on our *top* suspected terrorist list?"

Zack said nothing.

Erin lobbed the report onto the table. "From what I see so far, he looks to be a straight and narrow person, an upright American citizen."

"Yeah, and right on target," said Zack, refuting her.

"Only a genius could have found *all* these people that fast," said Brad. "He has connections, and it's our job to stop him from asking more questions. The world is definitely not ready for the truth about the Marshall Islands."

Erin sighed. "There's only one thing on his record that's off."

"What?" asked Zack and Brad, in unison.

"There's a story he wrote a few years back that won an award. Something about the Annapolis firehouse burning down."

"I think I know that story," said Zack. "Something about the mayor out there, ah . . . Jake Malone."

"That's right," said Erin. "There was a scandal about Mayor Malone and a mistress. The rumor is Channing provided his cover for that story. Who knows, maybe he's feeding this reporter guy, Channing, the list of *our* top secret names. I haven't ruled it out yet as a variable."

Zack squinted his eyes, deep in thought. "The only problem is that Mayor Malone is *everybody's* best friend in Washington. He's the only politician I know who doesn't have a single enemy."

Brad smirked. "Yeah, and everybody knows he owes Channing a huge favor."

BEING A RESEARCH ANALYST at a major Wall Street house has its advantages. Scheduling quick meetings was one of them. All Nate had to do was call the company's chief financial officer and mention the number of shares of stock First Global Investments held in the company, and soon he would be given access to its records and key personnel. Indeed, just a little knowledge of the Sarbanes-Oxley Act provided countless miracles for him when in a pinch with a bull-nosed accountant. (Following the Enron debacle, all chief executive officers were personally responsible for accurate financial reporting under Sarbanes-Oxley.)

After a relatively quick phone call to the chief financial officer (and a quick reference to Sarbanes-Oxley legislation), Nate was immediately given a time slot with Henderson Duvall, to "discuss whatever public financial information was deemed necessary to share."

TEN MINUTES BEFORE 9 O'CLOCK ON MONDAY, Nate parked his rental car in the first visitor's parking space of GenXY Corporation and confidently headed to the receptionist area. As he entered the building, he immediately saw a digital sign, welcoming him to the business, a courtesy practiced by most large firms. A chipper young woman in a buttoned-down white blouse welcomed him as he gave her his business card.

"Hello . . . Angie," Nate said, after quickly reading her name plate. "I'm Nate Baschard. . . . I have an appointment to see Mister Henderson Duvall."

Angie said, "Let me page his office. I know he's expecting you."

"Okay."

"Can I get you a cup of coffee or tea?"

"No thanks," Nate answered, removing his laptop from the carrying case. "I'm fine."

Angie glanced at him, and pointed to an outlet in the corner of the room. "Why don't you have a seat and make yourself comfortable. You can plug that in over there. The WiFi is free, and available to everyone."

"Thanks," said Nate.

For twenty minutes, Nate sat on a leather couch and read an article in *Science Today* about the ethics behind gene splicing in animals. The article was written by Klaus Hausman, a bio-ethicist in Berlin who warned against the risks of "the ease of flipping the binary switches of junk DNA." He warned: "the risk of changing the DNA code could end up greatly exceeding the anticipated benefits of junk D.N.A, about 96% of a DNA molecule's structure. I can't over-emphasize this risk. Junk DNA could theoretically be more damaging than all the nuclear weapons in the world. I believe there is a great risk of radically changing our slow methodological evolution for the worse."

"True, we might be able to eliminate genetic-based health issues. And, true, we may be able to speed our evolution into a productive direction. But it is *at least* equally likely that we will unleash changes we had no clue we could unleash. Further, those changes could end up spawning the undoing of mankind as we know it."

AFTER MEETING WITH HENDERSON on the finances of GenXY, Nate was shown into a laboratory, where Rita was comparing cell structures on four large, overlapping flat-screen computer monitors. When Nate and Henderson entered the room, she didn't even look up, being deeply entrenched in her work.

Nate had done well in manipulating Henderson to let him see Rita. Obviously, he could not just walk into GenXY and ask to see its leading scientist, so he had to maneuver with his questions to gain access to her. He knew he had only a couple minutes to get to the heart of why Gabe had her business card, leading to why Gabe had contacted her.

Henderson was fidgety, a subtle indication that he would only permit Nate to speak with Rita for a few minutes. Henderson said, "Rita, I'm sorry to bother you, but this is Nate Baschard, an analyst with First Global Investments, a company which is one of our company's *biggest* investors and definitely a strong advocate for the biotech industry."

Rita did not budge from staring at her computer monitors, continuing to observe the cells' developments. Her voice was without feeling or inflection as she spoke. "Hello, sir. Is there something I can help you with?"

Nate cleared his throat. This was not going to be easy. He decided to jump immediately to the core of his dilemma, hoping to draw Rita away from her intense absorption in her work. "I've read about the ethics of these types of experiments concerning junk DNA. It's a highly interesting topic, even for a layman."

Rita continued to stare at the cells and to take notes. Then she turned to finally face him with a bright smile that caught Nate off guard. "You're referring to the latest article in *Science Today*, the one by Klaus Hausman. His junk DNA rhetoric has turned some heads within the field, as well as that of some rather vocal politicians."

Nate returned her smile, knowing he had finally grabbed the attention of one of America's leading biotech scientists.

With stunning green eyes that had a hint of yellow, Rita broke many geek stereotypes. Her beautiful light brown hair, reached halfway down her back. It was impossible for him to not notice her slim figure, despite the lab coat she wore. He knew she was a smart scientist, but Rita Perez was certainly not what he expected. He caught his breath.

I could be attracted to this woman on a personal level, Nate thought. But this visit was for business, and he was not about to let personal feelings interfere with his career.

"I'm sorry, I didn't get you name," said Rita, removing a clear, rubber glove and extending her hand towards Nate. "I'm Dr. Rita Perez."

They shook hands. "I'm Nate Baschard, an analyst with First Global Investments. I've studied some of your company's work, and respected it enough to buy a few thousand shares of your stock. Now I can see why my personal investment is paying off." He panned the high-tech equipment and nodded, approving of it.

"Why thank you. A number of us contribute to our company's scientific breakthroughs and patents. Frankly, the financial side of the business is Greek to me. I'm always the one spending the money and they're the ones selling what little I discover. I really don't see how we make all our money, though I haven't given it much thought."

"You're being too hard on yourself again," said Henderson as he edged towards the door, ready to end Nate's little tour. "It's *your* work that's keeping stockholders like him happy."

Nate knew he had one final opportunity to find out Gabe's interest in her. "I get interviewed pretty frequently," he said. "Last week a reporter asked me about my business philosophy, so I told him I believe business solves the world's problems. Ultimately, capital naturally shifts to sectors with steady expansion."

Rita tilted her head. "My philosophy is different. I believe it's science that unites our world. Doesn't sound money follow sound science?"

Henderson opened the door, signaling for Nate to leave.

Nate leaned toward the door. "That's why I have a retirement portfolio, dedicated exclusively to stocks like GenXY, for issues wrapped around topics like these."

Rita shifted as she stood. "Come to think about it, a reporter called me last week about my retirement options, too. You never really know the true motives behind people these days."

As Nate and Henderson left the room and walked down a long corridor, he wondered what else Rita knew. Ironically, Rita wondered the same thing about Nate.

PENETRATING THE PENTAGON WITH A MISSILE may be nearly impossible (given the recently installed defenses), but a phone call might be able to do far more damage. Nate could not barge his way into the Pentagon, so a phone call had to suffice. From reading Gabe's notes, Nate knew Gabe and Harland spoke on the phone for about twenty minutes, an unusually long time for a phone call into the bowels of the nation's most secure building.

For the next three days, Nate routinely dialed the number four times a day from his mobile phone, always at different times, with the hope that eventually someone would answer, considering the odd fact that there was no voicemail. Finally, a heavy voice answered.

"Pentagon Office of Ethical Weapons. Major Harland Parker here."

Unhesitantly, Nate spoke. "Major Parker, this is Nate Baschard, Research Analyst with First Global Investments. It seems you and I were both called by a Gabe Channing, the president of The Channing Group regarding a retirement story he is conducting. Are you familiar with it?"

Harland paused before he answered, looking at a stack of phone records. "I see by my phone records, you have called my line twelve times. What is it that you want?"

"Gabe Channing's call was a peculiar one. My sector of specialty is biotech. I've contacted a few other people he called and you were next on my list. I was wondering what linked us all together. Does your job involve biotech in any way?" asked Nate.

Harland paused. "Are you calling me about that article on retirement planning?"

Nate answered, "Yes, but I don't know why he's really calling people, and I'm hoping you have some more information for me."

"I don't know a thing about that," said Harland. "Besides, I'm not authorized to discuss non-job related subjects on a government line. I have to go. Goodbye—"

"Wait!" Nate pleaded, but it was useless. Harland was gone.

NATE'S TECHNIQUE WITH HARLAND WAS UNSUCCESSFUL, leading him to use a different tactical approach with Sandra O'Callahan. Although her business card revealed she was a legal analyst with Watchdog Group, he began with a simple search on the internet, a tool Nate used frequently while conducting research, especially about intriguing people. He simply put her into the search engine and discovered there were only three people with that unique name in the mid-Atlantic region, and only one worked with The Watchdog Group.

Further searching revealed she was into skiing, just like him. It showed she was in her twenties, and that she was actively dating, or at least trying to date on one of those matching services, making her profile quite helpful. Within minutes, Nate knew her published likes and dislikes. If he could meet her, he now thought he knew enough about her personality to cleverly push her right buttons, not to mention which buttons to avoid. Her work address was in Dupont Circle, in Washington, D.C. Now the problem was how to casually meet her.

UNSURE OF WHAT WAS MOTIVATING HIM, but inspired by an insatiable curiosity, Nate re-reviewed his photographs of Gabe's business cards and files. Taking photographs was his way of recording many of life's important moments. With his father dead—killed in Iraq during Desert Storm—and a mother in Wisconsin he rarely saw, Nate developed a habit of recording whatever caught his fancy with his cameras.

When Nate got home, he pulled up the file of photographs and notes on his computer and zoomed in on them one at a time. Aside from himself, the most interesting person whose business card he had was that of Sandra O'Callahan. Her position as a legal analyst was inconsistent among the other business cards, which were primarily of biotech people and military types.

He was not in the mood to over-think a phone call. Instead, he merely picked up his cell phone and made the call to her office, triggering her voicemail.

"Hello, this is Nate Baschard, a research analyst. I received a call from a Gabe Channing last week and believe you have, too. It may sound presumptuous on my part, but I believe there is a peculiar reason this reporter has contacted a number of people, including you and me. Please call me at this phone number so we can talk about Mr. Channing and the increasingly profitable biotech sector."

HARLAND HAD BEEN WORKING DILIGENTLY for six straight hours in his office at the Pentagon when there was a knock on the wall—not on the door. Since visitors rarely came to his area in the basement, anyone appearing at his door definitely wanted to do more than start a flip conversation about the weather or the Washington Nationals.

Seeing the rank of the knocking officer, Harland stood and snapped to attention, saluting him. "Yes, sir."

Before him stood Admiral Ernie Ritten. "At ease, Major. . . . Sit down."

"Yes, sir," said Harland, sitting as upright as possible in his wooden chair.

"We understand you have been communicating with civilians about some of the files in this department."

"Excuse me, sir?"

"We don't have a lot of time, and I know you're busy, so I don't want to waste anyone's time with small talk. Am I making myself clear?"

Harland swallowed. "Yes, sir."

"Now, what do you know about Nate Baschard, and what do you know about Gabe Channing?"

BEING A LATE RISER, Sandra was never happy to greet the morning, though she was always eager to work late. At 10:01 a.m. she listened to her messages, paying special attention to Nate's call. Ironically, it was not his words that intrigued her, but the odd clicks in the background during the call. Her ear was acutely tuned to variations in tone, a trait she developed in law school while questioning witnesses. Previously, the clicking sounds made her think Gabe's phone had been recording her. Yet, when she had called her girlfriend to meet for lunch, she noticed the same clicking. Now she was certain she was being monitored.

Nate's reference to Gabe convinced her that Gabe's earlier phone call was also tapped. Now, if Nate's call to Sandra contained clicks—and if Gabe's call to Sandra contained clicks—why would they both want to record her? The trouble was that up until the call from Gabe—no other call on Sandra's phone contained those same quick, muffled sounds. Now it seemed that *every* call clicked, whether the calls were incoming or outgoing.

Sandra was serious about her job, passionately trying to marry the entities of government and business to ethically solve world problems. She had been a crusader for many years, willing to be arrested if a superior viewpoint needed to be triumphantly emphasized. But why would a journalist and a financial guy want to tap *her* phone? Were all her calls being monitored, or just some of them?

SAD AND ALONE, Gabe sat at the bar. Such was his life, a writer only popular in his own town, never married and no kids either. In some respects, Marti was not only his best friend, she also may have been his *only* friend, though there was always his "Mistress." He sloshed his ice tonight, a little more slowly than most other night, not certain of the value of his life during retirement.

"You seem down tonight," said Marti.

"Nah," said Gabe.

"Usually you swish your ice after the second drink. Today you're swishing after the first."

Gabe downed what remained of his drink. "I'll have another, doll."

Marti paused. "It's been years since you called me 'doll.' . . . What's wrong, babe?"

"It's been years since you've called me 'babe.'"

Marti's bar was pretty empty, at least by the standards of a Tuesday night. Moments like this gave the two of them additional time to reminisce. "I've seen and done a lot in my life, and what do I have to show for it? What good are those hundreds of newspaper articles today, anyway? What did I accomplish?"

Marti cleaned a glass in the sink. "Wow! Where did all this originate from?"

"I mean it, Marti. What *have* I done in my life? The world's become too formulaic, and it's really not supposed to be that way; at least it shouldn't be."

"I know." She handed him another drink.

"There were several occasions when I could have written stories that could have really changed Annapolis, maybe even perhaps Washington, D.C. . . . I mean, how many newspaper stories have ever really made a significant difference in our country?"

"Just one."

"What?"

"Just one, I said."

Gabe was confused. "I don't understand."

"Not everything needs to be so obvious. Sometimes change comes slowly. I mean, how long has it taken you to write this retirement story?"

"Like a year."

"And how far along are you?" Marti asked.

"Oh, it's still just in the note phase."

"How many pages?"

"Hell, I don't know, Marti. Lots of pages."

"How many . . . specifically?"

Gabe sighed. "Ten. . . . Maybe twenty. It depends on how you count them."

Marti looked around to be certain no one was listening to her. "No one who works here knows I own this bar but you and the hotel owner."

"Yeah, so what?"

"I've been pulling some strings and talking to the hotel management. They're willing to pitch in for a dinner for you and all those people on your list that you've contacted."

"I've only interviewed four people."

"Well then, including you, that'll be dinner for five. I'm sure the hotel can cover dinner for just a handful of people, at least for good friends of mine. I have an allowance I can use from time to time."

"One guy probably isn't going to make it, though."

"Okay," said Marti. "We can set a place for him anyways."

Gabe was grateful, even if her generosity was apparent. Reluctantly, he agreed that bringing everyone to the restaurant would create a solid deadline by which he would definitely finish his story. Her idea was perfect!

GABE SAT ALONE, staring at his IBM. "I can't finish this story," he said to himself. "I still don't know enough about retirement and I've interviewed a ton of people in my lifetime. I'm stuck."

He sat, pecking away at his keyboard, slowly turning letters into words, then sentences, then finally into a paragraph. Progress was finally being made!

SANDRA AND NATE AGREED TO MEET at an Irish bar in the Dupont Circle area of Washington, D.C., an ideal location because it was loud and Sandra didn't trust discussing details over a telephone.

They sat on high chairs in a corner section of Biddy Milligan's, a pub with a counter that sprawled around much of the bar. A petite waitress with dark brown eyes approached them. Nate always seemed to notice the eyes first.

"Can I get you another round?" asked the waitress.

Nate looked at Sandra, who shrugged. "Sure," he said. "We'll do another."

Nate's internet search of Sandra aided him in pushing her right buttons. Over the past forty-five minutes, she had only now started to warm towards him. Two people making their living in different competitive worlds, they seemingly would have little in common.

"I still prefer New York over Washington," said Nate, looking out the window. "I think it's hard to find a cab here, compared to New York."

Sandra pointed out the window. "One . . . two, three, four . . . five . . . six and seven. There. That's seven cabs in Dupont Circle in just the past twenty seconds. It's the easiest place to find a cab in the District."

The waitress arrived with their drinks, then left. Nate and Sandra clinked glasses. "To Gabe."

Sandra grimaced, "To Gabe? The man who tapped my phone?"

"No," said Nate. "To the man who introduced us, indirectly."

Sandra returned to her aggressive questioning from earlier in the evening. "How do I know it's not you who bugged my phone instead of him?"

Sandra was now playing Nate. Similarly, she had also done an internet search on him, doing some sleuthing of her own. His background was clean, with not even a speeding ticket.

"I told you I didn't bug you," said Nate. "This Gabe guy seems pretty odd, though. I mean, he's been going to the same hotel bar every day for the past twenty or thirty years."

"Yeah, I've been to that bar, too," said Sandra. There was a long pause. Then a tractor-trailer passed by, filling the window with an advertisement about Aspen, Colorado, distracting them from noting the coincidence that they had both been there before.

"I love skiing in Aspen," said Nate.

"You ski in Aspen?" asked Sandra.

"Yeah, it's awesome," said Nate. My favorite place to stay is at the Green Mountain lodge, overlooking the slopes"

"Mine, too! That's amazing," said Sandra, her romance warning system starting to signal "alert!"

Nate sipped on his beer. "Yeah, I think looking at the mountains at sunrise from that location is one of the most beautiful on earth."

Sandra smiled. "I love that sunrise. It's one of the best nature spots I've ever seen, too, aside from maybe the Redwood Forest in California. The only problem with it is how expensive it is. I've never seen a place that charges an extra $75 more per night, per higher floor."

"That's the way they designed that place," said Nate. "It's profitable for them. Plus, the lower floors don't have the same great views."

Sandra's intent had been to talk about the bugging of their phones. Regardless, she was in no mood or condition to complicate her life any more than it already was by starting a relationship. Her Brazil trip was approaching and that was not an assignment she would even think about dropping out of. And, there was still the ambassador and the Marshall Island story to figure out. Since college, she had virtually turned off every man she had met, and here this Nate was hitting all her buttons perfectly. Almost, "too" perfectly she thought to herself. "So, do you really think someone's bugging our phones?"

"I don't know," he said. "What I do know, though, is I have all Gabe's business cards for this assignment and nothing adds up. Sure, I know he wants to meet with us now, but I'm still not sure if he's the dumbest reporter in the industry, or just plain lucky."

"He's brilliant," said Sandra, acting a bit inebriated. "Anyone who can tap all these phones has got real connections, no pun intended."

Secretly, her suspicion of Nate was rising. How did Nate get all of Gabe's business cards? And—better yet— why did he have them in the first place? Besides, Nate was starting to seem a lot more complicated than he was appearing to be.

Nate chuckled. "Yeah."

"It's not like he's a dumb cable technician or something, or someone who gets your internet connection up from a remote location when it's been down for a few hours."

"I think we need to stay in touch somehow without being monitored," Nate replied.

"I agree. What do you suggest?" asked Sandra, once again wondering about Nate's motive.

"Let's exchange phone numbers of trusted co-workers. Then, we could call each other on unmonitored lines."

"Perfect. Works for me."

Nate and Sandra simultaneously pulled out their cell phones and each pulled up the names of trusted friends. After exchanging the numbers via a cocktail napkin (to avoid the possibility of being bugged, they thought), they agreed to inform each other if they discovered anything new.

When the check came, Nate reached for it. Sandra countered his move by saying the next time was on her. As they walked out, Nate realized he was somewhat attracted to Sandra, and vice versa. They looked at each other for a lingering moment, shook hands, and then headed home their separate ways.

ERIN LOOKED AT BRAD. Erin said, "This Nate Baschard guy needs to be watched real close. He contacted Major Parker; he visited Rita Perez; and then now he's meeting with that Sandra O'Callahan chick from The Watchdog Group. Even if Gabe doesn't connect the dots, this Nate guy might!"

"I agree. We need to alert Zack A.S.A.P. Record those numbers they just exchanged. These two are starting to act suspiciously *together*," Brad replied.

DEAR DIARY, May 13, 1982.

I'm writing this during a severe storm just north of the Marshall Islands. Hugo says it's not a tropical storm, but it's pretty bad. I think we are all feeling a bit seasick. Amy and I have been in the cabin for almost the entire day. We haven't been able to eat. The rain and wind have damaged the boat's electronics, so we can't even radio for help. Like these guys would even admit needing help! I'm scared and hope we don't die.

That sounds lame. "I hope we don't die," but I'm not feeling exactly poetic right now. I'm just scared out of my mind."

We seem to be taking in water, too. I don't know if it's rainwater or a leak. Hugo thinks we need to find a sheltered cove to anchor in. Our maps aren't much help—not enough detail. I don't think the boat can take much more of this.

It's not clear if the boat itself is damaged or not. Hugo says we'll make it, but the boat definitely needs to be repaired. I hope we'll be okay.

UNIT DISPATCHED
CHAPTER SIX

AS THE BUSBOY WIPED DOWN THE TABLE and covered it with a white linen tablecloth, John, a waiter at the Marina Hotel, polished a knife with a cloth. "They're going to be here for hours," said John. "It'll definitely be a long evening. These aren't the type of people who just come and go. Gabe said they have a lot to go over."

"How many people are coming?" Carley asked.

"Four. Maybe five," said John. "He said he doesn't think the fifth guy's going to be here at all, but he wanted a place set for him, just in case. The reservation is for seven o'clock."

Carley shrugged. "I hate when people don't know how many people are coming for dinner."

"People? Gabe made the reservation."

"*Gabe?*"

"Yeah, Gabe."

"Really?" said Carley, polishing a base plate with a damp cloth. "It's unusual for Gabe to pay for all this. I mean, this is our nicest room, and he booked the whole thing? I thought it was under the reservation of the house."

John grinned. "It is. It's Marti's treat."

"Marti-i-i? I've never known Gabe to have his own room, except for the time when he was with the mayor. And that's been over a year now."

John began to fold napkins. "I think she owes him and now that he's retired, Gabe isn't invited to much anymore. He's definitely out of the loop and I think she felt sorry for him."

'What about that story he's writing? He's been working on that thing for like a year now. Doesn't sound like he's ever going to complete it at this pace."

John smirked. "No, Marti tells me he's about to finish that story. He called all the people he interviewed, to get them all to sign disclaimers or something. He doesn't want to get sued, especially on his first freelance job."

"How long have they known each other?" asked Carley.

"These people?" he asked, pointing to the settings at the table.

"No, Gabe and Marti?"

"Twenty years," said John.

"Damn, I'm not even thirty years old. How long have you worked here?"

"Eight years," John answered. "Hard to believe, huh? When you're in the same job for *that* long, you get to know a lot about people. A whole lot."

A busboy approached a table with a group of businessmen.

"Who's the new busboy?" asked Carley.

"Juan," but he doesn't speak a word of English. Marti says management hired him just today. She didn't even have a say in the matter. First time that's happened since she started managing the bar ten years ago. Odd, huh?"

"Yeah, real odd. . . . Oh, and get a load of those suits he's talking with," she said, motioning past the ferns and towards a table near Gabe's seat at the bar. "He looks like he's saying something to me."

"Maybe they speak Spanish," said John.

"Yeah, maybe," said Carley as she started to slowly head over in their direction. As she started to get within listening range, all of a sudden one of the suits caught her movement and the conversations ended abruptly. Then Carley called out to Juan," Hey, you . . . ah . . . Juan."

"No Hablo Inglese," he replied, then headed into the kitchen.

AS HIS MOTHER WALKED OUT THE FRONT DOOR with young Sterling, Harland had an uneasy feeling in the pit of his stomach. He knew Sterling would have a great time spending the weekend at his grandma's house. She always spoiled him rotten. But this time, well, he felt something odd. He gave Sterling a big hug and told him to be good for his grandma. He knew he would; he always was.

Following behind them, Harland stepped out of his Capitol Hill townhouse and headed to the Metro, the subway system in Washington, D.C. Wearing a dark, blue suit and a striped grey tie, and carrying a thick stack of files, he was all dressed up for Gabe's dinner party, though he told no one he was going there other than his mother. He figured he didn't know anyone who cared anyhow. Still, he thought, first impressions were important. As he walked to the subway entrance, his mind wandered back to the events that had convinced him to accept Gabe's invitation.

Making phone calls to reporters was certainly not a habit of his. The saber rattling from the security at the Pentagon was all he could handle. He had rehearsed the scenes in his mind several times over the past month, remembering how each of the four calls had gone as he reconstructed each conversation in excellent detail. During none of them had he said anything important or even remotely relevant to national security—not to Gabe, nor to Nate. His conversation with Gabe was minimal, maybe five minutes at most. The other time was merely a voicemail from Gabe. When Nate called, he declined to give any information. Everyone in the Pentagon knew sharing information was prohibited—and dangerous. The fourth call was a voicemail message from Gabe to attend a party, an invitation Harland had planned to decline until the brass rattled his saber by rattling theirs with a visit to the basement.

Harland was as loyal to the government as they came. Following in his deceased father's footsteps, Harland would never have even considered doing something that could be considered reckless, which made him all the more upset—unnerved in fact—when an admiral with a higher rank, no less, accused him of being disloyal. Once Harland was accused of disloyalty, it crossed the line.

The stacks of paperwork that could never be properly read, the thousands of hours of work that was needed to honorably evaluate their proper intent could wait.

Never in his career had he had the stereotypical "knock on the door." Now, he no longer felt safe, especially in the quiet quarters of the Pentagon's basement. He was already an owned man, a man who owed his career to the government, and his future, too.

Harland's fear was that if the admiral was sent, then the D.O.D. must have sent him. And if the general sent him, then his career path was, at a minimum, on hold. And, he deduced, that if the general was unhappy with him for *thinking* he was being disloyal, then he would never gain his trust again. But why would a brief conversation and a simple voicemail ruin his earnest and loyal reputation?

Soon Harland was on the train to the New Carrolton stop, where he planned to take a taxi for the last leg of his journey. Since Harland did not own a car, public transportation was his usual form of travel. To him, it was inexpensive, efficient, and safe compared to car payments, maintenance, repairs, insurance, parking, and gas.

GABE SAT AT HIS BARSTOOL at 6:30 p.m., waiting for his guests to arrive. He was dressed in his best suit: a seersucker with padded elbows, a tie and semi-polished shoes.

"Get a load of those shoes," said Carley, sarcastically. "You're the best dressed man in Annapolis."

Marti turned to face Gabe, immediately pouring him a Jim Beam and Coke. "Why the nervous face, Gabe? This should be a big day for you."

"I've just got a lot on my mind," said Gabe, looking around the room.

"You mean like our little wager?" smirked Marti, still hoping to collect on their bet.

"Yeah, that and a whole lot more. I'm getting old, and with this writing stuff and all well. These people are pretty important."

Marti shook her head. "By the way, the room is now ready for you. All you need is the people and we can start."

"You know I'm thankful for all the strings you pulled for me, right?"

Marti handed him his drink. "Don't worry baby, you'll be fine."

As Gabe raised his glass, Jasmine looked over at him. "Name a song, Gabe."

Gabe thought for a second before he answered. "How about that Grateful Dead song, you, know, 'Ship of Fools'?"

"Sure thing," she replied, launching into a bluesy rendition of it.

AT 6:31 P.M., A RED LIGHT PULSED on a color monitor, drawing the immediate attention of Brad at the Homeland Security Department. Brad was busy attacking his egg salad sandwich, something that remained uneaten once he saw the light blink. To him, his job dedication was a way of life, not merely something just important to do.

H.S.A. had a practice of monitoring their internal people with top-secret clearances. Since Gabe had contacted several of the names on the terrorist watch list, including someone in the Pentagon, Major Harland Parker became the greatest concern of the H.S.A., due to his high-level clearance and the background of his father's apparent death.

"We have a hit," said Brad into a radio, swallowing another bite of his sandwich then washing it down with some lukewarm coffee. "Major Parker just got onto the Metro in Capitol Hill. He's probably heading to New Carrolton. Copy?"

"Copy and confirmed," said Unit 53-A from the New Carrolton train stop. "I'll be waiting for him."

"Ten-four."

WEARING A DARK GREEN BLOUSE AND A LONG GREY SKIRT, Rita walked into the bustling hotel bar at 6:45 p.m., carrying a briefcase on her way to meet Gabe. Being shy, Rita certainly was not a fan of small talk. She was far too dedicated to her job to waste the time that romance required. Her research into the mysteries of the genetic code intrigued her far more than any man ever had, or could, or so she thought.

"I'm here to see Mr. Channing," said Rita. "I believe he's expecting me for dinner."

Gabe swirled the ice in his drink, then rose to shake hands with her. "Hello, Rita. I'm Gabe Channing,

President of The Channing Group. Thanks so much for coming."

"Hello and thanks for the invitation." Rita glanced at the bar, seeing Gabe's briefcase, wondering if their whole meeting was planned at the bar.

It was a thorough enough glance that Gabe quickly responded. " I have the Seiler Room reserved for us, just past those ferns. They'll be a small group of us in there."

"Group? How many are coming?"

"It's just you and me, and two or three others," Gabe answered.

Confused and wary, Rita wrinkled her nose. "Why are there so many people here—all at the same time—just to sign a disclaimer?"

"It's my first freelance article and I thought I'd share my new start with all of you. It's not every day a man restarts his career as a writer."

Rita saw no sense to press the issue further. "There was a man who visited my office last month, a Nate-something. Is he one of your guests by any chance?"

Gabe's eyes widened. "That's interesting that you know his name. It makes no sense how he would even know to contact you."

"He said he's a stockholder in the company where I work: GenXY."

As they spoke, Sandra O'Callahan, dressed in a black cocktail dress, black pearls, and heels walked into the bar. Listening to an I-Pod, she was cute enough to draw the attention of two men wearing Washington Nationals caps. Their heads turned as she passed.

"I'm sorry," said one of the men, wearing his cap backwards and pretending to almost bump into her accidentally as she passed. "I didn't realize you were passing behind me."

"That's okay. I—"

"May I buy you a drink at least? It's the least I can do for such a pretty, young lady."

Sandra stared at his cap, noticing the hunting pin fastened to it.

"Do you hunt?" Sandra asked.

"Why yes, I do," he replied.

"I'll pass," she said. "I'm a vegetarian, and I think killing animals—except in self-defense—is cruel and barbaric."

"Here comes a live one," said Marti as she handed Gabe another drink.

Sandra approached Marti at the bar. "Excuse me, ma'am. I'm here for a dinner reservation with Gabe Channing, President of The Channing Group."

"That's me," said Gabe, his ego getting a much-needed boost, especially with the two gorgeous young women standing by him. "You two are a little early, though there's only a couple others coming. Why don't you both have a drink . . . on me."

"Oh, your treat tonight, huh?" Marti sneered, a ray of jealousy emerging. She then turned, quickly heading to take care of another customer, the paying kind.

"You know how it goes sometimes," said Gabe, talking to both women. "It's not every day I can treat such lovely ladies . . . and even a couple gentlemen to a first-class dinner. Nate Baschard should be arriving in a few minutes. There's also a Harland Parker who may come, he's a captain or major or something like that who works in the Pentagon."

Sandra ordered a margarita while Rita asked for a glass of pinot grigio.

HARLAND EXITED THE TRAIN AND SWIPED HIS CARD, triggering another red light to flash. Immediately, Brad got onto the radio.

"The rooster has flown the coop," said Brad, emotionally. "Need confirmation from kitty hawk."

"We confirm," said Zack.

"Ten-four," said Brad.

"Calling Unit 53-A. Come in 53-A."

"This is 53-A. Copy."

"Proceed with your mission," said Brad.

"Ten-four."

AS HARLAND WALKED THROUGH AN UNDERGROUND TUNNEL, two teenage males, each wearing a Washington Bullets jacket, ran past him.

"Hurry," said the taller teenager. "We're going to miss the start of the game."

"I am hurrying," said the other guy, running as fast as he could.

They ran through the tunnel, passing Harland as they sped towards two yellow cabs waiting near the curb.

"Open the door," demanded the first boy, banging on the window of the first cab. "We're going to miss the start of the game."

Instinctively, Harland walked to the second taxi, opening its door.

"Where to?" asked the driver in a thick Russian accent.

"I'm heading to Annapolis. The Marina Hotel."

"Yes, sir," said the driver.

The vehicle started moving and then swerved suddenly to avoid hitting the second boy who had carelessly run into the street, heading to the other door in the back of the cab.

"Happens all the time," said the cabbie. "Stupid kids. They think they don't need to look before running into the road."

"Yeah," said Harland. "That was close."

" You don't need to worry," he said. "I'm a great driver."

"Good. I've got enough on my mind right now as it is."

As their cab took off, the second boy's voice could be heard, trailing off into the background as he also began hitting the window. His voice growing louder and his anger more vehement with each blow. "Open the damn door! I said open the damn door!" Both boys began yelling loudly, pounding hard on the cab's back windows, but to no avail. With the doors firmly locked, the driver apparently did not want their business.

Harland's cab drove through the parking lot and eventually came to a traffic light. Nervous from all the excitement, Harland reached into his small briefcase and pulled out a copy of *Stars and Stripes*, a popular military magazine that he had loyally read for most of his career.

Unbeknownst to both Harland and the driver, the other taxi had also left the train station, following them without picking up a fare. "The rooster has escaped," the driver barked into the radio.

"What?" said Brad into his radio. "What happened?"

"Pigeon problem."

"Damn," said Brad, off the radio. Then he looked at Erin, who was standing next to him. "What the hell are we going to do now?"

"Keep up the heat," she answered.

Brad returned to the radio. "Keep on him," he said, abandoning protocol.

"Ten-four," said the driver-cum-agent, hitting the gas pedal heavily. He drove faster, breezing through one red light . . . then another.

In spite of the agent's reckless driving, neither Harland, nor his cab driver, noticed. Harland looked at his watch: 7:00 p.m. He knew Gabe's dinner party began at seven, but only now did he realize how late he was going to be. The peculiar situation with the teenagers and the cab had made him jittery. Living in Capitol Hill—with all its security—he was more protected from the reality of danger in downtown Washington, D.C. and unaccustomed to the reality of violence surrounding the nation's capital.

"What's the status on kitty hawk?" Brad asked.

The unit delayed his response.

"I repeat: what is the status on kitty hawk?" Bread repeated.

"He's still in flight," said Unit 53-A.

"Come in Unit 39-R. Thirty-nine-R, come in."

"Copy. Thirty-nine-R."

"What is the status on firehouse?" Brad asked.

"I'm just now on location," said 39-R, looking at Gabe's house from his Suburban.

"Is the eye blinking?" Brad asked.

"Negative."

"*Negative?*"

"I repeat: negative," answered 39-R.

"What!"

"I need more time. . . . Traffic problems on Route 50."

NATE WAS EIGHTEEN MINUTES LATE, but Gabe didn't mind, enjoying his long conversation with the two women, basically the only women—aside from Marti and Carley—he had spoken to in months. It was Gabe's turn to enjoy his all-expenses paid night out at one of Annapolis' finest establishment. However, now that Nate had arrived, his tone would have to become more business-like.

"You're sitting in the same place you were last time I was here," said Nate, removing his coat, then straightening his tie.

"I own this chair," Gabe said, feeling confident.

"What do you mean, you *own* that chair?" said Nate. "You don't own that chair."

"Yes, I do," said Gabe, proudly. "I literally own this chair."

Sandra was incredulous. Although Carley was quite busy with the Friday rush, Sandra had no qualms interrupting her to ask a simple question. "Excuse me, miss. But does Gabe literally own that chair."

"Yeah," said Carley. "It's true; he bought it—"

"Look," said Gabe, pointing to a small gold plaque affixed to the side of the stool. "I told you so. I bought that after I had my ten-thousandth drink. I'm not a liar."

John, the maitre d', approached Gabe, overhearing a portion of their conversation. "It's true. It's his chair. Everyone asks him that question, too, so don't feel bad about it. And it's also true he doesn't lie, well, unless there's a fire involved. . . . You're table's ready, *Mister Channing*."

"Thank you, sir" said Gabe, straightening his tie and adding a sense of formality to the night's proceedings.

"Any word on that fifth guest?" asked John.

Gabe glanced back at the bar. "No, I don't think he's coming. Must have had trouble with his commute.

Then Nate's phone rang—somewhat loudly—causing everyone to pause and look at him curiously. "Sorry about that," said Nate, looking at his display pad. "I meant to turn it to vibrate. . . . Oh damn, it's Spelling on that promotion."

The phone rang again. "A promotion?" asked Gabe, standing to walk into the dining room.

Nate answered his phone. "Hello?"

"Hi, Nate, glad I finally reached you," said David. "Have you decided to take the promotion yet?"

"You said I had until tomorrow to decide."

"Um, ah-h-h. I got another call today from a investor in alternative energy, and I told him I'd get back to him today because he'd be one of your accounts. It's important that I get your answer now. This is a big account—quite big, too. He's on hold for now."

"It's kind of loud in here," said Nate. "I can't hear you."

"It's a great opportunity," said David, louder and louder. "What's your answer? I need to know right now, Nate. I need to know . . . right . . . now."

The noise in the bar nearly overpowered David's voice, though Nate could understand him enough to follow his logic. "I can't hear you," said Nate, lying. "I'll call you back later."

As the group waited for Major Parker, each began to suspect that something wasn't right. Small talk about "clicks" on the each person's phone. Their list of peculiar incidents overlapped beyond that, too. Some had different mailmen, too. In time, the random occurrences began bothering everyone.

IMMEDIATELY, David Spelling phoned Brad.

"Yeah?" said Brad, who sat in his Chantilly, Virginia underground office. "Did he accept?"

"No."

"That's odd," said Brad, staring at his computer monitor. "You're sure?"

"Positive. . . . Then do what you have to do."

"Ten-four," said Brad, reluctantly hanging up his phone.

ZACK IMMEDIATELY GOT ONTO HIS RADIO. "Big Mama calling Blackbird One."

"Blackbird, here. Copy."

"*All* of them," said Brad.

"Ten-four."

DRESSED IN ALL BLACK, Unit 39-R parked in front of Gabe's brick house in his black Chevy Suburban and once again walked to the back door and easily entered the unlocked door. It was the second time he was in the house, making his job easier. He activated the powerful night vision system on his cap and walked confidently to Gabe's circuit breaker to turn off the proper circuit.

He then headed to Gabe's office—which was more organized this time—and saw Gabe's keyboard. He focused his light on the same inset light fixture in the middle of the ceiling, carefully moving Gabe's desk beneath it to stand atop it to once again slide the fixture downward. Fortunately, the camera was still where he had planted it a few months earlier, undisturbed.

From inside his coat, Unit 39-R removed an electrical device that re-softened the putty and allowed everything to be removed without leaving a trace. Then he slid the light fixture back into place, making it appear that the original lighting from when the house was built some fifty years earlier had never been disturbed. He returned the I-Pod video into his pocket and carefully placed the desk and items back into their original locations. His movements were smooth and calculated, and his observational skills were exact. There was no way Gabe would know an intruder had been in his home, let alone put a camera above his head and then removed it a month later.

However, his concern was not what Gabe would think, or what Gabe would notice. Unit 39-R had only one concern: could a private investigator—or an outside independent authority—notice there had been changes to this home? Would an unsuspecting police officer notice there were changes? It was no longer his concern what Gabe would think, for he expected Gabe would never return to his house anyway.

AN ANNAPOLIS POLICE CRUISER passed by Gabe's house and stopped behind the Chevy Suburban. Officer Lenny Dempsey looked at the license plate, noticing federal tags. He got on his radio, calling Annapolis police headquarters. "I'm in Quadrant three, with a suspicious vehicle at 1143 Elmhurst Avenue. Federal tag HH1430. . . . It's Gabe Channing's house."

"Gabe's house?" said the dispatcher. " That's odd. Let me check it out and get back to you."

Officer Dempsey waited patiently, continuing to stare at Gabe's house. He noticed Gabe's light was out in his living room, a light Gabe *never* turned off.

"Requesting backup," said the officer, removing his seatbelt and tapping on his gun holster as he headed out of the car. "Requesting backup. . . . Do you copy?"

"I copy," said the dispatcher. "Back-up is less than two minutes away."

FROM ONE HUNDRED YARDS BEHIND, the Unit 53-A driver followed Harland's cab. Then, as they exited the highway in Annapolis, he crept closer in the fog, though still without the awareness of the other driver or Harland. His approach remained close until they approached the Annapolis State Circle. When Harland's driver stopped, Unit 53-A removed a gun from under his seat and aimed it at the back window of Harland's car.

The Annapolis State Circle is a rotary, excessively difficult to manage with its multiple lanes and seemingly illogical traffic patterns peppered between close, tall buildings. Unquestionably, it's difficult for anyone to maneuver, even an experienced driver. Now, with an assassin known only as Unit 53-A working secretly for the U.S. Homeland Security Agency, the Circle was about to become one of Harland's worst nightmares.

Harland read from a map he had printed out from the internet. "My map shows the hotel is just around the corner, point two miles on your left."

"I'm new at this job," said the cabbie, lighting a cigarette. "I've never been to Annapolis."

"I never trust Washington cabbies for directions," said Harland, proud that he was prepared. "It looks like you just loop this Circle—if you can—then veer right over there."

Unit 53-A's cab drove faster, hoping to hit Harland's cab and send it spinning into one of the buildings, perhaps killing Harland in the process or, if necessary, hopping out and finishing the job during the ensuing chaos. What he had not planned on, though, was for Harland's cab driver to stop short at the light, and then to put the pedal to the metal, to head into the busy rotary. Flustered, the cabbie dropped his cigarette and bent down to find it, accidentally hitting the accelerator in the process. As he reached for his gun, Unit 53-A suddenly found himself speeding out of control.

Harland's driver jetted into the rotary, causing the pursuer to carelessly miss his car, and sideswipe a new black Suburban on the right side, then crash against the wall of a church. The crash was ear-piercing, instantly jarring Harland, whose nerves were already tense. Their car slowed, the taxi driver looping the rotary to inspect the crash.

Since they were basically the first at the accident scene, Harland and his driver viewed the gruesome details, with blood all over from the cuts inflicted by the windshield. The cabby's clearly broken neck added agony to all the gawkers. With the cab stopped, they both quickly exited the cab to see if anyone had survived. As Harland looked into the cab, he spotted a handgun with a silencer on it next to the driver's mutilated and crumbled body. The Suburban driver, a heavy-set man wearing dark glasses and a dark suit, was badly shaken but apparently uninjured, aside from the fact that he was slowly rubbing his left elbow.

"Are you okay?" Harland asked, gently touching the man's shoulder as he looked at his elbow.

"Ye-yeah," the driver answered. "I- I think so."

"I didn't see him coming," said Harland. "I just heard the crash. It was—"

"Holy crap," said the cabbie. "Look at *that!*"

"Are you sure you're going to be okay, to make out the police report and all?"

"Yeah, I saw the whole thing," said the Suburban driver. "Why didn't he stop? He should have stopped."

Soon four or five people approached the injured driver, who was now the center of attention. "I saw the whole thing," said a local businessman, who ran out of his shop. "That cab just blew right through the light, then pounded right into your SUV before hitting the church."

"He was going faster and faster," said a woman holding a child in her arms. "I saw it all. It was unbelievable."

"She's right," said another well-dressed man holding hands with a woman, a little younger than him. "We both saw it. Came from out of nowhere."

Harland scanned the assembly of people, a growing gathering of now about twenty, including three yellow cab drivers. Then he looked at his watch: 7:31 p.m. He was now really late for Gabe's dinner, and even more certain his life was in danger.

The young man looked directly at Harland. "Did you see anything?"

"Not a thing," said Harland.

Harland then looked at his cab driver. "How about you?" asked the young man.

"No, no, nothing, nothing at all," he said, shaken by the close call.

Almost as one the growing group then moved towards the now-demolished yellow cab. The businessman got there first, stopping still a couple feet from the driver's window.

"He's dead," said the businessman. "He's definitely dead."

The young man inched closer as most others dropped back at the sight of fresh blood. "How do you know, maybe he's . . . no, no, he's, ah, *definitely* dead. There's not a doubt in my mind."

"Poor bastard," said the businessman as he dialed 911 on his cell phone.

Many in the crowd were quiet, though one woman sobbed, creating an eerie sound that mixed with distant approaching sirens.

Harland pulled himself together and turned to his cab driver. "I'll walk it from here," he said, reluctant to leave but equally nervous about staying. "Here's fifty bucks. Keep the change. I have an appointment to keep. It's just up the street."

"Yeah, yeah, I'm out of here," said the driver. "I saw nothing."

Harland walked the remaining distance to the Marina Hotel, more convinced with each step that he was the target of that dead man's gun. "I could have been dead," he said to himself, still thinking furiously. "I *should* have been dead. . . . Someone definitely wants to kill me."

THREE SQUAD CARS on silent approach gathered in front of Gabe's house while another pulled around to the service road behind his house. Then three officers— each with their right hands firmly on the guns in their holsters—crept towards the house. In their left hands each officer held a powerful, long, silver flashlight. Several lights flooded into Gabe's house, illuminating the otherwise dark house.

A dark figure inside the living room started toward the back door.

"Stop in there," shouted Officer Dempsey. "Freeze! Police!"

Dempsey got onto his radio. "Intruder inside house confirmed."

An officer opened the back door, gun in hand, while another officer flung open the front door, which was also unlocked.

Unit 39-R immediately threw up his hands. "I'm F.B.I.!" he said. "I'm Agent Unit 39-R. Don't shoot. Don't shoot."

"Yeah, sure you are," said Officer Tony Simitti, sarcastically, his gun laser light aimed at the intruder's heart.

"My badge is in my right pocket," said Unit 39-R.

Officer Tony Simitti reached into the man's pocket as two more red lights hovered on the man's chest. He then removed a badge. "You *really are* F.B.I. What are you doing in Gabe's house?"

Unit 39-R did not answer.

"We still have to take you in," said Officer Simitti. "Police protocol until your creds clear."

"Got it," said Unit 39-R.

"But why *Gabe*?" asked Simitti as he removed handcuffs from his belt. "He's a harmless reporter."

Unit 39-R was smug. "Hmpf. Harmless my ass."

Simitti handcuffed one hand. "What do you mean by that?"

Unit 39-R was quiet.

"Answer the question," he asked again.

Unit 39-R remained quiet.

Simitti radioed into headquarters.

The desk sergeant called the captain, who called the mayor. Then the mayor made a few calls and within minutes the word was out. Gabe Channing, a retired small-town reporter, was on the Homeland Security Agency's list of wanted bioterrorists.

CHASE IN ANNAPOLIS
CHAPTER SEVEN

WITH A POWERFUL ELECTRONIC BUG hidden under the bread, the busboy nonchalantly placed the breadbasket in front of Gabe. The signal was transmitted back to two black Chevy Suburbans parked outside the hotel restaurant where eight agents—four in each car—listened in. Each agent was a tall, solid male dressed in black clothing and loaded down with a plethora of equipment, including a short-barreled scatter gun, a phase gun, a pistol, and two knives.

The vehicles, themselves, were not suspicious, as federal vehicles from Washington, D.C.—only 28 miles west of Annapolis—were routinely seen in Annapolis being used by VIPs at high-profile events away from the intense media scrutiny in the District. On this night, they waited for final orders on how to proceed with the planned arrest and then transfer to a terrorist holding compound outside of the U.S.—of Gabe Channing, Rita Perez, Sandra O'Callahan, Major Harland Parker, and Nate Baschard.

GABE, NATE, RITA, AND SANDRA sat around a round antique oak table with one seat still empty, the seat reserved for Major Harland Parker. They were just finishing their first drink order when John, holding a pen and pad of paper asked. "Is your party ready to order, Gabe? I mean, sir."

Gabe shifted in his seat a little. "I guess there's no point in waiting any further for the last guest. Sure, I think we are all ready." Everyone nodded.

"And what would you like, sir?"

"You know *exactly* what I like: The Gabe: the plank roasted salmon with the wild mushrooms and asparagus tips."

John chuckled, because he knew Gabe usually ordered a corned beef sandwich on rye with extra mayonnaise. "I'm sorry, sir, but that is not available in the formal dining room."

Gabe replied, "Okay, give me a minute. Why don't you start with her." Gabe pointed to Sandra.

"I'll start with the Caesar salad and then move on to the pasta primavera," said Sandra. "It is vegetarian, right?"

John nodded.

"The strip steak," Nate began, "with the redskin potatoes and, ah . . . the house salad."

"I'll have the veal parmesan," said Rita, "and with extra cheese."

Sandra's jaw dropped slightly. She couldn't believe she was sitting at the same table as someone who would order veal. Didn't Rita know how the meat industry treated the calves they turned into veal? It was all she could do to not start a scene.

John, still holding his pad, looked over at Gabe.

Gabe had not read a menu at the Santa Maria Restaurant since it was bought out fifteen years ago by its current owner. Even though the menu had been completely revamped a few times, he kept demanding the salmon dinner whenever he ate in the formal dining room.

"Well, then, if you don't have my regular chow, I'll have the swordfish," said Gabe. "Cook it medium well, with extra lemon and a little cranberry sauce on the side. That's what I eat when you're out of salmon."

"And bring us a bottle of the house cabernet and chardonnay," said Gabe. "I have the feeling the wine is going to flow tonight, so we might as well start now."

John left the room, leaving the group alone for the first time.

Sandra said, "It's interesting this is the second time I have been at this restaurant."

"Me, too," said Rita, surprised at the coincidence. "The last time I was here, I attended a speech on stem cell technology during a conference."

"Come to think of it, I've been asking myself why you seemed so familiar when we had lunch together," said Nate, looking at Sandra. "I was here also but I got there a little late."

There was an uncomfortable pause as everyone stared at each other in wonder, due to this unlikely coincidence. Maybe retirement planning was not the real agenda.

MINUTES LATER, Harland walked into the dining room, still unnerved from witnessing that horrible accident and seeing the powerful gun next to the body. He was sweaty and visibly shaken. His white shirt was wrinkled and drenched in sweat, making him seem less of a soldier, and more like an average person.

"I think someone just tried to kill me," he stated as he sat down in the one vacant chair. His eyes glazed.

"Oh give me a break," said Sandra, panicky. "Now even *you're* buying into all this garbage. It's got to end. All of you are making it sound like the government is after us. They're not after *us* any more than they're after *anyone* else. It just doesn't work that way. Believe me, I'll be the first to admit that parts of our government are corrupt, there is not a doubt in my mind, but there is no reason for the government to be chasing after five ordinary people like us. I mean, what business does a reporter, a soldier, a businessman, a scientist, and a bleeding heart liberal lawyer know that could trigger such aggressive actions by a government like ours? We're nothing to them, just a bunch of worthless peons. It's the tycoons they want or the journalists in mass media, and I'm not talking about retired ones, either, Gabe. They want insiders, reporters who have connections who will lie to the television viewers or their readers without a second thought."

Gabe shrugged his shoulders. "What about the clicks on the phone you accused me of? I wasn't monitoring you. I really wasn't. I hardly understand how to use an answering machine, let alone eavesdrop on someone else electronically."

"That's right. I forgot all about that. But who knows what that was. I've noticed a glitch with my mouse lately, too. This stuff is much more difficult to know for certain without hard evidence."

Harland sat down in his chair. "I have that problem with my computer, too. I've always had it. At the Pentagon we're told it's merely part of our military operating system. We're monitored all the time."

"Harland, why do you think they were trying to kill you?" Gabe asked.

"There was a wreck right behind the cab I was in. A real bad one, too. The guy must have gone into Annapolis Circle going about sixty. And . . . he had a gun in one hand with a silencer on it."

Gabe grimaced. "Sixty?" It's hard to take that turn at twenty let alone with a gun with a silencer. . . . What about you, Nate? Have you experienced anything odd lately?"

Nate chuckled. "Not at all. My boss wants to promote me, that's it. Oh, and I have noticed those same clicks on my home phone, and on my office phone, too, now that you mention it. And, that mouse thing."

"What type of a promotion?" asked Harland. "I don't mean to pry, since I really don't know you, or any of you for that matter, but when I'm telling you I think someone tried to kill me, I mean it. I'm not going to get into my personal reason for coming here, though until I hear what the rest of you have to say. What was with the promotion, Nate?"

Nate curiously tilted his head. "It was kind of odd, now that you mention it. My boss stopped my article about the biotech sector from appearing in the New York Times the other day, only to then take me out to lunch at a posh restaurant and offer me a promotion and a raise."

"I agree that's odd," said Gabe, scratching his head. "But I don't see any connection yet or any reason for surveillance, let alone deadly force."

"It was especially odd that he told me I needed to change sectors, from biotech to energy, since biotech is my area of expertise. If I declined he said I would be let go."

Harland was fidgety. "I could use some extra energy myself, right about now."

They all chuckled, except Sandra, who didn't find the comment humorous. "I was also offered a real plum assignment in Brazil. . . . I was working on a story about the Marshall Islands and government corruption."

OFFICER DEMPSEY AND OFFICER SIMITTI put Unit 39-R into the backseat Officer Simitti's patrol car, which was standard operating procedure when a criminal was apprehended. The officers then got into their respective cars and headed back to the station.

Dempsey held a cup of coffee as he drove to the station. In all, it was a boring ride from Gabe's house to the station, only to go through the actions of booking an F.B.I. agent whom they suspected they would have to release in a few hours. Then there would be the usual calls from the governor's office, questioning why a federal agent had been booked in the first place, even though he absolutely knew the procedure requirements of why he was booked. Regardless, the governor wanted to sound good for the surveillance cameras on him, making his activity seem more earnest to federal government types whom he suspected also listened to him 24/7. Since 9/11, all V.I.P.'s were under protection by the Feds and he suspected that protection included monitoring all communications. During the ride, Officer Dempsey used his personal cell phone to call the Marina Restaurant, a number already programmed into it.

"Hello," said Marti.

"It's Lenny. Is that guy who owns the stool around?"

"You mean Gabe?" asked Marti, wiping the bar with a washcloth. "Yeah."

"Lenny, what's up with that accident in the Circle? Everyone's been talking about it, even the people from out of town."

Lenny sighed. "I don't have the story on it yet. . . . Hey Marti, like I said, is that guy there?" (Lenny had not wanted to use Gabe's name on the radio.)

"You don't sound yourself. Gabe's not related to that guy at all, is he?"

"No, no," said Lenny. "It's something different."

Marti leaned against the wall, listening more closely. "Like what?"

"I can't say. Police business."

Marti's eyes grew stern. "Hell, I know your business more than you do. Why do you need, Gabe? Right now he's meeting with—"

Lenny sighed and cut her short. "We caught a federal agent in his house . . ."

"Damn! . . . So?"

". . . and he had a miniature spy camera on him. From what we can tell, he was removing it. Something's going on, Marti. If the accident is related, it makes all of this seem even stranger. Can you tell him to watch his back closely?"

"Does the mayor know?"

Lenny said, "Like I said, I'm trying to piece it all together. Just tell him to be careful. You know I am not saying those words 'be careful' lightly."

"You bet," said Marti, no longer wiping the counter.

"And there's something else," said Lenny.

"Yeah?"

"He's on the Fed's bio-terrorist list."

"Who?" asked Marti, her jaw dropping as she awaited the answer.

"That guy," Lenny began, "the one who owns the stool."

Marti hooted, dropping the washcloth to the ground. "Are you shitin' me? Gabe's no t-e-r-r-o-r-i-s-t."

"I'm not kidding whatsoever," said Lenny. "The Feds don't break into people's homes without a reason or at least what they think is a reason. Of course since the passage of the Patriot Act, they have been able to spy more on U.S. citizens."

MARTI WALKED INTO THE BACK ROOM, smugly carrying a tray with a Jim Beam and coke, knowing perfectly well how to influence Gabe, by using his favorite drink. As the conversation in the group intensified, Marti quietly walked up to Gabe and whispered into his ear.

"I need to talk with you, privately."

"You know I'm busy right now," said Gabe, reaching for the drink.

"No, no, no," she said, pulling the tray away from him. "You can't have this in here. Follow me, okay. It's important."

Gabe stood, addressing everyone in the room. "I'm sorry everybody, but I have to leave for a moment. I'll be right back."

SITTING IN THEIR SUBURBANS, the F.B.I. agents continued to monitor the room, listening to everyone through the electronic bug in the breadbasket. When Marti was taking Gabe out of the room was a cause for speculation.

"Where's he going?" asked one agent. "Why did she say it's important?"

"I don't know," said another.

"Well, we can't barge in there and cause a scene unless they're all together."

"Maybe he'll just be gone a minute. They know each other, he and that bartender woman. Don't worry about it. We still have some time before everything is in place."

Just then, another agent was being told about the accident on the Circle."

MARTI AND GABE stood together in the hallway leading to the kitchen. Marti was visibly flustered, though she had not yet revealed the reason why, causing Gabe to grow more nervous. "What's wrong, Marti?" Gabe asked. "You're as nervous as a cat in traffic."

"You know I share with you things I really shouldn't know and I don't want to get anyone else in trouble if I tell you something."

Gabe crossed his arms. "What, Marti? What is it? Spit it out."

"Lenny called. He said they caught someone in your house dismantling a wire tap or a camera or something. A Homeland Security guy? A Fed?"

"What?! Are you kidding?"

Tears filled Marti's eyes. "No, it just happened. I don't mean to sound paranoid, but that busboy who started today, Juan, I don't trust him. Nobody is ever hired without my approval. Even though I'm not in charge of personnel. management never hires anyone without my okay. I'm thinking maybe . . . he . . . ah."

Now Gabe was really concerned. "Do you think the Seiler Room is tapped, too?" Gabe asked as he panned the main dining room, looking for anything out of the ordinary.

Marti was in tears. "You know I don't believe in any of that crap, but I believe in you, Gabe. I don't want anything to happen to you. Then there's that horrible wreck down the street that Navy guy told me about when he was looking for you. He thought someone was trying to kill him. And I'm worried—"

They hugged, as old friends hug. Then they kissed each other, but with a soft and swift kiss, as if they were not allowed to kiss.

"I'll be okay," said Gabe as he held her tightly. "Please don't worry."

"There's one more thing," said Marti, tears again swelling in her eyes.

"Yes."

Marti cringed.

"What is it?" asked Gabe. "Tell me."

She hugged him, clinging to his back in a long embrace. "They've labeled you a bio-terrorist," she whispered into his ear.

"Oh come on," said Gabe. "I'm not a *bio-terrorist*," he whispered back. "They must have the wrong address or something. I wouldn't take it seriously, Marti."

Marti laughed a nervous laugh. "I hope your right, but at least promise me one thing."

"What's that?" asked Gabe, dabbing her tears with his thumb.

"Promise me you'll get out of here right now. Just head to a different restaurant or something. I'll take care of the bill and all. Just get the hell out of here."

"Why?" asked Gabe.

"Just promise me," said Marti, grasping Gabe's tie. "That's why."

"Okay," said Gabe.

"Go into that room, and close the door behind you. Then head out through the back exit in your room. I'll have Holly wait for you with the hotel van. And don't say anything . . . in case they really are listening."

"Okay. I promise. I'll go and I won't say anything."

"And, Gabe?"

"What, Marti?"

"Nothing."

"Thanks, Marti. You're a real friend."

TRUE TO HIS WORD, Gabe headed to the room and shut the door behind him, motioning to everyone that they all needed to head out through the back door while acting as if nothing weird was happening. It was an odd scene, with Harland still sweating and Sandra wanting to shout out loud. They all seemed to understand Gabe, even though he didn't say anything, because when someone acts with such urgency it's tough to say no.

A few seconds later, Marti and Carley pushed the heavy dessert cart in front of the thick oak door of the back dining room. As Carley walked away, Marti pretended to slip and fall, knocking over the dessert cart and spilling it all over the floor. As she bent over to try and clean them up, she slipped. Swearing loudly like a sailor, she claimed to hurt her ankle and didn't want to be moved or touched until an ambulance team could help her.

The agents monitoring the dining room chatter noticed then that the room had gone dead. Either their equipment was malfunctioning or the pigeons were about to change everyone's plans.

Then they got another call, saying the agent who was removing the bugs from Gabe's house was arrested. The plan to proceed quietly was starting to unravel.

THE TEAM OF EIGHT MEN from the Suburbans hurriedly entered the restaurant and headed immediately to the back dining room. Although they never revealed any weapons, their dispositions spoke of powerful firearms and a take-no-prisoners attitude.

Jasmine once again repositioned her microphone, making sure to point the end of it at the door to the dining room.

When they finally got to the door, the slippery floor, and injured woman created a real barrier as the first two slipped and fell on top of Marti, who then screamed in pain, followed by more vocabulary typical of the Navy. The next few agents tried to jump over them but their takeoffs were hampered by the slippery floor and they ended up as part of the mess, too.

Once they untangled themselves, the next problem became opening the locked door (which opened outwards), because they couldn't get traction. One man brazenly removed a weapon looking like a sawed off shotgun and blasted off the lock, causing a flurry of panic through the restaurant. All the patrons dropped quickly to the floor. When the agents eventually entered the room, it was empty. Surprised, they rushed to the opposite door and found themselves next to a dumpster in the back parking lot. Now that their targets were gone, headquarters was really going to be pissed, they knew.

DEAR DIARY, June 18, 1982.

When the sun set today, there was an ever-changing array of colors and shapes across the water with the branches of the palm trees gently swaying in the tropical breeze. A few meters away from me a beautiful pair of parrots just landed in the branches of a bougainvillea. Every day since the wreck we've had perfect weather, just like this.

Amy found a sign with the name "Enewetak" written on it with black paint. I can see another island in the distance, though we won't be able to get a closer look at it until Hugo and Jason fix the boat, which is still heavily damaged from running a-ground.

Almost every day, Amy and I hike all the way around the island, which takes about three hours to cover at a somewhat leisurely pace. Fortunately, the tropical vegetation with its vast assortment of fruits is abundant. Oddly, we haven't found any animals aside from birds. There isn't even any sign of a lizard or a muskrat!

Our only trouble is the availability of fresh water, which has been a serious problem for us. Thus far, we have lived off of some water that seems to be flowing from an underground source. The area looked weird, though, like it was some kind of manmade structure. We tried digging, but everything we tried to use just broke.

Today Jason finished a series of changes to a third hut, which is serving as somewhat of a kitchen or living room for us, away from the other two huts which we use as bedrooms. Although we're essentially marooned on this island, we have come to rather like our lives here. We all hope to be discovered by a passing ship, but if we don't we almost don't even care, aside from all of us wanting to talk to our families.

I don't miss going to work and couldn't care less about the news or even knowing tomorrow's weather report. All the conveniences of a "normal" life seem so stupid now. "Don't worry!" That's my new motto. Just relax and everything will take care of itself.

ON THE RUN
CHAPTER EIGHT

THE ELEVEN-PASSENGER VAN drove slowly in the fog as Holly held the steering wheel with a tight grip. Holly was jovial and kind, having diligently worked for the hotel for the past thirteen years. She knew all the main streets in the Washington, Baltimore, and Annapolis triangle, traveling nearly every day to the local airports of Dulles, Reagan, and BWI. Guiding discussions was yet another of her many personal skills. Whether it was politicians, dignitaries, athletes, or businessmen, she would drive them from the hotel to where they wanted to go. In the process, she would pick up interesting tidbits of information she used in her chatter with other clients.

Gabe jumped into the front passenger seat as Nate, Rita, Sandra, and Harland sat in the next two rows of seating. None of them were in a mood to talk, except for Gabe, who loved the excitement, not to mention that soft kiss from Marti. He felt old feelings being rekindled. Finally Marti had showed him she cared for him. Maybe two decades of Jim Beams and sandwiches had given her reason to like him. Though he was never much of a tipper, he believed his smile and smart talk helped to carry her through each night of work. He knew her smile and comments helped him.

Holly finally broke the silence, looking at Gabe, whom she had known throughout her years of working at the hotel. "Marti says I can have the whole weekend off. Since I already don't have to work Monday and Tuesday, that's five days for me. And here I don't have a single idea of what to do."

She glanced at Gabe, who was in deep thought.

"So where are we off to, Gabe? The funny thing is Marti told me to not bother to bring the van back tonight. Now what am I going to do with this van that I can't do with my own car?"

"I don't know, Holly," said Gabe. "I just don't know."

"Now it doesn't matter to me if you don't know where to go, because I'll just keep driving until I have to fill her up. But I do like to at least have an idea of where I'm going. But, like I said, I can just keep going around in circles for as long as you want."

"No, no circles," said Harland, a voice from the next row of seats. "I think some cabby tried to kill me at that circle thing in Downtown Annapolis about twenty minutes away."

"Oh jeepers," said Holly, taking yet another turn. "You saw that wreck? I pass through that circle about six or seven . . . hundred times a day and I've never seen anything like it. That car was way up into the State House area. He must have been going like full speed into that thing."

"All I know is it scared the crap out of me. I even saw the mutilated body."

"Damn!"

"Yeah, it could have been me, I'm telling you. It happened right behind the cab I was in. That's how I got into this mess—"

"The same mess we're all in," said Nate. "This has got to be the strangest day I've had in years. Even my boss—the same guy who hates my guts—offers me a raise and a promotion today, only a couple days after he killed the biggest story of my career."

"Well, I cancelled a date to be here tonight, just to get a look at Gabe's story. And here we didn't even get to eat. I'm hungry," moaned Sandra.

Rita sat quietly in the back of the van. She had no interest in talking, and no one else seemed to want to invite her into the conversation, either.

Holly smiled. "Gabe, you know so many people. You've got to be the most popular man in town, even more so now that you're retired."

"Thanks," said Gabe, looking out at the Chesapeake Bay. "I really haven't done much since I retired. I've not even been on my boat much, except to check on her. You know, make sure she would be ready for a nice, long cruise. Maybe after the article I am working on is accepted, I'll take her out."

Holly turned, just as instructed to do. "I never knew you had a boat, and I've worked at the hotel for years.

"I built it myself, years ago," said Gabe, proudly.

Harland's eyes widened. "You built yourself your own sailboat?"

"Yes, I did," said Gabe. "I built it when I was in my late twenties, after I served in the Navy. That's all I did back then, every day for three or four years, before I started at the *Triangle*. I had her fully provisioned about a month ago, when I made a decision to eventually head out to the Caribbean."

"I wish I had a boat, a big ole' sailboat" said Holly. "I'd sail out through the Bay and into the ocean, not giving a care about anything else in this world except for my kids and my mom, and the Good Lord, of course."

Gabe nodded. "Holly, take a left turn here then head down to Starfish Marina. Maybe that boat's where we can pass the time until we figure out what the hell is happening and get our thoughts in order."

HOLLY TURNED DOWN A HILL and passed the Starfish Marina sign, which was barely visible in the fog. "Where to from here, skipper?"

"Drive as far in as you can," said Gabe. Then he turned to face Harland. "Yeah, I built my boat from a design I read about in a Navy manual. I improvised a little though."

"Now I don't know much about boats," Holly began, "but from the looks of the boats at this marina, it doesn't look like you used a starter kit. . . . Which one is it?"

Gabe pointed to a 45-foot catamaran at the end of the dock.

Holly stopped the van and everyone shuffled out and gathered in a little huddle on the gravel parking lot.

It was a beautiful summer night, with a cool southern breeze in the air, combined with a light fog that made everyone feel refreshed as they looked out into the calm waters.

Surrounded by sail boats and cigar boats, the marina was an intriguing place to visit. It differed from Washington, D.C. because the nation's capital was not all that accessible by water, aside from the Potomac River. The Annapolis harbor—all lit up at night—was a peaceful sight to see for the group of six.

Gabe automatically straightened his tie. "I'm sorry it's not been such a great night for any of you, but maybe some time on my boat will help things somewhat. I know it's an understatement to say, but it's not been the evening I thought it was going to be either."

"We never got our dinner," said Sandra. "I'm not a big complainer, but I'm hungry, people."

Nate rolled his eyes, for Sandra was indeed a complainer, and a talker, someone who seemed to always put her opinion into a conversation regardless of whether it fit or not.

"There's plenty of food on my boat," said Gabe. "Just follow me."

The group paraded through the gravel, then out along a wooden pier.

"My family in Argentina would often rent a boat like this," said Rita, motioning towards a cigar boat near the end of the pier. "Even though they'd spend most of their time quietly making wine, when they got out onto the water, they liked the speed."

"What did you like, though?" asked Gabe.

"Sailboats," said Rita. "I love the idea of harnessing Mother Nature: a strong wind and a full sail. I'd try to remind my father, it was the wind that made his wine taste so good, but he wouldn't agree with me. He didn't like to talk about the vineyard when we'd be out on the water."

"I like the speed boats, too," said Nate. "At least in the movie I like them. But I've never been on a boat of any kind."

"Never?" said Sandra. "You spend too much time in those skyscrapers."

"At least I don't live up in trees like a monkey."

"I would have continued living in that tree if I hadn't been struck by lightning," said Sandra.

Nate smiled. "How many people, the first time you meet them, tell you they tried to live in a tree? And she said it in just the few minutes you were out of the room in the restaurant."

"Here she is," said Gabe. "That's my Mistress."

"Really?" said Holly, slowing sliding her hand on the side. "It's so beautiful."

"Real nice," said Harland, even though he was staring at Holly. Holly blushed as she caught Harland's look.

For a moment, they were all transfixed on Gabe's forty-five foot sailboat, staring at the word "Mistress" painted in large, black Old English-styled letters on the boat's stern. It was a boat, built of dark wood, but with a mast painted gold.

"Why the gold on the mast?" Holly asked.

"Those are my Navy colors," said Gabe.

"I don't see a registration number," said Harland, looking all around the boat.

"That's right," said Gabe, unraveling a thick rope, that held the boat to the pier. "Hey, Nate, Harland, give me a hand with this. I never registered her. She's my mistress. A secret. Expensive. And not visited nearly enough. Get it?"

The three men unraveled the rope as the women stood to the side and watched.

"I don't have a good feeling about this," said Sandra. "And trust me, I know when my gut starts acting up."

Gabe fired up the engine, and turned on his running lights as Harland and Nate got ready to cast off.

"Don't worry," said Gabe. "My Mistress is in perfect shape . . . even if her captain isn't."

WHILE THE OTHERS WENT BELOW, Gabe was alone on deck, slowly motoring out into the Chesapeake Bay. He did not like the feeling in his stomach, either, as thoughts of federal agents in his house weighed heavily on him. Surveillance was something meant for a paranoid Nixon-led era when Watergate and Vietnam dominated newspaper headlines. Back then, somewhere in each paper were stories of surrendered civil liberties. Homeland Security: it sounded almost Nazi-ish. Americans never referred to the USA as their "Homeland." Why was the government suddenly bugging him? He hadn't done anything wrong and the only radical person he knew was the mayor. And even he wasn't a radical; he was a liberal!

Those days during the Nixon era were not a time for happy spirits, in spite of tales from Woodstock. Privacy was surrendered in the name of government privilege and "safety." The introduction of television to mass audiences had shifted people away from believing the truth in front of their eyes, and instead believing the spin of televised news.

Accepting what Marti had told him from Officer Lenny Dempsey was difficult for Gabe. Why would they bug his house? And why the need for a camera? What were they watching? What possible need was there for them to watch his home?

The more he pondered it, the more the Vietnam era flashed before his eyes, somewhat of a post-traumatic disorder sparked deeply in his subconscious. During the Vietnam War, Gabe served, though not in the frontlines, but in the front pages of the *Stars and Stripes*. He saw Vietnam as a civil war, not an inner war of guns within the country's borders, but as a war of ideas, where outside opinion was the enemy. Yet, the guns were real and many of his friends' names were written on the wall at the Vietnam Memorial.

As he stared out into the fog with Annapolis' yellowish lights blurred against the foggy night-time sky, he remembered the yellow jar of business cards atop the mahogany bar, holding its random collection of people with unknown names. Now four of them—plus Holly—were crewmates on his boat. They were all following his lead right now, though no one knew where they were going—not even him.

When he was a writer, Gabe would have to create random stories on blank white sheets of paper. At the beginning, all he had was an idea, and from that idea would emerge a story. When the story finally was published, fresh ideas would enter into the minds of his many loyal readers, the majority being people he had never met.

Gabe figured he was starting a new story. Blank white pages were in front of him. Now, he just needed to start writing a story, a story that hopefully would have a happy ending for the party aboard his Mistress.

HAPPILY, the five passengers discovered wine, beer, Jim Beam, and enough canned goods for a crew of six to last a month at sea. There was even Russian caviar! In time, they all sat quietly and just enjoyed the sailing.

AS RITA SIPPED WINE from her large glass, her thoughts shifted to her home in Argentina and her family's wine business. The evening was still young, as it was now only 9:05 p.m., a little over two hours after she had planned to meet with Gabe and the others, giving her consent for his retirement story. However, now that all seemed like a distant thought at this juncture in the evening, with all of them heading off to sea.

Over the entire evening, Rita was the most quiet, only revealing her short story about home, the boat her parents would rent, and the vineyard. She did not like the idea of going out to sea, but what else could she do? She didn't need to work weekends, though she usually did. Her life was a boring one, aside from her research. As the others had spoken of their great successes of late, with great job promotions, she kept thinking about the computer monitors she would stare at for hours on end, recording any unusual developments in the cells. It was all she could do to pass the time in her lonely life.

She had not said anything to the others, even as she pondered how unusual it was how they all had gathered. Why had Nate and Sandra been offered such impressive promotions? Why had Harland almost been killed, or even why did he think he was a target? Why did Marti give Holly the weekend off? And why was Gabe, a simple hometown journalist, reluctant to return to his home?

The pattern of events against the others was irregular. Only her patterns were not. There was nothing unusual about her life. She seemed the most sane, the most simple, like the person with the least purpose of being there in the first place. She didn't see how she fit into the puzzle. What information did she have of such importance? There was nothing great to her past that connected her with this group. Her life was composed of merely watching the movements of animal cells as they divided, trying to isolate the genes that caused adaptation. As much as she tried to think about it, she felt she did not belong in this group. Well, at least she did not yet understand her place amongst them.

Instead, to pass the time she played a game she had invented along with her brother on her laptop: De-evolution, a genetic game fashioned like Tetris, though it would switch on parts and switch off parts of the supposed junk DNA then, via a projected alternation alteration, reconfigure them into a probable future.

NATE WAS ENJOYING HIS FIRST EXPERIENCE on a boat despite being nervous. Sipping his wine as the others gabbed, he thought about the promotion David Spelling had strangely offered him out of the blue. This was a most confusing turn of events, considering he had thought he was going to be fired—for his success, no less. Now he found himself on the run with a group of strangers and the potential of a big raise and promotion to face when he got back to New York.

Taking a few days off, if this trip did amount to a few days off, would be a good thing for him. He didn't have to be at work in New York until Monday afternoon, anyway. What harm could a short boat trip be?

His career was now looking like it was going to take off, and with Rita on the boat he could finally grill her with his biotech questions. There was plenty of time to talk about work later. Even if he did take the promotion and switch to alternative energy, he still believed in biotechs and information from her could be personally quite profitable.

With that promotion, he could even afford his own boat now. He could have his friends on it whenever he wanted. Of course, he would need to make a few friends first, but with more money would come more friends, right? People liked to flock around successful people with money. Certainly with getting a fifty percent raise, he could have a boat, maybe even buy his first apartment in New York, overlooking Central Park.

It's not like he couldn't afford to buy something now, he had plenty of money. But he never had any time or reason to buy anything. Then his money would increase, and he would hope for a better place to buy. He would almost make a decision on a new place, then his salary would advance even more, further delaying his buying decision. His problem was he spent so much time thinking about Wall Street that he never had time to think about himself. But with this promotion, he was sure that would all change.

Maybe, he thought, just maybe it was time to start looking for a woman to get seriously involved with. A bigger apartment, a boat, and a bigger personal portfolio sounded a bit empty without someone to share it all with. As he sat there thinking, he caught Sandra's eye and they both smiled, then quickly moved away.

HOLLY KEPT THINKING about her daughters and her mother, even as she drank a beer. She knew they would be safe tonight, as they didn't expect her to return until morning, after her shift ended. For now, she had the time to head out to sea.

She was happy Gabe's boat was abundantly stocked with beer and wine, and an entire case full of Jim Beam. Alcohol was naturally not permitted on the job as she drove, but she decided to consider this time off the clock, though technically she was still on it.

It was also Holly's first time on a boat, though she did not want to admit it. Over the years, she learned to keep her opinions to herself, as best she could. She did not want to sound too stupid or inexperienced, especially in front of a military man like Harland. She wanted to be as sophisticated as possible, which is why she used the beer cooler for her beer. It added a nice touch, she thought.

SANDRA HAD DECLINED most of the canned goods Gabe had offered her, because they violated her strict vegetarian diet, but she was enjoying a glass of cabernet. Tuna, sardines, and cream of crab soup had no place in her world. Fortunately, she discovered plenty of dry goods like beans and pasta and some cheeses in the refrigerator, as well as a good assortment of soups she could eat, perhaps a couple week's supply if the others stuck with their primary meat-based diets.

She found it odd that Gabe had so much food and alcohol on his boat. What would he need with it all? She assumed he was single because he was not wearing a ring and never mentioned a girlfriend. Why all the stash in a boat? And why was the boat called "Mistress?" It was such an odd name for a boat. What need did a bachelor have for a mistress? A mistress was something for a married man, wasn't it?

Sandra also thought about her promotion. Surely she could spend some time in Rio de Janeiro and "carnival" popped into her mind. Exotic, sexy. Hot. Steamy. Yes, Rio could be hot. It could be the perfect time to get reacquainted with some of the activities she enjoyed so much at Smith College. It was a surprise for her that Smith had so many free thinkers (and doers). Since college, she had adopted the straight and narrow, but in another country she could do as she pleased. Indeed, Rio would be fun.

HARLAND HAD BEEN ON BOATS several times, though always in uniform. He was similar to his father in that regard, always taking a trip when one was offered.

He thought about his father, a man he thought about every day. Harland seemed always surrounded by death. His father's photo reminded him of death, as did his wife's. How many men are widowers, especially military men? But, he did have his son, a source of daily joy.

In spite of their troubles, the boat ride nevertheless filled Harland's soul with peace. The waters calmed him, as he was sure it calmed his father in the Marshall Islands. Peace is not easy to find, especially in a dead-end job processing complaints in the basement of the Pentagon.

As Harland sipped his cold beer he wondered if this craziness would be straightened out. Was that guy really trying to kill him? If he went back now, would someone else try to kill him? And who was that guy? Was it really the Feds?

GABE REMAINED ON THE DECK as the boat headed out into the Bay, whose waters were smooth and peaceful today. The remaining five spoke among themselves in the galley below.

"It's pretty nice in here," said Holly as she sipped from her beer. "It's sure been a different kind of evening than I expected when I clocked in this morning."

"That's for sure," said Sandra, sipping her wine. "This has been one of the most confusing nights of my life, and believe me, I've lived through some pretty extraordinary things."

"So he called each of us just because we all threw our business cards into that jar," said Nate as he walked in on the conversation underway. "Talk about dumb luck."

"Reporters are all lazy, at least most of them," retorted Sandra. "I've got a million things to do and here I am on a boat going to God knows where with a bunch of people I barely know. . . . You're nice people, I think. In fact, I can't think of a better group of people to spend time with on a boat tonight," said Sandra, realizing how stupid that must have sounded.

Harland sipped from his Heineken. "At least he picked a good night to do this. That seems true for all of us. I told my mother I'd be gone all night, so she expected to watch my son until morning."

"Oh, I have two children, too—both girls," said Holly. "They are six and eight, Elise and Pamela."

"My son is five. His name's Sterling, named after my dad."

Sandra wanted to roll her eyes, but caught herself. Any thought of children made her ill. "I just don't get it!" Sandra blurted. "Why do you suppose we all had the same bad luck to find ourselves where we are right now? Just because of some stupid ethics speech and a glass bowl in a hotel bar in Annapolis?"

"Ethics and science go hand-and-hand," said Rita. "Scientific knowledge is usually good, but it can go too far, like when human embryos are killed."

"Pro-life, huh?" asked Sandra.

"I'm certainly not pro-death," said Rita.

"Then why did you order veal?" asked Sandra, changing the subject.

"You don't mind working on animal research, though?" asked Nate of Rita.

"Animal research is good—to a point—it has historically helped save human lives. But any experiment to kill humans to save humans is obviously counterproductive. It's that simple."

"It's all the same to me," said Sandra, combing through her hair with her hand. "Killing animals is no different than killing people. Death is death. And the calf killed for your veal dinner sure isn't saving anyone."

"Do you remember *anything* from that ethics speech?" asked Nate. "He was the speaker, anyway? Admiral Owens something."

"Nelson Owens; Admiral Nelson Owens," said Harland. "He's pretty well-known, at least, within the weapons and ethics fields. My father met him once, at the Marshall Islands."

"The Marshall Islands?" blurted Sandra. "That's the most corrupt place on earth. Well, maybe not *the* most corrupt place, but certainly the most corrupt place the U.S. deals with as an accredited nation. Who would ever want to be involved with on the Marshall Islands?"

"Why do you think it's corrupt?" asked Nate.

"It's just a gut feeling," said Sandra. "I was meeting with the ambassador to the Marshall Islands, getting ready to write a big exposé on its corruption. And then I got this promotion to go to Brazil, which is making me put my story on hold."

"Oh. A lot of biotech research originates from there," said Nate. "I don't know why, though."

Rita moved forward in her chair. "After World War Two, the United States conducted most of its atomic testing research out there. Every week for years they detonated atomic bombs near the Marshall Islands. Kwajalein and Roi Namur. It was not a good period for ethical research in bio-technology."

Harland blinked. "That's a pretty messed up place in the world. There's been some weird reports from out there."

"Like what?" asked Holly.

"Part of the Marshall Islands is off limits," said Harland, tilting his head slightly. "It's still a pretty secret place for the military."

"I know it's always in the news regarding ethics," said Sandra. "You can never get a straight answer from anyone out there."

"I get reports about it all the time," said Harland.

"Like what?" asked Sandra.

Harland scoffed. "Odd reports from a bunch of drunken soldiers. Nothing to put any faith into, though."

Rita was quiet, as she listened, fixated on the discussion.

"Being drunk can be fun," said Holly as she looked at Harland. "Pass me another beer. And come and sit here. . . . Tell me about your boy. . . . You got a wife?"

Everyone chuckled.

Harland opened the refrigerator and handed one to Holly. "Like I said, they're just stories drunken sailors tell. Nutcase stories of sea monsters and strange creatures." He then smiled at Holly and plopped down next to her.

"Anything dealing with deformed humans?" asked Nate. "Like in the movies?"

Harland was serious. "No, not like the movies. It's more complicated than folk tales of Ulysses passing a bunch of Sirens. Their stories cause, ah, complications, for the military."

"What happened to those reports?" asked Sandra.

"I look at them every day I'm on the job," said Harland. "But that's only the beginning. When I get a report that is odd, like one reporting on Marshall Island whackos, I have a to make a report about that report, reporting that the report exists."

"That's sure a lot of reports, there," said Sandra, half joking and half serious.

"It's serious," said Harland. "Some of those people get locked away."

"What?" said Rita, finally commenting.

"I'm telling you, once they file one of those reports, they shut those guys right up. . . . Then I add their names to the report of people who claim that there are sea creatures out there."

"You're crazy," scoffed Nate. "Those things only exist in the movies."

As Nate was thinking that the people filing those reports really did need to be locked up, Harland was secretly holding the report his father filed. He wasn't sure if now was the right time to bring it out or not.

ON DECK, Gabe was nervous as the motor in his boat hummed quietly. He still had not decided what he was going to do, let alone where he was going with these people. He had no ideas, no plan, no assurances. Thus, in doubt, he waited and poured himself another Jim Beam and Coca-Cola.

He could hear the other five below talking gibberish, as far as he was concerned. He knew everyone had their problems, but his problems were present, too.

His hands were on the controls and he was quiet, with time to think. Why was Homeland Security at his house? And why were the police there, too? And why didn't Mayor Bolton call him? He wasn't happy about the situation, let alone all the change the situation and the havoc was making with his life.

Unsure of what else to do, Gabe turned on his scanner, tuning in to the Annapolis police department, which had a frequency that could be picked up anywhere on the Chesapeake.

"All points bulletin. I repeat. All points bulletin. We're on the lookout for Gabe Channing: 65 years old. 210 pounds. 5'9-1/2". Salt-and-pepper hair. Consider him armed and dangerous. He is traveling with four others: Nate Baschard, Sandra O'Callahan, Rita Perez, and Major Harland Parker. Major Parker is also considered to be armed and dangerous."

Gabe was aghast and indignant. First of all, he was only 199 pounds, not 210. Secondly, his hair was not salt and pepper grey. He was not armed, although with a deck of cards he could harm his own wallet. He hadn't shot a gun since he was in the Navy. And the only gun he owned was no longer even mechanically workable because it's unique bullet-type had been discontinued.

Gabe began to think hard. Again, he wondered, why were the police after *him*? He had done nothing wrong. He couldn't even imagine what he could have done wrong, had he even wanted to do something wrong.

Gabe left the wheel and rushed down the stairs, yelling, "Turn off your phones!"

Everyone stared at him.

"I said, turn off your phones," Gabe repeated. "There's no turning back."

"What the hell are you talking about?" asked Sandra, alarmed.

"It's over," said Gabe.

"What's over?" asked Nate.

Gabe sighed. "Your lives. My life."

Harland rubbed his face. "What? This is bullshit. What the hell is going on? When am I going to get back to my son?"

"Never," said Gabe.

"Never?" asked Harland, disbelieving.

"We're being hunted down by the government," said Gabe. "Now turn them off, immediately!" Just like in the restaurant, the authoritative way Gabe first spoke made them all comply, though they didn't quite understand why.

Holly set down her beer, two empty cans already in front of her. "Now, I don't know what you'all are doin' and I don't know how I got mixed up with you'all, but I want to go back to shore. I've had all the fun I care to enjoy."

Gabe eyes grew serious. "Pardon my enthusiasm, kids. But something's wrong. Really wrong."

"But what? What have we done? We do we have that they want?" asked Rita as she reached into her coat pocket and made sure the laptop was still there.

"Well, I don't have all the answers, but what I know is we either have something they want or know something we shouldn't," answered Gabe, looking worried.

"But we still hardly know each other?" said Sandra, protesting.

"Exactly my point," said Nate. "The only thing we have in common is that jar we put all our cards into." Nate looked pointedly at Gabe.

Gabe looked down at the floor.

"We've been talking," Nate began, "and we realized we all met you through that jar on the bar, putting in our business cards for the free dinner for two at the Marina Restaurant."

"Yeah," said Gabe, reluctantly.

"That means we're in all this trouble because of you," said Sandra. "I have a job to start next week, I don't need this crap. I want off this boat."

"Me, too," said Nate. "What about my promotion?"

"There's no promotion," said Gabe. "Those are just bribes, distractions. Something's wrong. We need to get out of here."

"That's for sure," said Holly.

"Where can we go?" asked Harland. "Are we heading anywhere right now?"

"No," said Gabe, then he paused to recollect his thoughts. "Look, I don't know a lot, but what I do know is every person with any sense in Annapolis knows I wouldn't harm a fly. Hell, the only harm I've done to anyone in forty years is harm to myself, and my liver. Now there's an all point bulletin that just came across on the police band saying I'm armed and dangerous. I got a bad feeling none of us can go home again."

"You mean *I* can't go home?" asked Holly. "No one knows me. I ain't done a thing."

"Yes you have," said Gabe. "You drove us to the Bay. That makes you an accomplice. And all you others were specifically named in the broadcast."

Holly stared in dismay.

"I think I understand his point now," said Sandra. "I was wondering about that job to Brazil. The Amazon project. It made no sense to me."

"Why do you say that?" questioned Rita.

Sandra scratched her head. "Well, I hate to say it, but according to most people I know, I'm bad luck. And in the last couple months I've suddenly had all the luck in the world. A great job. Then a great new project. Then I get a promotion. I've never had such good luck before."

'Where's that good luck now, Sandra?" asked Gabe.

"That's what I thought," said Nate. "I haven't met many vegetarians before you."

"At least I don't kill things," said Sandra, pointedly. "I stick to my principles. Suddenly I've had all this good stuff happen. It's not like me. I'm in this world to protect the planet, to do good. To stop corruption. I don't want big business to continue to pollute the world. The biotechs are some of the worst, particularly all that pollution crap going on at the Marshall Islands."

"Biotechs are fine," said Nate, putting a sailor's cap on as he looked over at Rita.

"You don't know what you're talking about," said Sandra. "Biotechs are the worse culprits."

Rita just listened, not revealing information she knew.

"It's about profit," explained Nate. "As long as biotechs make a profit, they're doing their jobs. It's not about what's good or bad, right or wrong. It's about money. Making money."

"You telling me you don't care about our planet being destroyed so that some greedy people in power can get even richer?" scoffed Sandra. "You don't look rich to me. Maybe just stupid."

Nate shook his head, surveying the others.

"I know you don't understand this," Gabe interpreted, trying to keep them on topic to get them to understand the gravity of their situation. "But we can't go home—any of us—or we'll be arrested. It's guilt by association. You can never go back. It's no coincidence: cameras in my home, Harland's near death by a cab driver, Sandra and Nate's promotion, phone taps, new mailmen, and who knows what else. What I don't know is why Rita's with us. But biotechs and the Marshall Islands keep coming up."

Rita remained quiet.

"I'm not connected to any of this," said Holly. "What do they want with me?"

"It's by association," said Gabe. "Like I said, you're with us now."

"Gabe, you're a friend and all, from the restaurant, and I've known you for years. But nobody knows I'm with you except for Marti," Holly pleaded.

"Just trust me on this," said Gabe. "I'm a veteran. A Navy veteran. I've seen a lot in my days. Life is not all it appears to be."

"Quit with the crap," said Sandra. "I don't want to stay on this boat forever. Can't you take us back to Washington?"

"If I take you back," began Gabe, "you'll be arrested and never get out of jail. They own us now. I'm telling you, without a doubt in my mind and with forty years as a reporter backing me up, we may never be able to go back. Life will never be the same for us.

Sandra said, "Well, I don't know what we should do about all this crap, but I do believe we need to actually remove the batteries from our cell phones, so H.S.A. won't be able to track us." Reluctantly, everyone followed her advice.

There was one point everyone agreed on: nothing needed to be decided immediately, because no one needed to be anywhere until the next day. Unsure of what to do, or where to go, they decided to wait until morning to make a decision.

DEAR DIARY, August 21, 1982.

This morning, when I was with Hugo in our hut after our walk, we began kissing and cuddling. He said my skin was rough. He complained about it, saying the salt water isn't good for me and that the sun is even worse. With all the swimming I've been doing, that's not going to be easy to change. My skin moisturizer is almost gone. Maybe some coconut juice will help me. Although I love the water, I love Hugo, too.

I then told him all this time on the island has made him extra hairy, which I thought was funny, though he didn't laugh. Nothing is funny to him anymore. He said he doesn't care about all the hair he's growing. HE said maybe his body was helping to protect him from the sun and that I should do more to protect my skin.

He and Jason aren't even working on the boat much anymore. At this rate we could be stuck here for the rest of our lives. But who cares! We actually like it here. Don't worry, be happy!

Amy and I have been fighting lately. She's starting to act real strange. Her eyes dart from side-to-side, like she's non-stop suspicious. Now she tilts her head when she's trying to listen. Her nails, toes, and hands are growing long and sharp. I can't figure it out?

SAILING TO THE TRUTH
CHAPTER NINE

ALL NIGHT, Gabe stayed awake with a bottle of Jim Beam as the others slept, giving him time to think in the haven of the safe seas. As more police bulletins were sent out, he continued to wonder why there was no search for him on his Mistress. Apparently, he was on the boat so seldom that only Marti and the dockhand knew the boat existed.

With the government, planes had the best surveillance, followed by cars. But the least surveillance was over boats. A boat could remain relatively obscure, providing it did not interfere with other boats.

SANDRA WAS THE FIRST TO RISE, heading immediately to the deck to talk with Gabe, who was now drinking a cup of coffee and listening to the police scanner. He savored his coffee, roasted fresh with lots of cream. The coffee tasted better to him today. Maybe it was just the familiar smell of the salty ocean water that made everything feel a little better, or maybe it was watching a glorious sunrise. Whatever the reason, Gabe was happy.

"I've been giving it some thought," said Sandra, as she wrapped her arms around herself, feeling the cold wind.

"There are jackets in there," said Gabe, pointing to a bench. "It gets cold out here. And there's fresh brewed Java."

Sandra opened the bench and removed a bright blue jacket. "I don't like any of this. I'm in this world to do good, not to be chased after for doing something bad, especially something I'm completely in the dark about. Why are we in trouble with the law?"

The local police scanner interrupted, "We now have a description of Sandra O'Callahan: 5'3, 120 pounds, with long blond hair. Considered armed and dangerous."

Sandra's jaw dropped. "What? Armed and dangerous? I helped organized a march last year in Seattle against the Second Amendment. This is unbelievable!"

"It's been going on all night," said Gabe. "They haven't said anything about Holly yet. I don't think they know she's with us. Rita is the one they talk of the least. Harland's got the most problems. There's a shoot to kill order on him. It's crazy."

"What the hell do they think we know or think we did?" said Sandra, collapsing on the bench. "All we did was attend a speech on ethics almost a year ago. If it wasn't for that speech, we wouldn't even know each other."

"I think it's more complicated than that," said Gabe. "I don't believe any one of us knows too much. I think it's what we all might know *together* that's the problem."

"What do you mean?"

"Separately we're not impressive, but together we're quite a rare breed: a reporter, biotech scientist, a stock analyst specializing in biotech, an advocate, and a Pentagon guy reading reports of sea monsters. My problem is I can't figure out how we fit together."

Sandra put her head in her hands. "They're acting like we're building a nuclear bomb, or developing Anthrax or something."

"Actually, two of us are in biotech," she continued. "Maybe it has something to do with that."

Gabe nodded. "Yes, I think it does. The main question is, what do the two of you know . . . or even the five of us know . . . that the government thinks we know? How could seemingly innocent individuals be in so much trouble and not even know what they've done to get there?"

Nate emerged on the deck. "This biotech sector can get pretty interesting. It goes up and down on the market, but in spurts overall."

"Hey what's your take on this trouble we seem to be in?" asked Gabe.

"Well, I don't invest in anything that's harmful to the planet or to mankind," said Nate. "At least according to my definition," he added, noticing Sandra was standing there.

Gabe said, "Now, that causes a problem for me, because I think some of these biotech firms are secretly practicing genetic engineering, though that's just a hunch. I mean, what are the implications on future generations if we change the genetic code, just to further science? There are massive ethics problems involved here."

Sandra began pacing. "I was about to have a promotion, a big promotion."

"So was I," said Nate.

Sandra pointed a finger in his face. "Hey, I listened to your perspective, now you listen to mine: I believe in natural environment evolution, with an anti-big business bias, with minimal scientific-government meddling."

Nate chuckled. "Can you give me that again in plain English?"

"All I know is that we're sitting here on this dumb ass boat putzing around in the water as if we're planning to stay here for the rest of our lives. None of us knows why we're here. We can try to figure it out. I mean, we can spout out all our biotech thoughts, but we don't know a damn thing really—"

The police scanner began again, "We have a confirmation. The following people are confirmed to be on the wanted bio-terrorist list: Harland Parker, Gabe Channing, Nate Baschard, and Sandra O'Callahan. No confirmation yet on Rita Perez."

Sandra began pacing faster. "What! Me! A bio-terrorist? I got a 'D' in biology, and that was just luck."

"No wonder Rita's still sleeping," retorted Nate, sipping on a cup of coffee. "She's not been declared a bio-terrorist yet." Looking over at Gabe, he added, "really good coffee."

Harland joined them. "I don't know what any of you know, but it's time we all start doing some serious confessing. I've got a son at home, and I want to know if I'm going to ever see him again. And if you all have someone you love, too, then you best start talking."

"Why don't you go first," said Gabe. "There's a shoot to kill out on you."

Harland cleared his throat and began speaking, removing something from his pocket. "I need to come clean about something. I have this letter, from my father, just before he died. Here it is. My dad was bitten by some strange creature out near the Marshall Islands. The teeth marks looked human, but, oddly, that was the only part that looked human, they told me. He died the day after he sent this report. I am reviewing 20-year-old reports and I came across this," Harland sat there staring in disbelief. "Then came the knock on my door."

"Obviously," said Nate. "They probably don't even know about that report, let alone what it says."

"Exactly," said Harland, wondering how Nate knew that. "Well, I'm not exactly sure why this Admiral came a'knockin, but I think it had something to do with the Marshall Islands."

"It's not a country known for it's ethics," said Sandra again.

Harland continued, "Well, like I was saying, this report was weird, but it sounded valid to me. And there was another report from that same time period by an admiral who reported having seen sea creatures out there: Fish people, bird people, cat people. People who were not people, but animals, half and half. I didn't believe that one and shredded it, but now—"

"There were rumors," said Gabe, looking at a compass. "I was a sailor and I had heard about those sea creatures, long ago, though I never saw one myself."

"Were you ever stationed at the Marshall Islands?" asked Harland.

Gabe shook his head. "No. Guam, but not the Marshall Islands."

Harland continued. "I'm telling you, I've read thousands of reports—honest reports from officers, but the only time I've read about those sea creatures was in reports that date back to the seventies or eighties—and then only on the Marshall Islands."

"Keep going," said Nate. "I have my own Marshall Islands story, but I want to finish hearing yours first."

"Me, too," said Sandra. "But, yeah, keep talking."

"Well, some of them, the older ones, are about the bird and cat creatures. It's the sea creature rumors that persisted, though."

Suddenly, Rita and Holly emerged from below. It was only 8:15 a.m. still quite early for a Saturday morning at sea. Holly broke in. "I can't say good morning unless someone tells me this has all been a bad dream."

There was no response.

"Oh, boy," said Holly.

"Wait a minute," said Rita. "Did I just overhear something about strange creatures in the Marshall Islands?"

Sandra picked up where Harland had left off. "What I know about the Marshall Islands is that their government is as crooked as can be. For example, after the Exxon Valdez spilled millions of gallons of oil at Prince William Sound in March 1989, Exxon renamed the ship the 'Exxon Mediterranean,' and then later the 'Sea River Mediterranean'. Then they shortened the name to S/R Mediterranean, then simply to Mediterranean still flying under the beloved *Marshall Islands* flag, even though she's been prohibited by law from entering Prince William Sound. Trust me, if the ship responsible for one of the largest environmental disasters in the history of the world still sails out of there, then something's definitely wrong."

The police scanner interrupted. "Attention all units. It's now been confirmed that Rita Perez is also on the wanted bio-terrorist list. Female. 33 years old. 5'6" 135 pounds. Brown hair. Hazel eyes. Suspect is considered to be armed and dangerous. Orders are shoot to kill."

Rita's gasped, her complexion turned pale and she almost fell to the deck. Fortunately for her, Nate caught her. Without a sound, she sank on to the bench and breathed slowly. The news was a grim reality she was not prepared to face, causing a silence to fall on all aboard.

"A bio-terrorist?" she said, tears flooding her eyes. "I'm a scientist. A sci-sci- scientist. I work in a laboratory, with cells. Animal cells. Well, some type of cell." Her voice trailed off. She began sobbing.

Nate took a long swig of coffee, emptying his cup and looked at the other five people, each quiet. Lost. Confused. His motions seemed anti-climatic under the circumstances, the sudden intensity of the situation that was turning into a fear. Everyone was now watching everyone else and wondering how this horror had happened. What was next?

BRAD'S FACE WAS GRIM as he took a bite of his doughnut at 8:48 a.m. at the underground facility in Northern Virginia. "They got away, sir."

"How is that possible?" asked Zack.

Erin was frustrated, too. "Detainments originating in public places cause, ah, complications. As you know, we can't shoot someone in a public place without it, well, turning into a public relations nightmare."

"Did they *all* get away?" asked Zack. "All *five* of them?"

"Yes, sir," said Brad, looking at a timer that read 15:30:01, the time since the cab driver had crashed at Annapolis Circle.

Zack's eyes grew hard. "We are not supposed to be a sloppy department. We're the most efficient department in our government, the country's best. . . . What the news on the cabby?"

"D.O.A.," said Brad.

"And Unit 39-R?"

"He's still in detention in Annapolis," said Brad.

"Why is that?" snapped Zack. "He should have been released immediately!"

"Mayor Bolton, in Annapolis, is giving us some trouble," said Brad. "He's got to be the one behind this mess."

"I'm not so sure," said Erin. "He's not one to advance."

"You know Bolton," said Brad. "He's a maverick. Plus . . . he likes this Channing guy."

"Bolton likes everyone," said Zack. "I want more from you."

Brad handed Zack a document. "Here. You should have this."

Brad scanned the document, a newspaper story from 1999 about the mayor's reaction to a fire at the fire station. "What's this?" he asked.

Zack answered, "Channing wrote that. It won a contest, at the Washington Press Club. Best story in '99."

"Yeah?"

"Well, the rumor is Bolton was with his mistress that night. Gabe somehow knew it, and he covered for the mayor by writing a long story about his reactions. Everyone in Annapolis ate it up."

"An alibi," said Zack.

"That's my point," said Brad. "It was the mayor's first term and the beginning of his career. He owes Gabe. He's not going to let Unit 39-R go without a fight."

"It's trouble for us," said Erin.

GABE LOOKED OVER AT RITA. "Tell us what you know about all this bio-tech crap."

Rita's hazel eyes were bright. "All of evolution is parroted through embryonic development. When you were an embryo you had gills, evolving through the entire evolutionary spiral of our species. You have genes which are repressed. Natural selection suppresses the currently unneeded ones. With the adoption of a simple reactivation, the entire evolution is changed. The genes are still inside all of us; they're just suppressed."

Holly shook her head, "You'all talkin' too much about things none of us really understand."

Nate crossed his arms. "The business sector is already making money out of this. Big money. I've watched it happen for years. I don't buy into this creature stuff, and, seriously, I don't need to ever buy into it. But if the market believes it, that's all I need. Money makes the system work. If the market believes in them, then the market will respond favorably. If the market wants advanced vitamins, then the business world will give them what they want."

Rita continued. "I disagree. We're playing God, messing with a genetic code we haven't begun to fully understand. Any scientist can easily switch on a bunch of genes in a mostly binary sequence. But how many scientists consider the consequences? Do scientists really consider what the DNA code actually holds? The danger to our race, the risk of tampering with what we are, no one monitors that. Some of this stuff could profoundly change us. Who's monitoring that? Government? And *who* in the government? What about the experiments occurring in weak economies around the world?"

Sandra said, "Why are we being targeted this way?"

"What are you saying?" asked Harland.

"Well, should we call their bluff?" asked Sandra. "Or should we take the government's claim seriously that we are bio-terrorists? Oh come on, that's bullshit. And now we're all going to jail? What about Guantanamo Bay? That's a jail and those people *still* aren't charged with a crime. I'm telling you, you can't beat the government when they claim you're a terrorist or anything, for that matter."

"Why can't we?" Holly asked.

"They can claim whatever they want, then put the claims under classified information status until law enforcement officials buckle under endless red tape," said Harland.

Nate scoffed. "We're not going to get arrested. Well, we will get arrested, but the charges will be dropped. It happens all the time. In the end we'll be fine."

"Are you sure you shouldn't just turn yourselves in?" suggested Holly. "Maybe it will help you get out of jail faster."

"We don't get extra points if we turn ourselves in," said Gabe.

Nate squinted his eyes, gazed at Rita, then back to Gabe. "What do you mean, we can do whatever we want? We can't do whatever we want. Or *can* we? Explain that!"

Gabe checked his boat controls, reconsidering the position they all were in due to the scene in Annapolis. "I've reported on a lot of arrests over the years. This situation is odd. We're normal, common people, for God's sake. The media attention around us will be enormous. In a sense, they're stuck. There's been a death already, and a bad scene at the Marina Restaurant, now we're sitting on a boat doing absolutely nothing."

Rita scoffed. "We should move this forward. I, ah, I have to admit something. I have a program written by my brother with gigs of data here." She reached into her jacket and slowly pulled out her laptop. "This little device identifies where each new DNA segment *begins* and where the previous one *ends*, by knowing where to start in the re-sequencing—the evolutionary sequence."

Harland was all ears. "Say, is that really true?"

Nate's eyes widened. "Are you telling us you know how to make one of those creatures?

Rita showed almost no expression when answering. "That's right."

"Now are those blue creatures you can create in your little laboratory, or yellow ones?" asked Gabe, jokingly.

Rita said, "In all seriousness, all I know is that those cells are not completely human. They're part-human, and part something else."

"What do you mean by something else?" asked Sandra. "Just so you know, every day it's my job to sort through facts and lies. How big is the company you work for? Because it's not sounding realistic to me, creating some creature then selling it on the mass market."

"I didn't say that," retorted Rita. "I'm saying I'm not actually sure they're even actual human cells I was working on. All my testing shows is that they're mostly human, like 95%."

"How do you know they're not monkey cells, then?" asked Holly.

Rita shook her head. "I've tested the DNA against every known species. It didn't match anything we've known about. The closest match was with humans. And they're *definitely* not human cells, though they're closer to human cells than to anything else."

"I hate to change the subject," Nate began," but I'll bet some businesses would pay some pretty big bucks for that knowledge . . ." It seemed to the others that when Nate opened his mouth, dollar signs always came out.

"Wow, that's for sure," said Sandra, rudely interrupting.

Nate continued, ". . . and I'll bet under the right circumstances, some foreign governments would handsomely pay for what you know, a lot more than GenXY is paying you."

"That's not my goal," protested Rita. "I'm a scientist."

"Okay, I respect that," said Nate. "But remember we've met before, when I visited GenXY. Your stock is rising at unprecedented rates—"

"Yeah, along with a lot of biotechs," said Sandra, again interrupting.

Nate continued,"—so it's my guess that various insiders know that information and are beginning to—"

"Profit off of it," finished Rita. "Yes, that's definitely true. That explains all the money out there, including those frequent trips by all those admirals to the Marshall Islands, and a few other island nations in that area. That Henderson, my boss, and some government officials have been talking together, real secret like."

Harland sat up on the bench. "That would explain all those crazy reports I've been reading. I'll bet those are sea creatures they're talking about on those Marshall Islands."

"Now you people are just full of crap," said Holly. "I've heard plenty of outrageous stories in my life, but I think the wine from last night has finally done you'all in."

Everyone turned to Gabe, clearly the oldest person in the group, and—being a reporter—probably the most skeptical. "I don't mean to start believing in these boogie men, but when I was in the Navy, we used to detonate all these atomic bombs at the Marshall Islands. It didn't even make sense. We just kept exploding them day after day—"

"Contaminating all the water and soil, for sure," said Sandra, interrupting.

"Yeah, that's what I was thinking," said Gabe. "For certain, we killed most all the marine life in those parts."

"And probably all the sea-monsters along with it," said Nate, half-joking, half-serious.

The police scanner came to life again, "The orders on those five have been affirmed—use deadly force if necessary. They cannot be allowed to escape."

Sandra's eyes raised. "I think we're on to something here. And even though I don't believe in sea monsters, and I don't understand DNA, I think we need some outside help, and I have some friends in high places in other countries." Sandra stood and walked toward the front of the boat. "Is this boat up for a sailing voyage, Gabe?"

Gabe nodded, eyeing her speculatively.

"Because I think we need to head to New York City, to the United Nations. We need to make plans for ourselves, and right now there's no hope but in what Rita has said."

"What are you suggesting?" asked Nate.

"Yeah," said Harland. "Please explain."

"We need to somehow stop the United States government from making these creatures, and I'm certain some of the other countries in this world will want to put a stop to what our government is doing."

"How do you know our government is making them?" asked Harland. "Maybe they want to destroy them, especially if what Gabe said is true, that they used atomic radiation to kill them off."

"There *is* money involved," said Nate. "And where there's money, there's—"

"Corruption," said Sandra, staring directly into Nate's eyes for the first time. "If there's one thing I've learned in my life, it's, if the United States government is involved, and big business is interested in a project—"

"And stocks are rising," said Nate, interrupting.

"Then corruption is right around the corner," finished Sandra.

"By preserving the DNA and killing off all sub-human creatures."

"The government and the biotechs will control just about everything."

MISTRESS HUGGED THE COAST, as Gabe kept a firm grasp on the steering wheel. He was in his full glory, sailing the six people aboard in the Atlantic Ocean, on a mission of world importance to the United Nations. They were lost souls, now. None of them could return home, as arrest was imminent if not outright extermination. They were labeled bio-terrorists, though they were still not completely certain as to why. But aside from that, with the sails high and the wind at their backs, sailing could not be more fun.

Hugging the coast had one specific benefit: Holly's cell phone access remained active, even as everyone else's phone remained off. Since Holly was not a bio-terrorist suspect, her having a functional cell phone would not create a problem as yet, and did allow some discreet calls outbound as well as inbound.

"They don't know you're with us," Sandra said as she looked at Holly, "so you're safe. You're not a suspect . . . yet."

All of a sudden, Nate jumped up. "We're all going to be millionaires!" he shouted.

"Don't tease us like that," said Holly.

"I'm not kidding," said Nate.

"Do you swear we'll be millionaires?" asked Holly.

"It's probable," said Nate, "though not definite. All I know is that there's going to be several businesses quite interested in buying your information, Rita. Don't you agree?"

"I don't know about that," said Rita, still unsure of anything.

Nate grinned from ear to ear. "How about a million for each of us?"

"What?" asked Sandra, in disbelief.

"You mean each of us?" asked Harland.

"Including me?" said Holly. "What do *I know* that's worth that type of money?"

"That's a lot of money," said Gabe, over his shoulder. "Sure, there will be lots of governments and businesses interested in what Rita knows, even if it's not marketable yet."

"That's true," said Harland. "We *could* sell it, but we should be doing this to help our planet, not just for a profit."

Rita agreed, nodding.

Gabe continued, "You know, all our accounts will be watched and tracked from this point forward. We can't even touch a penny without the Feds knowing."

"See!" blurted Nate. "We need that money to live off of. With a million bucks, invested at eight percent, we'll each make about eighty grand a year. It's not that great, but it's not a pittance either."

"Speak for yourself," said Holly. "I'd love to have a pot load of money like that."

"Of course we can sell it," said Nate. "But first let's see how good Sandra's contacts are."

"My contacts are fine," said Sandra.

"Well, then make your calls now," said Nate.

Unthinking, Sandra reached for her phone, which was still off.

"No," said Gabe, grabbing her hand. "You can't use your phone. They'll track us down. Use Holly's phone. And we should probably all lock ours away so we don't accidentally turn them on."

"Yeah, she's not been named on the police scanner yet," said Nate. "Use Holly's."

"Good point," said Harland.

"Alright," said Sandra.

"Well, here goes nothing," said Holly, handing Sandra her cell phone.

Sandra pulled out her own cell phone, put the battery back in, and scrolled through a few entries. Then—using Holly's—she dialed the number of Jacob Btok, ambassador to the Solomon Islands.

IMMEDIATELY, Brad jumped up and grabbed his phone to call Zack. "Sandra's phone just went live," said Brad. "She's somewhere in southern New Jersey, near the coast. . . . Shit, it just went dead."

"Well, let's center the operation there, then," said Zack, wondering why the group—if they were still moving as a group—would be in Jersey. Zack then dialed tech support and asked for an historical correlation between each member of the group and New Jersey.

AFTER THREE RINGS, the voicemail began, "This is Jacob Btok, with the Embassy of the Solomon Islands. I apologize for not taking your call, but I promise to return it when I can. Thank you."

As the voicemail message began, Sandra announced, "Voicemail."

"Hang up right now!" Gabe shouted.

Instinctively, Sandra complied.

"Why?" asked Nate.

Gabe's eyes widened. "Because we're being hunted as terrorists. Remember? Leaving any message for anyone right now, using our real names is not a good idea."

"He's right," said Nate, cursing himself for not thinking of that. "Call the next one."

Sandra shook her head. "How do we know we really have these mutant cells here? It's not like we're certain we're on to something."

"Keep making the calls," said Rita. "I'm certain enough. I've spent years on this project. They're definitely not animal as I know it, something I didn't grasp at first. They must be from these sea monsters from the Marshall Islands."

"Or some type of mutant creature," said Nate. "Obviously, if they're not animal or human, then they're something in between. And if they're something in between—"

"Then there's value in them," stated Harland.

"Yeah, lots of real value," said Nate, his eyes gleaming at the thought.

"So, we're talking millions here?" questioned Holly.

"Millions," said Nate, rubbing his fingers against his thumbs. "Maybe even more."

Sandra punched through her cell phone entries again, and dialed another number. " Jonathan Summers? . . . It's Sandra O'Callahan, with WatchDog. . . . I'd like to meet you regarding a matter related to the Marshall Islands. . . . Well, it is, ah, about genetic engineering. And it's critical we talk. I'm going to be in New York tomorrow night. Are you available? . . . Great. . . . Well, by the docks. . . . Sure, yeah, if the other ambassador wants to come, he's welcome. . . . Yeah, if you want to bring them all, you're welcome to."

"Yeah, I know I'm on the bio-terrorist list. . . . Yes, the U.S. government is trying to find me. And yes, I believe the U.N. needs to know what the U.S. government is up to."

Sandra hung up the phone and stared at everyone.

"What did he say?" asked Gabe.

"He said they'll meet with us."

With that news, Nate jumped up again, singing *If I had a million dollars*. Everyone laughed, because he sang so silly. It was the first time they all had laughed since they had fled Annapolis.

DEAR DIARY, October 3, 1982.

They've all changed so much. Hugo now has thick, black hair and mumbles more than he speaks. He has become depressed, and it seems to be escalating. He no longer wants to kiss me or make love to me. Meanwhile, I'm as excited about it as ever. What do I do? I keep going for long, lonely swims. It seems to help, relaxing my mind and relieving me of my frustrations. Amy keeps growing and stands maybe a half meter taller than she did only a few months ago. Jason is losing weight and has oily skin with tiny soft things growing out of it. I'm the only one who hasn't changed.

Their attitudes are changing, too. They look at me differently, no longer like I'm a long-time friend, but like I'm a stranger. I'm getting a creepy feeling.

My days now are mostly spent in the water. I like the fish; and the vegetation I used to love now tastes bland to me. Actually, I've started eating raw fish and shellfish. I think they call that Sushi in Japan. My swimming ability has improved over the past few months, and I'm becoming quite good at holding my breath under water with my lungs developing accordingly.

Well, to hell with them then! They can fight and argue among themselves. For me, I have the sea—something I *oh so* love.

UNITED NATIONS PAYOFF
CHAPTER TEN

THE GENETIC BREAKTHROUGH came in 1944, when a scientist named O.T. Avery, together with two of his colleagues, studied a substance that was capable of changing one strain of bacteria into another. This was deoxyribonucleic acid, commonly known as DNA. In time, genetics studies evolved, always adding further scientific knowledge to the existing knowledge base. Eventually, scientists were able to unlock the genes, altering the normal development of specialized cells, through a science commonly known as stem-cell research.

Through stem-cell research, cells were captured and harvested during their early stages of development, before they developed into more specific types of cells such as bones or nerves. For instance, cells from a tiny human embryo were captured and studied before the embryo developed a heart, fingers, hair, and teeth. The idea was that cells in their early stages of development were more scientifically powerful than cells that had begun the specialization process, like a diamond in a large, raw form can—through cutting—become much more valuable than when it was in its undeveloped stage. However, in maximizing its potential, an uncut diamond must be properly studied. What is the proper way to cut the diamond, maximizing its profit? Will a bad cut shatter the entire diamond? Can diamond flaws be removed during cutting? Or, will flaws be *created* during cutting? And just like diamonds, it was believed that once a specialized cell was cut—similar to a cut diamond—it could never return to its earlier state of existence.

In the next stage of genetic engineering through stem-cell research, scientists believed it might be possible—in theory—to encourage the stump of an amputated arm to grow into a new one by de-differentiating its cells and then allowing them to grow and differentiate again. Scraps of embryonic tissue or fertilized ova could be directed into the production of hearts, kidneys, and other organs.

The raw science was more complicated. If a new DNA helix found its way into a sperm cell or an egg cell—replacing the existing helix and from there into a fertilized ovum, all the cells of the new organism would possess those original cellular blueprints, thus affecting the new organism as a whole, and not just some of the individual cells.

The blueprint of each cell was mainly a component of binary analysis. Cells either advanced in one direction or another, depending on which switches were turned on or off during DNA manipulation. The most valuable cells were the early cells in an organism's life, not the later cells, the opposite of what a laymen would think—as with the diamond. Even simple manipulations to the early cell's environment could be used to increase the probability of a particular outcome—or conversely—diminish the probability of a particular outcome. Through a small difference in heat, a totally different type of person might be produced, as the environment in the womb was highly sensitive to chemicals and mutagenic agents.

One small change in a cell's developing life would become greater and greater as each cell perpetuated itself in future replications. Any chemical change to the genetic code would alter the final human who was born. The presence of any different enzyme introduced early enough in a cells development, always distorted the chemical workings of the cell (even slightly) changing the person into a somewhat different living organism.

Although most chemical changes created only slight differences in a person (like a difference in hair color or the length of one's fingers). Other chemical changes could affect development in multiples, like the body developing a third eye, or an extra arm).

Other mutagenic agents—similar to those introduced via the atomic experiments on the Marshall Islands, following WWII—were able to introduce massive doses of DNA, restructuring energy into the early development of cells. It affected countless sperm and egg cells in many thousands of people. The rule was: any change to the structure of sperm or egg DNA would change the development of human life in the current generation and all future generations.

Scientists speculated about the potential future consequences to individuals who were routinely exposed to genetic changes. How did vaccines affect cell development? Did genetically engineered foods change the cells in the stomach? Did they flow into the blood and possibly the brain? Still, most of the speculation remained unexpressed since concern was equated with cost—and cost could *cost* the scientist his job.

ONE OF THE BIGGEST PROBLEMS with genetic study is the lack of an enforceable, consistent ethical code. Was it unethical to raise the heat of a laboratory womb three degrees instead of two degrees? The question is absurd! Only after many tests spanning decades would the answer be known, and even then, organisms would have been created violating later ethical rules. Then those laboratory samples (or were they humans?) could be further altered, creating even more ethical risks and with it, creating further deviation from the scientific norm.

The thirst for scientific knowledge and commercial advantage was unquenchable. Hence, was it too late to stop the madness? Would the insanity of man drive *mankind* into destruction before knowledge could reach a necessary level of safety? What would be the consequences to the cells that developed into genetically modified people? Were they now a race all unto themselves? How could the new imperfections in the cells be minimized?

Could gene combinations create higher intelligence, artistic creativity, and therefore a greater humanity? Would people idealize a genetically modified body for themselves, in a new form? Would the day come when the ultimate goal would be attained of directing the evolution of people into superior forms intellectually and physically, creating a (seemingly) better and more advanced form of human life? Would it be ethical?

PASSING NEW YORK CITY VIA BOAT is a journey not taken by most people, but for those who do it, it is always an awesome experience. Watching the New York City skyline rise up from the sea was a dramatic experience for everyone. For Nate, it symbolized some of the greatest achievements of mankind. However, for Sandra, it was symbolic of how far mankind had gone to manipulate the natural environment of the world.

For Gabe, bringing in a crew of six was a dream come true. It brought back old memories of sailing around the world as part of the greatest Navy that ever floated. Being labeled a bio-terrorist was really as bad as it gets, but at least there was an adventure in the works.

Since Gabe had built his boat almost forty years earlier, he had only sailed it locally, aside from a few trips to New York decades earlier. Using the boat mostly on Saturdays and Sundays, Gabe had become quite a competent sailor. He knew how to sail a boat as few others could do, since most boats the size of his required a crew of three or more. In his earlier days at the Naval Academy, he was one of the Navy's finest, building small test models with hand tools, before machines took over much of the process.

Much as he loved sailing, the seriousness of their situation took away a lot from the otherwise pleasurable trip. Rita's explanation was sensible, and he trusted her, even though her knowledge of genetic science was mind-boggling at times. Understanding genetics was difficult for him, though he was able to handle a variety of stories, each with its own peculiarities.

Being a rebel as well, Gabe had never registered his boat, with Mayor Jake Malone giving him ample legal shelter. Why would a legal technicality be a problem for him? Gabe's problems were never with the law.

As he approached New York Harbor he yelled "coming about" and swung the boat toward the east. Realizing that ever since 9/11, New York would be monitored, he decided to head east toward the Hamptons. Out there on Long Island one more sailboat would blend in with all the others. All he needed to do was to find an out-of-the-way marina.

Four hours later, he steered and docked his boat against ragged tires, bumping the boat against them as he grinned in anticipation of the upcoming adventure. He exited the boat and paid the $100 docking fee. He returned to the Mistress and found his passengers in a lively discussion of sea creatures and mutants. He poured himself some Jim Beam and Coca-Cola and settled in. Now it was time to wait for the ambassadors to arrive.

FOUR MEN, TWO IN TRADITIONAL ISLAND ATTIRE, and two in dark suits and dark sunglasses, arrived at Gabe's boat. Everyone on board had spent the day relaxing, sunning, and drinking wine and liquor, they were feeling good, which was understandable, since it was now just 4 p.m.

Ambassador Summers, Ambassador Btok, and two bodyguards announced their arrival. The ambassadors entered with all the presence of men of power, though privately each was skeptical of the reason for being there on that boat.

After all the formal introductions were made, Sandra began the discussion. "I know it's short notice, but it's extremely important, and you know I wouldn't call you—"

"Yes, unless it's important," said Ambassador Btok, nodding. "I trust you, Sandra. You've done good things for us, and I'm here because you asked for me."

"And me," said Ambassador Summers, looking at the bodyguards. "The islands stand as one."

The two nameless men nodded, expressions of total disinterest on their faces.

"What's going on?" asked Ambassador Btok. "What is so important that we couldn't have discussed this over the phone?"

Harland was quiet. Rita said nothing. Seeing an opening, Nate moved into his Wall Street salesman persona.

"Well, gentlemen, first we had the Dark ages," said Nate. "Then there was the Renaissance Age. That was followed by the Age of Exploration and the Industrial Age. Then the Robber Barons and the Information Age."

"And now what?" asked Sandra, playing with her necklace out of nervousness.

Nate smiled. "Oh, my friends, it's now the Genomic Age, the age of genetics and research, the age of stem-cell research. The age of scientific engineering and hybrid development. We're here to see the dawn of something we have never seen before, something that will change life on Earth like it has never been changed before, and something that will sustain us for the rest of our lives."

"Or destroy us all," Sandra added.

"Well," Ambassador Summers began. "Of what value are we? I don't see why two small South Pacific territories are to be involved."

"Nor I," said Ambassador Btok. "Enlighten us."

"It's about genetics," said Rita, finally finding her voice. "We're here for the truth. We need to show you the truth, the truth of genetic engineering."

"I'm a soldier," said Harland. "I believe in my country, and all it stands for. And yet it's my country which has put me—all of us—into this situation. I'm here because I know the truth, and the truth is in all this genomic—biotech—or whatever stuff. Rita's findings: it's in reports I can't show you, classified reports, and in sector research I can't understand."

"That's true," said Sandra. "I can show you what he's talking about, but it's not something I can explain easily. It'll take some time."

Ambassador Btok subtly looked at his watch. "We haven't a lot of time. How about an executive summary right now."

Gabe spoke up. "Gentlemen, I don't mean to assert myself on your agenda, or your time, no less. But I do want to tell you I believe beyond a doubt that there could be something special on Rita's laptop you need to see.

"Is this true?" asked Ambassador Summers, looking at Rita, then at Sandra.

"It's true," blurted Sandra, frantically trying to impress upon them the importance of Rita's findings and how they could be used destructively. "We have reason to believe, all of us, that the United States government is creating an advanced soldier, for military purposes."

"They want to be able to defeat any other army, not only with technological prowess, but with scientific might," said Harland, following Sandra's lead. "They want to develop a soldier who is advanced—" He looked at Sandra for help.

"Genetically," said Sandra. "Right, Rita?"

Rita was hesitant. "That's basically true. It certainly seems that way. I've . . . well . . . I've discovered through my research that I've been working on what seems to be human cells and then killing them, killing human embryos—all the while thinking they were animals. As someone from your culture should respect, I believe any killing of an embryo is an absolute death of a human life. A murder, no less."

"Well, I don't know about that," said Nate. "But what I do know is that much of U.S. industry has billions to gain by having a scientific technology like this developed. That's what we found out when we were on the boat sailing here. I didn't believe it before, but now I'm convinced sub-human creatures have actually walked the globe."

"That's crazy," said Ambassador Btok.

"No it's not," insisted Nate.

"Harland's right," said Sandra. "We're convinced, all of us, that our government is secretly creating an advanced form of life, a life form that we never before have seen, or could imagine."

"Mutant humans," said Harland, mumbling. "They're real! They killed my dad, right over there in your Marshall Islands."

"It's true." said Rita. "I have all the information on this laptop. It has all the technology you'd ever need from laboratories, that proves the U.S. government is tampering with life, like it has never tampered with anything before."

Incredulously, Ambassador Btok looked at Ambassador Summers, the other two men standing silent. "This sounds like some science fiction story!"

Ambassador Summers looked at Sandra. "Why do you believe in these things?" he asked.

"I just do," answered Sandra, looking directly at Ambassador Summers. "The story of Harland's dad, us being bio-terrorists, Rita's research, Nate's numbers, even my findings."

Gabe was scribbling notes in his ship's journal as they spoke, not contributing to the conversation going on, though listening intently.

Sandra was serious. "They're out there. That's why the U.N. secretary general traveled to the Marshall Islands for his last vacation, isn't it?"

Ambassador Summers was serious. "We know there was extensive testing at the Marshall Islands after WWII. They were releasing atomic energy into the atmosphere and sea many times every year, with bomb after bomb being tested."

"I've read the reports," said Harland. "Hundreds of officers have seen these things. They certainly exist."

"I don't believe it," said Ambassador Summers.

Ambassador Btok put his hand on Ambassador Summers' shoulder. "I've heard those stories, too, but I always heard it was the tales of drunken soldiers, not officers. U.S. officers, too, right?"

"That's right, sir," said Harland. "From Rita's laptop, I've seen all I needed to believe that they exist. Somebody could make those soldiers if they wanted to."

"Outrageous!" said Ambassador Summers. "Jacob, we need to leave now!"

"Not so fast," said Ambassador Btok, again holding Ambassador Summers' shoulder. "I've known Sandra for ten years. Her father and my father were good friends. I know from experience she wouldn't say anything that's not fact."

Gabe continued scribbling in the journal, though no one on the boat noticed.

Ambassador Summers abruptly removed Ambassador Btok's hand off his shoulder. "I can tell you with complete certainty that there are no creatures on our islands. This allegation is absurd." His anger showed.

"What about the dramatic rise in biotech companies that have research facilities out there?" pursued Nate. "All those companies don't suddenly start rising at the same time unless something big is happening. And they all are working on Marshall Islands projects." (Nate was bluffing, hoping no one would catch it.)

Ambassador Summers' anger suddenly wilted, looking at the dock and the swaying boat as he held a long silence. "What's your price?"

Nate grinned. "One million dollars, each. American dollars. With $100,000 each in cash, and the other $900,000 in individual Swiss accounts."

"I'll see what I can do," said Ambassador Summers, who then abruptly turned and left the boat, followed by Ambassador Btok, and two bodyguards.

Sandra shouted, " Ambassador Summers!"

He turned around, facing her from a distance. "I know you're a man of your word. No one is to know where we are. That is absolutely imperative." She spoke with an authority never before seen by the others, inferring the two of them had other dealings which were understood between them.

"You have my word," said Ambassador Summers, who then turned and left.

"And mine, too," said Ambassador Btok.

FIVE SECURITY COUNCIL REPRESENTATIVES (each in a seemingly identical blue suit), sat around an oval table at the United Nations building in New York City. The senior officials of China, Russia, France, England, and the United States sat grimly as Ambassador Btok and Ambassador Summers stood. Ambassador Summers took the lead, as he concluded his summary of the situation at hand.

"Now I ask you, gentlemen: how do we handle this?" asked Ambassador Summers.

"Is the demand of six million for the technology?" asked the Ambassador of China, a question requiring an interpreter to translate the request into three languages.

"That's correct, sir," answered Ambassador Summers, nodding. "Their demand is one million dollars each for the technology. Six million American dollars in all."

"There are only five on the bio-terrorist list," said the American Ambassador. "Who is the sixth person?"

"I don't know, sir," said Ambassador Summers. "I'm just repeating their specific request."

The ambassador from China remained silent, showing little emotion.

The ambassador from Russia folded his hands. "Who will then own this information from the scientist's laptop?"

"There is no information," scoffed the ambassador from the U.S. "It's a useless hand-held computer gadget. They're bluffing."

The interpreters struggled with the words "gadget" and "bluffing," repeating the word several times.

"Perhaps there's been some sort of misunderstanding," said the ambassador from the U.K. "This idea of the U.S. wanting a new breed of soldier sounds like science fiction to me. I mean, why would the most superior military in the world require a genetically modified soldier. What exactly *is* a 'genetically modified soldier'?"

The ambassador from China lifted an eyebrow, still saying nothing.

"Why should we trust the Americans," demanded the ambassador from France. "It's been our understanding for decades that the Americans are the first to lie, and the last to tell the truth."

"This is ridiculous," said the ambassador from the U.S., pounding his fist on the table. "This girl's—excuse me—this so-called scientist's story is a farce! She's a below-average scientist at a mediocre laboratory. The idea of these "creatures" is a total fairy tale!" The interpreters spoke frantically, each into his or her own microphone, which then went through multiple translations and then into a headpiece worn by each of the ambassadors. "This nonsense needs to end, with the pay-out being a violation of U.N. and United States policy. I repeat, this technology does not exist. It's invented out of greed."

"I have heard tales and I believe it does exist," said the Russian ambassador, tight-lipped. "Soldiers with wings. Others with gills. Some who can run at the speed of cheetahs. Night vision, like owls. Indeed, not even I had fathomed that could become a reality. It was our thought only that biological weapons were meant to be released into the atmosphere, or the water, not induced under controlled conditions."

"We all know the effects of a ground war," said French ambassador. "To occupy is to win."

The U.S. ambassador's forehead was beaded with sweat. "There seems to be a consensus among all of you to negotiate with these people, these bio-terrorists—"

"They're heroes," said the Chinese ambassador, breaking her silence.

"Greedy terrorists!" rebutted the U.S. ambassador, leaning into the table.

The Ambassador from the U.K. raised his hands. "Fellow ambassadors, we must be able to reach a diplomatic agreement."

"I agree with our Chinese friend," said the French ambassador. "They're heroes because they seem to be exposing a secret hybrid weapon system. This is genetic warfare."

"These people are bio-terrorists in the truest sense of the word," argued the U.S. ambassador. "I tell you they have no technology of any value, they're attempting to profit by extorting false information. . . . It's an empty threat."

"It seems you're developing a biological weapons system: hybrid warriors capable of harming the world. Perhaps we should launch a full-scale investigation, with weapons inspectors entering these laboratories in Rockville, Maryland?" asked the French ambassador. "I'm sure the American media would have a laugh at your country being the victim of its own games for a change."

"Soldiers that fly!" The Russian ambassador was now grinning. "I'm sure that information would come with quite a price among international weapons merchants. It's a biological race you are beginning. I guess those rumors of sea creatures in the Marshall Islands were true, after all. And this group is coming to the U.N. not arms merchants. And if their information is useless then why are you trying to knock them down with shoot-to-kill orders?"

"This technology should be owned by all members of the U.N.," said the ambassador from China. "Is that agreed?" She gazed around the table.

Everyone nodded, except for the U.S. ambassador, who was looking ill.

"This meeting is groundless and out of order," said the U.S. ambassador, his fist slamming on the table. "Our veto will stop any deal from progressing."

The ambassadors agreed to a thirty minute recess during which they all contacted their respective government leaders. When they returned, the U.S. ambassador recognized that an international scandal could unfold, further damaging the U.S. standing in the world community. Then he agreed with the others and dropped the veto threat.

During the recess, he contacted H.S.A. and notified them of the contact between the group and the two ambassadors. Zack immediately initiated a full-scale search of all the hotels within 50 miles radius of Manhattan.

THE NEXT DAY, twenty-five armed soldiers stormed GenXY in Rockville, escorting twelve computer programmers and sixteen people in moving companies through the laboratory. Their orders were to make an absolute sweep of all technology in the building and completely vacate the building of its 125 employees within 72 hours.

The same procedure was duplicated across the Marshall Islands and all other biotechs involved with Project M.I.X., with the order closing six facilities, employing 700 total people. Similarly, computer programmers were ordered to remove and destroy most articles in the labs, with only a minimal amount of information (mostly cell technology) being shipped to the Pentagon via air transport carrier.

Each person who worked in each of the facilities was then ordered home the next day, a permanent change accompanied by an immediate three-year conditional severance package for all workers, with the accompanying order being that no one was to talk to media or family about any details at the facility. Any violation thereof would be treated as either treason or see them labeled as an "enemy combatant," and relocated to Guantanamo.

The orders were considered over-the-top for employees who were mostly scientists, but the severance package made the decision a natural one for everyone.

ALMOST EVERY PAGE IN GABE'S JOURNAL was filled as he wrote vigorously with a ball-point pen. The discussion with the two ambassadors provided the inspiration for him to change the direction of his story, from a story about retirement to one about the cell technology being developed in Rockville.

Oddly, much of the biotech story overlapped neatly with the retirement story. Since Gabe had his original notes with him, making some basic changes was rather easy. Knowing how to quickly transpose appropriate material was a skill most writers developed. His sources, Nate, Harland, Sandra, and Rita stayed the same. Just change the quotes from investments to biotechnology and the story flowed!

Gabe liked the tone of this story—a big government exposé—and not merely a trumped up story with a mayor about a fire station fire. It seemed his boring life of writing was about to change.

The more Gabe thought about this new storyline, the more he liked it because it had the potential to be purchased by a national publication. It was a story with "legs," which also meant it was fun to write. After all, how many people really cared about retirement articles except people who were recently retired, or people planning to retire within the next decade or so?

He continued to work diligently, doing his best to create a sensible story out of what seemed to be science fiction. The retirement story was already 1200 words, enough for a magazine, though it wasn't organized properly. Now with the extensive ambassadors' quotes, it was over 2100 words. Although a magazine story required 2000 to 3000 words, Gabe would have to do some editing to make it solid enough.

In light of the story change, Gabe was finally motivated to complete it. He figured by morning he'd be finished and then able to use Holly's phone to sell the story to some national publications. He was working late into night, when he suddenly remembered a story he wrote maybe 20 – 25 years ago. He started rummaging through some old notebooks he had never taken off the boat when he moved into his house. Then he found what he was looking for: old notes from a conversation he had had at the bar with an admiral!

He realized that he could blend the old (unpublished) story with the new one. After a few hours of cutting and pasting, he knew the story was ready to publish.

MARTI STOOD BEHIND THE BAR, and threw a broken glass into a garbage can. "I can't stand it anymore," she said. "I just miss him so much. I need to know what's happening."

"It's only Monday," said Carley, drinking a cup of coffee as her 5:00 p.m. shift began. "I'm sure he's fine."

Marti tried to hold back her tears, but was unsuccessful. "Every day for the past thirty-some years, Gabe's sat in that chair at this time. You could set your watch by him. He's never late, never early. Always right on time. And today he's not here again."

"Maybe he just took a few days off."

Marti shook her head. "No. Holly didn't show up for work either. She was the one who drove them to wherever they are."

"I know you love him, but give it a rest," said Carley, glancing at four customers as they sat down at a table. "Maybe you should take a vacation. Give yourself a breather."

"I don't know. I'd still be worried."

"Don't worry," said Carley, patting her hand. "He'll call. All men call eventually and God knows he'd call you first."

STEAM POURED OUT as Zack poured his third cup of coffee this particular morning. He reached for a spoon and dumped a large scoop of sugar into his cup, stirring it quickly and causing some of the coffee to spill. Brad approached him, holding a small stack of photographs.

"These are from the surveillance camera at the Marina Restaurant," said Brad. "There are only five of them seated at the table."

"Then why the six million?" asked Zack.

Erin said, "Something seems fishy. Five people don't ask for six million dollars for just a fishing trip. There's got to be a sixth person in on this deal, and maybe someone with some serious authority, too."

"None of us know either," said Brad, starting to sweat. "But I agree, there's six of them, fine. Not five. They're traveling with someone else. They must have another government insider we don't know about yet. We've got to find out who it is."

"And we will," Erin added.

AREA CODE 702 BLINKED ON HOLLY'S PHONE DISPLAY, a Las Vegas number. "Hello?" said Gabe, everyone else in the boat gathering around the first call to come in, in hours.

"We want the story," said a man on the other end. "It's Jason Shaw again, with Playboy Magazine. We want the exclusive on it, though. Can you do that?"

"Sure," said Gabe. "I had a feeling you'd call back. What price are you offering?"

"Are the ambassador quotes solid?" asked Jason.

"I'm an award winning journalist," said Gabe with a confident smile.

"We know that," said Jason. "Okay, the story pays $30,000, deposited directly into your account upon receipt."

Gabe's eyes widened. "Really?"

"How much will they pay?" asked Nate, whispering.

Gabe pressed the mute button. "Thirty thousand dollars."

"Ask for a hundred grand," said Nate.

"You've got to be crazy," retorted Gabe.

"Trust me. This story is a killer."

"I can't," said Gabe, shaking his head.

Nate reached for the phone and deactivated the mute. "Sir?"

"Yes?" said Jason. "Who's this?"

"I've been working together with Gabe, calling various publications. We have another offer higher than that, and, frankly, the credibility of Playboy—"

"And the pictures," said Sandra, glancing at Rita and Holly.

"The offer's thirty grand," said Jason. "It's all I'm authorized to offer."

A "low battery" message appeared on the phone display. "Crap," said Nate, carelessly. "Wait a second, I have another call."

Jason paused, along with Nate, as he hit mute.

"What should we do?" asked Nate to the group.

"What's his name?" asked Harland.

"Jason Shaw," said Gabe. "Why?"

Harland rubbed his chin. "I know that guy. There was a story about him back in June."

"How do you know?" asked Sandra.

"I'm a subscriber," said Harland without embarrassment.

"You go, big boy!" said Holly, hitting Harland's back as she chuckled.

"He's a big wig out there, I'm certain of it," said Harland. "Tell him $100,000 or nothing. And I mean it. If they want your story about sea creatures, they'll pay for it. They'll kill for something like this."

Gabe reached for the phone, and deactivated mute. "Jason?"

"Yeah."

"It's Gabe. I appreciate the offer, but I'm not willing to risk my career over $30,000. Seriously. I've been contacting other publications about this story for months."

"I thought it was originally a retirement article," said Jason.

"Do you think, as an award-winning journalist I'm going to leave messages around the country telling them I'm writing about a top-secret government operation?

That's absurd! My professional integrity is just too high for that bullshit. The price is $100,000. take it or leave it."

The "low battery" light blinked again.

"One second," said Jason, followed by a brief pause. "We'll take it. But we need the story immediately."

"I'll put it in the mail today," said Gabe, giving the group a thumbs-up.

"Mail?" asked Jason. "Can't you email it?"

Gabe stared at the journal, with his chicken scribble all over it. "No, I'll mail it. It'll take . . ."

"Three days to Nevada," whispered Nate.

". . . t-h-r-e-e days to get there," said Gabe.

"Then it's a deal," said Jason. "Can't you overnight it?"

"I'll see what I can do," answered Gabe. "I'll have to charge you an extra twenty bucks then."

Jason sighed. "Sure. It's a deal then.

Great!" said Gabe.

Jason said, "After we get the story, and if the quotes are as good as the ones you told me in our last call, then I'll transfer the money to your account."

"Thanks," said Jason.

"Thank *you!*" said Gabe.

HOLLY PLACED THE ARTICLE into an overnight delivery envelope and dropped it into the pick-up box. Since Holly was the only person not wanted by H.S.A., she was the natural choice to leave the sail boat, and run a few quick errands.

She then flagged down a cab and headed to an electronics store, where she purchased six phone chargers, twelve pre-paid phones (each with 5000 minutes of usage), and a laptop plug. Minutes later, she flagged down another cab and returned to the sail boat.

She was smiling when she re-entered the boat. "I'd never want to live around here," she said. "Traffic's a mess. And all the lines are long." She removed the backup computer battery and then handed the pre-paid phones to Gabe. "Here you go."

"Great!" said Gabe.

Gabe handed a phone to everyone on the boat.

Rita immediately connected her new cell phone to the laptop and then turned it on, careful to press the option that prevented it from using it's own signal. She then logged into her bank account file, and noticed a pending transaction for $68,931.14.

"That's odd," said Rita. "There's a pending transaction in my bank account."

"It's probably a year's salary," said Harland. "H.S.A. probably closed down your company in Rockville and paid you a year's salary. It's government policy to do that in time of war."

"War?" blurted Sandra. "There's no war."

"Yes there is," said Harland. "Ever since 9/11, we're under a declaration of war, which is technically the case until we return to Level Green."

"But we've never even been down to Level Blue," said Sandra. "It's been at Yellow forever, except when they want to change the media topics, then they bump it up to Orange."

Harland shrugged his shoulders. "Look, I don't make the rules, I just know them. It's my turn with that."

Harland reached for the laptop and plugged it into his pay-as-you-go phone. He then logged onto a public website for civilian use that he used to monitor his status as a military employee. After a pause, he was connected. "I've been court-marshaled. How- how is that possible? I haven't done anything!"

"Could be another one of your military rules," said Sandra, smirking.

Disturbed, Harland shook his head. "I must really be a bio-terrorist then."

"Definitely not," said Nate. "There's not a doubt in my mind I've been fired. Spelling's been on my ass for months now, ever since I started pushing to publish my work on the bio-tech sector that was rising so quickly, with all those firms associated with the Marshall Islands."

"How about you?" said Harland, looking at Sandra.

Sandra dialed her office from her phone. "Hello, Zula? It's Sandra. . . . No, I'm going to be working from home all week. I would have called earlier but I was just too busy working. . . . No, I'm feeling great. Did anyone ask about me today, any calls? . . . Just one? . . . No, tell her the position is closed. Okay, I gotta' go. See ya."

"So much for ethics," said Nate, sarcastically.

Sandra rolled her eyes.

ON WEDNESDAY, the same two bodyguards from Monday morning arrived at the boat, each carrying a briefcase handcuffed to his wrist. Without introducing themselves, they went inside the hull and opened the briefcases. "It's all there: one-hundred thousand dollars times six. The remaining nine-hundred thousand times six has been deposited in unnamed Swiss accounts. Here are the account passwords to access the money."

The man handed six cards to Gabe. "On each of these is a Swiss account number and a password."

"Thank you," said Gabe. "We're really not bio-terrorists."

"That's not my determination to make," said the bodyguard. "I've done all I can."

"What about asylum?" asked Sandra. "Has any country offered us asylum yet?"

"The ambassadors said they will make a few more calls," said the bodyguard. His eyes turned to Rita. "We need your laptop now."

"Here it is," said Rita, showing the man her laptop and briefly punching some keys on it. "It's all there, and a beta version of the program, too, that my brother designed."

The bodyguard grinned shyly. "Now I need you all to sign this contract, confirming you have no current backup, and will immediately destroy any backup if you discover one. Otherwise, you agree to surrender all the money."

Rita quickly signed the contract, followed by everyone else signing their contracts. Rita then handed her laptop to the bodyguard. "It's all the data I have," she said.

Silently, the bodyguards unlocked the handcuffs on their wrists, leaving the briefcases on the boat. They then turned to leave, never to be seen again.

A FEW HOURS LATER, Holly held her money in her hands and stared directly into Gabe's eyes. "Are you sure no one knows I'm involved?"

"To the best of my knowledge," said Gabe, reassuringly.

"Cuz' everyone knows I'm not a bio-terrorist," said Holly. "I don't even know anything about science." She looked wonderingly again at the money, holding a few stacks of cash in each hand. "It's just so much money. I have never even seen this much money before. I don't even know what to do with it all or where to start."

"You could always go shopping," said Sandra, her eyes smiling.

Holly smiled back. "I don't want to be on the run like you'all are going to have to do. Nobody is going to suspect me. I haven't done nothin' wrong."

Nate raised his eyebrows. "Then why did they just give you a million dollars? Obviously, someone is going to have you on some list. I don't think any of us are actually safe anymore. Once they put you on a list, then your life is never quite the same, even if they do give you a million dollars to make it seem like life's better again."

"Why do you say that?" asked Holly, still holding the stacks of cash in her hands. "It's a million dollars. All of my problems are going to be gone now. I don't have a worry in the world anymore."

"I don't think you're understanding the big picture," said Nate. "The U.N. just paid out six million dollars for a one thousand dollar laptop. What they're going to do with that information is going to change not only your life, but the world as we know it."

"Like how?" asked Holly, feeling a twinge of worry start.

Nate stood. "I've been tracking these bio-techs for years now. They're all growing, across the world. And whether or not Rita even recognized it, she has pinpointed some type of breakthrough that not even she fully understands yet, but for six million dollars, all the world's governments are now going to have access to that technology."

Now, Sandra was worried. "What he's trying to say is none of us know exactly what they're going to do with the information on Rita's stupid laptop, but what we can guess is that supreme technology in the hands of greedy businessmen and ambitious politicians is a recipe for disaster."

Holly was stubbornly oblivious. "I don't give a damn. I'm taking my money and heading back to Annapolis. You'all can do whatever the hell you want, but as for me, I'm gonna' live it up."

Holly then carefully folded her money into her purse and started to walk off the boat.

"Why don't you wait a couple days," suggested Harland, reaching for her arm.

"No. I'm leaving," she said, hopping off the boat. "There's no reason for me to stay here any longer. I've got the money. I'm out of here. Thanks for the memories."

"Please don't," said Harland. "It's too risky."

The others were watching, unsure of how to react, their faces worried.

Harland held his breath.

Holly kept walking, heading to the parking lot. She waved without looking back.

DEAR DIARY, November 18, 1982.

Today I watched Hugo's eyes change. His expressions were unemotional and his eyes were chilled, fixated on me in a way I cannot explain. In most respects, he is still a man, looks like a man and usually speaks like a man (when he speaks) and thinks like a man, I guess. But I feel like he's changing somehow.

They all look so different, which is really scaring me. I have never before lived with such constant fear. From their looks, I am the only one who is still me. I'm getting a little freaked out here!

I know Hugo no longer feels any emotion. He hasn't told me he loves me for months, and all his jealous feelings are gone. All his former ambition has evaporated.

Jason is singing and whistling all the time, and makes the most beautiful sounds. He is the only happy one but spends all his time looking for food.

Amy is too tall now to sleep in the hut. She just lays on the ground at night, not even bothering to cover her lanky self. She stopped writing her poetry long ago.

I'm feeling angry lately, and all of them are getting on my nerves. Their peculiar looks and erratic behavior are disturbing. Also, for the first time in my life, I am losing my desire to write.

My skin keeps getting rougher and now it's almost scaly. I must have picked up some kind of skin fungus or something. It must have something to do with the water in this area, which makes sense since I'm swimming so much, sometimes even now at night. I go out and just swim for hours and hours and hours.

SHOPPING
CHAPTER ELEVEN

MARTI STOOD BEHIND THE BAR, barely able to speak as she wiped the marble counter with a white cloth. It had been three days since she had seen Gabe, and the reality of seeing his stool empty again at 5:15 p.m. was too much for her to bare. Tears filled her eyes, as she tried to hold them back.

Gabe had not contacted her, and she had no way of contacting him. On Friday night, she had taken a cab to the marina to fetch the van, because she did not want the police to see it by the water and to suspect he had gone out to sea, even though none of them knew he had a boat. For her it was a simple ride to the marina in a cab where she used her spare set of keys for the van. Then all she had to do was drive the van back to the hotel.

Marti wondered why Gabe headed for his boat. She assumed he would feel safe out on the water, but perhaps she just knew him better than she was willing to admit. However, it was over the weekend that she really began to worry. And now that Holly hadn't arrived at work on Monday, Marti was beside herself. Were they okay? Did Homeland Security arrest them? Did they suspect them of heading out on Mistress? Were the cops going to start questioning her? Would she ever see him again?

It was her assumption that he would head to the Caribbean, because that's where he had been planning to go. Maybe it was her guess or just good intuition, but she felt laying low would appear suspicious. Gabe had told her he was really pissed off with this Homeland Security crap when she pulled him aside in the restaurant. He hinted that his story was going to take a drastic turn.

Marti wiped away a tear, believing Gabe would soon be drinking tequilas in another bar, and worried profusely that she would never see him again. Suddenly the Marina Restaurant was no longer that important to her. Her savings totaled almost sixty thousand dollars, certainly enough to live off of for a while. What to do with her ownership interest was a whole different matter. As each minute passed, a spontaneous trip to the southern hemisphere was sounding like a better and better idea.

That's when the phone rang. "Marti, it's Gabe."

"Oh my God! Are you okay?" The tears were now from relief.

"I'm fine. I can't talk long, but I wanted to tell you not to worry."

"Where are you?" Marti asked, tears of joy filling here eyes.

Gabe paused to chew on some peanuts, staring briefly at his pre-paid mobile phone. "I, I don't want to say. I just wanted to tell you not to worry."

"Dammit, Gabe. Are you in the Caribbean or did you head north?"

"Well, ah, ah—"

"Don't bullshit me," hissed Marti. "I know you went to see your Mistress. Now, where are you? And don't bullshit me around here."

Listening to the phone tap, Brad's eyes came to life. Channing had a mistress, and he actually went to see her! Zack would love to hear about this later!

"I can't! Listen, your phone may be being monitored. No more names or questions about locations or who may be involved. Nothing, okay?"

"Okay," Marti responded, trying them to calm herself.

Marti reached for the list of over 500 popular Caribbean docks that she had found off the internet over the weekend—all a weekend's sail from Annapolis. Many names contained asterisks to pinpoint docks that were small and would be easier to dock a medium-sized boat.

"Dammit, Gabe. How are we going to . . . communicate?"

"I don't know right now," said Gabe.

"Then how am I going to find you?" Marti asked. "I, I, I've got to see you. I can't stand it anymore."

Brad added another log entry: Marti needed to be followed. He then placed another call to Zack which went directly into voicemail.

"I'll be in touch soon. Trust me, babe. Don't try to find me, okay?"

"Okay, Gabe. . . . Be safe. . . . I love you."

"I love you, too, Marti," Gabe answered and then before disconnecting, quickly added, "And don't tell anyone about my Mistress. Understand?

"Yes, darling, I got it," answered Marti.

Marti stared stunned at the phone in her hand. It was a strange exchange because neither had ever used the word "love" before in a conversation.

A FEW MINUTES LATER, Holly arrived for work and punched her time clock, then approached Marti who was still standing behind the bar.

"What's wrong, Marti?" asked Holly.

"Holly!" said Marti, dashing around the side of the bar and hugging her. "Are you okay?

"I'm fine," said Holly, smiling. "I just got in this morning."

"From where?" asked Marti, tears still in her eyes. "Where's Gabe? Is he really okay? Where did you guys head to?"

"Oh, I don't remember. I just got my money and left. I figured nobody knows who I am anyway, so I took my $100,000 and got the hell out of there."

Marti wiped her tears, changing her tone. "What $100,000? You don't have $100,000."

"You're right," answered Holly. "It's really a million. The $100,000 is in cash and the other $900,000 is in a Swiss account. Marti, I'm a millionaire!"

Holly began jumping up and down, holding Marti in her arms. Marti was still confused but jumped with her. "What about Gabe?"

The commotion caught Jasmine's attention. She was working on a jazzy version of "Blowing in the Wind," a Bob Dylan classic.

"Oh, he's worth a million, too," said Holly. "They're all worth a million bucks, though nobody knows I was involved, which is awesome!"

Marti was in a daze. "Who's they?"

"Homeland Security. My identity was never known."

"But where is Gabe. Where did you guys sail to?"

"Oh, I don't know, Marti. I still can't believe it. I never thought I'd be a millionaire."

"Well, I guess you are."

Holly smiled, weakly. "But what should I do with myself? I don't know what to do with myself anymore."

"Please, Holly. I need to know where Gabe is. Can't you tell me anything, anything about your trip?"

"Sorry, I don't remember a thing." Holly was evasive.

Marti's voice quivered. "Nothing, dear? Do you remember the port, or the dock where you went?"

"I'm sorry. I just don't."

"Somewhere in the Caribbean?" Marti reached for a pad of paper. Holly shook her head. "Do any of these names sound familiar? Marti showed Holly a list of northern communities known for sailing?

"That one," said Holly, nodding.

"Which one?"

"Hampton. I, I remember seeing a sign somewhere. Hampton. Yeah, that's it."

Marti hugged Holly. Then Carley walked in.

"I passed by earlier," said Carley. "I don't mean to interrupt you, but did I hear you say you've got a million dollars?"

"That's right," said Holly, happily. "Now what am I supposed to do?"

"What I'd do is buy a bar," said Carley, happily.

"I just can't—"

Marti smiled. "One hundred thousand dollars. Cash."

"Ah, I, I don't have a hundred thousand on me."

"I thought you said you did."

"Well, I spent $600 on a plane trip home, first class, so I'm a little short of the $100,000."

Marti didn't hesitate. "That's okay. I'll take whatever you have. It's close to $100,000, in cash."

"But why would you sell the bar?" asked Holly.

"Well, I've been listening to Gabe for a long time," said Marti. "I know he has a lot of odd concepts, but he's a good journalist. . . . Lately he's been talking about the world ending, about science taking over, about people changing in weird ways."

"Wasn't he writing a retirement story when this all started?" asked Carley.

"Yes, he was," said Marti. "But then he started talking to these people. All of them were somehow involved with biotechnology, in matters great or small. He's writing about changes in the world, something I don't understand, but changes that will make things as we know them have, well, no real value anymore. I really think he's onto something big now. This next story is going to go national."

"It's a deal," said Holly, not hearing most of what Marti just said. "I'll take the bar."

"Now that includes operations as is," said Marti. "There's a small operational debt, nothing big. "That would need to be cleared."

"Like I said, I'll take it."

All three women hugged. "I'm heading to the Hamptons," said Marti. Then she looked at Carley and Holly and added, "Now don't tell anyone about this. Nothing! You understand!"

Carley and Holly both moved their hands to zip their lips. Then both laughed.

Sensing something important was being discussed, Jasmine aimed her microphone at them, though it was beyond its reach to catch sounds at such a low volume.

"And I am the owner of the Marina Restaurant Bar."

"And I'm still just a waitress," said Carley, wryly.

MARTI DROVE her old minivan north along I-95, then headed on I-278, across the Verrazano Bridge to the Southern Belt Parkway. A couple of times she felt like she was being tailed but the heavy traffic and thick fog made it easy for her to shake whoever it was that was following her. Finally she reached the small town of Patchogue. It was quite a drive, almost six hours, but Marti never second-guessed herself.

As she drove, she had plenty of time to think about a variety of personal matters, the uppermost one was about being with Gabe. She didn't understand why he was now considered a bio-terrorist. Hell, Gabe couldn't even boil an egg. Yet her instincts had taken over, and all she knew was she wanted to be close to him, to try and help.

She had reached a point in her life where nothing mattered anymore but the simple need to be with the person she cared for deeply. The needs of her job, financial stability, even her freedom as an American were suddenly all of lesser importance than being in the company of the man who filled her thoughts.

Marti had no children, no real family to speak of. Her parents were both gone, and her only kid sister, Dee, an estranged sister, lived in Maine. In the past twenty years she had spent more time talking with Gabe than everyone else close to her combined throughout her whole lifetime. In her heart and mind, Gabe now needed her help, and even if she couldn't do anything directly, at least she could be near him if anything was about to happen.

Zack McHenry started the conversation by swearing loudly into the receiver. "How could you have lost her?" he asked.

The agent on the other end of the phone grimaced. "Equipment malfunction, sir."

Zack slammed the receiver down, as the tail had lost her because the homing device had malfunctioned. What's next, he wondered.

MARTI PARKED HER CAR and reached for her suitcase and several quarters. Approaching the parking meter she stared at it. She became overwhelmed with the thought that she did not need to put any quarters into it. For some reason, she just felt that she would never return to that place again, she would no longer even need her car. Indeed, she felt her life was about to change forever. She fed the meter, thinking it would buy her—and maybe Gabe—some time before the cops called in her plates. She boarded the Long Island Railroad heading east. She would be in the Hamptons within the hour.

With relief and joy, she spotted Mistress at the third marina she checked out. With new determination she climbed on board. "You look familiar," said Nate.

Marti's eyes brightened. "I'm the bartender at the Marina Hotel, you know the one where you all slipped out the back before the Feds broke down the door."

Nate nodded.

Before he could ask his next question, Marti blurted. "Where's Gabe?"

"He's sleeping in the cabin," said Sandra, frowning at her. "How did you know where we were?"

"I'm not such a bad investigator myself," said Marti, flippantly leaving her suitcase on the deck, and heading into the cabin. "Don't worry, I'm not going to tell anyone where you are, because I'm not leaving until all this gets worked out."

MOMENTS LATER, Marti entered the cabin and found Gabe on the phone. He sounded confident, much more so than she was used to.

"That's hilarious." Gabe was saying, a glass of Jim Beam and Coca-Cola in his hand. "No, I don't have any problems at all with you running my article with the naked aliens as a go-along pictorial. I'm only sorry I can't be there to supervise the shoot. Sure, ten copies would be great to have. But hold them for me at your main office, okay? I'm in no hurry to get them. Thanks." He then hung up the phone.

Marti lunged for him, giving him a bear hug. "I've been so worried about you!"

"I told you I was fine. In fact, Playboy is going to publish my story."

"I see you haven't lost your sense of humor," said Marti, still hugging him.

"No, seriously. They're running it as the feature in their next issue, which comes out in a week."

"Oh, Gabe, that's ridiculous," said Marti.

"I'm telling you, next week my words will be surrounded by girls and guys in alien costumes—or at least what looks like costumes—from famous movies. It's going to be one of the most famous stories to ever hit the newsstands in the history of journalism."

"You're joking!" Marti smiled. "No bullshitting, remember?"

Marti's jaw dropped. She dropped her arms and stared directly into Gabe's face. "Now I *know* the world is ending. You're actually having an article published, and in Playboy no less?"

"You owe me a Mac," said Gabe, grinning.

"Don't get on me about that bet," said Marti. "What are you planning to do, sail around the world as you type on a laptop?"

Gabe shrugged. "Not a bad idea, actually."

"These charges against you are serious, Gabe."

"Don't worry about it," said Gabe "It will all work itself out in time."

"I don't think so," said Marti, shaking her head. "Whatever trouble you've gotten yourself into, I don't think an article in Playboy's going to do anything to help."

THE NEXT DAY, Marti, Rita, and Sandra headed to Main Street to do some serious shopping. All three were beaming with smiles. "I didn't think I'd ever get off that boat," said Rita, bending over to touch her toes to get a good stretch.

"That's odd," said Sandra.

"I guess my gut was wrong," said Marti. "What's weird?"

"All I know is I'm finally going shopping," said Rita. "I really haven't ever gone on a shopping spree for myself, certainly not with a million dollars."

"A million bucks!" said Marti.

"Yeah, and in a Swiss bank account, too," said Sandra.

"That sounds too good to be true," said Marti. "A million bucks each, just for a laptop?"

They headed up one street, then down another, which led them to the downtown area with lots of shops, many bearing designer names.

"Girls, I think we've found heaven," said Marti, looking around her.

"This reminds me of Georgetown," said Rita. "I wonder if I'll ever go back there. How are we going to beat this bio-terrorist charge?"

"I think the asylum plea will come through," said Sandra.

"But I don't want to leave the country, or go back to Argentina," said Rita. "I don't want to leave the States. I've come to like it here!"

Surveying the trendy names, Marti smiled from ear to ear. "Let's shop 'till we drop, ladies."

"Where did you live in Argentina?" asked Sandra of Rita as they strolled.

"Patagonia," said Rita. "My family owns a large vineyard down there."

Rita wine store.

GREEN IVY COVERED THE CHALLIS ENTRANCE to Hampton Wine and Beverage, a store with oak counters and a rustic pine floor. It was an old barn, converted into a wine store a half century earlier. On the Historic Register, the store was a reminder of the Potato farms that covered Long Island centuries ago. Being a wine store with a small vineyard in the background, it was grandfathered in as a farm, giving it a unique tax advantage. Consequently, Hampton Wine was a cornerstone of the neighborhood.

A middle-aged woman with long dark hair, stood behind the counter as Sandra, Rita, and Marti walked into the store. She glanced up from the book she was reading as the women entered. "Warm outside, huh," she said in a friendly manner.

"It's a scorcher," agreed Sandra. Then they laughed. The temperature was unseasonably high, reaching a near 80 degrees Fahrenheit.

"Definitely," said Marti, looking at the book a woman was reading. "At least it's not *Fahrenheit 451*."

Gabe's liquor cabinet was seriously thinning itself out, with the help of the six passengers, and the crewmates were becoming rather worried. The money lessened their initial worries. Even the threat from Homeland Security seemed less frightening now that they no longer had the laptop with the data on it. H.S.A. was too late, too slow, and too sloppy. Maybe money was the opiate of the masses. If they had done something terrible, then why had the United Nations given each of them all that money?

In their hearts, each of them believed Homeland Security was bluffing, at least that's what they hoped. They didn't believe the charges they heard on the scanner were valid. None of them were terrorists. Each worked in a normal job with a respectable paycheck and within an honorable career. No one maintained the belief that any of them were targets to be eliminated.

Each wanted to return to a secure life, a safe home, and a loving family or group of friends. Although Harland was the only one of the six with a child. Except Marti, they all wanted to return to their prior lives. No one wanted to flee the country and enter into a new world of uncertainty and doubt.

The women browsed the wine store, each viewing the wines and hard liquors. Marti was fond of the hard liquor. Rita viewed the wines. Sandra looked at the organic section.

"I can't stand it much more on that boat," said Sandra out of the blue. "I want to go home."

"Right on," said Rita. "We've been there for days. It's no fun to sit around and just wait to hear that you're not a—"

"I understand," said Marti with a warning look. "But maybe things will change soon."

Sandra rolled her eyes, then reached for the bottle of some Argentina Malbec, having a label identifying it as organically grown. "We're going to need something to carry us through for a while. And I swear, if I see one more bottle of Jim Beam, I'm going to flip out. That stuff is for old men."

"Yeah," said Rita, fixated on the champagnes.

Sandra approached the counter, holding the bottle of the Malbec. "Do you have this by the case?"

"Ah-h-h-h, let me check," answered the woman behind the counter.

"How many cases do you have?" asked Sandra.

The clerk raised an eye. "Let me check; give me a minute." She opened a side door and slowly descended a wide staircase to the wine cellar.

Rita smiled faintly, holding a bottle from her Patagonia Estates. "This is a wine from my family's vineyard. They carry several Argentinean wines here, all of them from the provenance where my family lives."

"That's cool," said Sandra. "I just asked for some organic Malbec from Argentina. It's a pretty good wine."

"Show me what you picked," said Rita. She smiled approvingly when she saw Sandra had unknowingly picked one of her family's wines. "This is good," said Rita, an idea forming.

"The people who own this store must like my parent's wine. See, they have six different wines from our estate alone."

"It's a small world!" said Marti.

Rita said, "I know the wines from that area because I grew up near there. The next closest vineyard has only three wines on their shelf."

"What's your point?" asked Sandra, sensing something.

"These people must have business connections to my family," said Rita. "Maybe we can use their connections to contact my family to help us get to Argentina for asylum."

"But I'm already working my contacts to head to Canada," said Sandra. "It should come through any day now."

"And what happens if it doesn't?" retorted Rita. "What are we going to do? Stay on Gabe's boat in South Hampton Harbor for the rest of our lives, or until we're arrested? We're on the run, and even if we do have a million dollars; we're still fugitives—at least in the eyes of the U.S. government. I wasn't born in this country, so I don't have the same civil rights that you have."

Sandra shook her head. "I still say there's something screwed up with this system. The U.N. popped out 6 million bucks for Rita's data."

"I have to agree." Marti nodded.

"I think I can convince her to use her phone, to call my parents," said Rita.

"Yeah, an *international* call," said Sandra. "Give it a whirl!"

The clerk opened the door, reentering the room. "We only have a few bottles left—"

"Great! I'll take 'em," said Sandra.

"Ah, okay."

Rita placed her bottle of Patagonia Estates on the counter. "Excuse me, ma'am, but I see you carry six wines from the Perez Estate in the Patagonia Provenance, in Argentina."

"That's right," said the clerk. "They're some of our best sellers."

Rita's eyes shifted from left to right. "It's rare for me to see my family wines on a shelf. Do you have a lot in stock?"

"Someone asked me that yesterday," said the clerk. "All of them are almost out. My supplier is away on a buying trip, so I can't place an order for a couple more weeks."

"I can call them for you," offered Rita, eagerly. "If you really need the order, I'd be happy to do it for you. It's my family's vineyard."

"I had no idea. I rarely meet any vineyard owners. . . . You would?"

"Sure," said Rita. "I can call now if you like."

"Ah, sure," said the woman, sliding the phone around. "I'm not sure where the number is, though."

"I know the number," said Rita. " I'll just need the shipping info."

"Sure." The woman handed her a business card.

"How many cases of each do you want?" asked Rita.

"I'll take five of each, plus an extra case of any other wines your family sells."

Rita smiled, then punched in the number. Her mother, Eva, answered in Spanish. Rita greeted her in the same language and went on to explain where she was and placed the order. She then briefly explained the trouble they were in while trying not to cause alarm.

"So, will you ask Ambassador Jose Barrata for asylum for the six of us?" asked Rita, staring out the window.

"This is really important. We need that asylum granted immediately. Please Mama."

"I'll see what I can do," said Eva. "How will I contact you?"

"You talk to Ambassador Barrata and I'll call you back as soon as I can, probably in a day or two. . . . Yes. . . . Don't worry, I'll be safe. I love you. . . . And say hi to Papa."

"Your wine will be here within seven days," Rita told the clerk. "Glad I could help."

A THIN STREAM OF SMOKE rose from a cigar in an ashtray at the Ninth Street Steakhouse in Washington, D.C., near the Capitol. It was one of the only locations where smoking was still not discouraged inside the District, though only cigar smoking was tolerated and then only in a private room. The thin stream lazily rose, filling the room with its pungent odor.

Zack would occasionally puff on his cigar, without speaking a word. His eyes were heavy, having had little sleep for days. It was his job to authorize the people who made arrests. And in spite of what he was hearing every hour from counter terrorism—that the five would be caught "within hours"—his reputation was now on the line. He hated being unable to make a seemingly simple arrest of five people who had become terrorists almost overnight.

Erin mopped her forehead. She spoke in a whisper, careful to not allow anyone on the staff to overhear.

"Don't worry about it, boss. We'll find them. They may be terrorists, but they're not sophisticated ones."

A waiter approached the table. "Another vodka and tonic, miss?"

"Sure," said Erin.

Zack just nodded, his expression a mixture of emotions.

After the waiter left, Erin folded her hands, avoiding eye contact with Zack. "We're going to get them," said Erin. "It's going to happen. I tell you."

Brad entered the room, out of breath. "I have good news. The Bureau has just obtained a tape from a surveillance camera in Baltimore. They have identified Harland Parker. He was in a stolen pick-up truck with Maryland plates."

Erin laughed. "How do they possibly know it's him. Half of Baltimore drives pick-ups."

"Face recognition software," said Brad. "It's correct within a million to one accuracy."

"Then we found the outlier," said Zack, lifting his cigar.

"I tell you, that technology is solid," said Brad.

Zack exhaled his smoke. "Keep looking. You know what's at stake."

"Absolutely, sir," said Brad.

Zack stared sternly at Erin. His jaw tightened. He was not a man of many words. His eyes spoke volumes.

"Absolutely, sir," said Erin. "I know what that data can do. Henderson explained it to me yesterday. He knows information about genetics Spelling doesn't understand, though Spelling's pretty good at his stocks.

He knows exactly what's going to happen when that technology hits the world market."

"When that technology hits the market no one on earth is going to be able to stop it," said Zack, glancing over at a priest at another table, eating with two nuns. "Even praying to God isn't going to matter anymore. . . . Even our faith in God will revert back to baying at the moon."

Erin noticed the cross hanging around Zack's neck and wondered where his faith had gone.

GABE PICKED THROUGH A BARREL OF LURES inside of Charlie's Sea Store. He was still looking for a deal, in spite of having $100,000 in cash. Still locked into old habits, he wanted to have a deal on everything. It was ingrained into his nature or was it in his DNA? Not accustomed to having so much spare money at his disposal, his habits were not going to change overnight.

Harland and Nate had done some shopping earlier. Nate had bought a short-sleeve polo shirt, running shoes and designers shorts for swimming and lounging about in. Harland was now dressed in a natural looking outfit, complete with boat shoes and a keychain for the keys to his house. Regardless, every time he looked at those keys, he wanted to see his son again.

"I'll need some fuel," said Gabe, talking to a clerk. "I'd like to fill it up—all three tanks and an extra one for back-up. Some food, too, of course. We plan to be at sea for a few weeks, maybe a month."

The clerk was unphased by the order.

"We're just passing through," explained Gabe, nonchalantly. "Do I get some kind of large-order discount on that delivery, by any chance? And can you deliver it for a discount? I mean, I'm buying all this stuff. Can't you give me a discount on that by any chance?"

"Yeah, I can take something off," answered the clerk.

"Thanks," said Gabe, sipping a cup of coffee. "Whatever you can do for us, I'd appreciate it. And here's a little list of some extras we'll need before I leave. . . . How long will it take before you can deliver?"

"For safety purposes, it takes a couple days for any delivery, whenever gasoline is involved," said the clerk. "You know, environmentalists and safety things."

"Can't it be done any faster?" asked Nate. "We're right here in your marina! We've got a lot of fishing to do in the next couple weeks, before returning back to work and don't want to waste any time."

"Going to sea's always been a dream of mine," said Harland, reaching into his pocket. "Come on, man. Can't you pull a few strings for us?" Harland handed the man a hundred dollar bill. "I really want to get out to sea and get home in time to see my son compete in his first karate tournament. You understand."

"I'll make some calls," said the clerk, taking the bill and glancing at the slip of paper Gabe handed him. "This the slip?"

"Yeah," said Gabe, flinging a fisherman's cap on the counter. "And add this to the bill, too."

DEAR DIARY, December 31, 1982.

Today I got into a huge argument with Hugo. I wanted to be with Hugo but he kept yelling at me. Then I tried to kiss him, but I kissed him too hard and he fell asleep and he started to bleed.

Jason and Amy began yelling at me and I tried to explain that Hugo was sleeping but they wouldn't listen to me. I don't even care about what happened. At least now I can swim more. Don't worry!

I think I'll try to get Jason and Amy to come swimming with me. There are some incredibly beautiful reefs about 30 meters down. I'll probably have to pull them along since they don't swim as well.

I wonder, how come they don't swim well? They look so strange lately. Maybe I need to watch them more.

CLOSE CALLS
CHAPTER TWELVE

GABE QUIETLY SAT AT THE TABLE in the galley of his boat, momentarily getting lost in the sounds of seagulls laughing loudly over the water. He was surrounded by the group and unsure of what to say. He was wide awake, having slept much over the past few days. He was also restless. They all knew that they could not remain on the boat for much longer without going stir crazy.

Surrounding them were many bags of clothes. Designer clothes, fine shoes, hats, bathing suits, toiletries, and tanning oils were heaped along the cabin's walls. They had spent a couple of thousand dollars each on goods, material objects that would comfort them as they waited for maybe a month or so until the bioterrorism claims were dropped. Having worldly comforts around them made them feel better. How else could they get to sleep each night, knowing they could not return home for an indefinable time period?

"The boat supplies should be here any minute," said Gabe, his elbows remaining fixed on the table. He bowed his head and folded his hands. "We need to leave here."

"Where can we go?" asked Nate. "It's not like we can just head home. None of us can."

"It's true," said Sandra. "I want to get back to D.C., but I know I can't."

"And I want to head home to see my son," said Harland, clinching his fist.

"You can't do that," said Marti. "After all of you left the bar, those Homeland Security people shut down half the restaurant. I swear they would have shut down the whole place if Mayor Bolton wasn't there that night."

"Bolton was there?" asked Gabe.

Marti nodded. "I know. What a coincidence, huh? He was having his usual steak with a couple of reporters that night. They want him to run for governor, but he always defers to any candidate from Baltimore."

"He hasn't changed a bit," said Gabe, grinning. "But I'm not sure even he can help us."

"My family can give us shelter," said Rita.

"Way down in Argentina," said Harland. "I need to be with my kid, not on some vineyard halfway around the world."

"Where else are you going to go, Harland," said Rita. "We'll be arrested."

"Definitely," said Marti. "I may even be arrested for joining you."

"Then why did you come?" asked Sandra.

"You know, when you run a bar there's a lot of talk," said Marti, pouring herself a drink. "But some of that talk sits with you. . . . Sometimes these old Navy guys come into the bar. They're higher ups, but regular customers for me. They wine and dine, sometimes even girls with them, spending lots of money. Well, usually one of them gets a little loud when they get drunk. On occasion, I tell you, this one guy, he repeated this a few times (so you know I'm not making it up), he has said that there are these cells in laboratories that they're researching, looking how to reverse DNA switching. Something like reversing the reversing?"

"De-evolution?" asked Gabe.

"At the Marshall Islands?" added Harland.

"And the cells are in Rockville right?" added Rita.

"And big business has a plot to develop them commercially and make a ton of money?" added Sandra.

"Because of all the profit involved?" added Nate.

"How do you know all of this?" answered Marti. "I thought the information was top secret, at least that's what those old Navy types kept saying."

"Hello?" called a deep voice from the dock. "Is anyone in there."

"Who's that?" asked Nate, jumping up.

"The supplies," said Gabe. "They're here."

Gabe walked out onto the deck and saw a man in a white T-shirt and a baseball cap on the deck.

"Are you Wilson, Mister Wilson?" asked the man.

"Well, yes," answered Gabe, now going by a fake name. "I assume you're here with the supplies?"

"Yeah, I have a whole truck of crap and other junk for you. It's like a month's supply for a good size party of land-lubbers."

"Great," said Gabe.

The man turned to head back to the truck. "Can you help me?" he asked.

"Sure."

THE SAILS WERE HIGH as the boat headed south, enroute to Argentina. It had been a week-and-a-half since they had fled from Annapolis, so the night-time sight of Ocean City within his binoculars bothered Harland. He and Gabe stood alone on the deck as Gabe sailed.

"Can't we stop in Washington?" he asked.

"It's too dangerous," answered Gabe. "You don't want to be in prison in Cuba for the rest of your life, do you?"

Harland was slow to respond. "How do you know they're going to do that? I'm not a bio-terrorist, and neither are you. I'm sure a lawyer can get us out of this mess."

"That's not true," said Gabe. "I just don't see an end to this. And they probably wouldn't let you near a lawyer, and that's if they don't shoot first and ask questions second."

"And neither do I," said Harland. "How are we going to get away from the U.S. government and still have a life to enjoy? How long can we just float around in a boat without getting arrested? I need to get back home. I really do, Gabe."

Gabe stared at the wheel. "I know. We don't have diplomatic immunity yet, but I think Rita's correct when she says her family can get us asylum until we work this out through some lawyers. . . . Just give it some time."

Harland paced on the deck, his binoculars still in his hand. "What if this takes another month, or even a year? I can't go that long without being there for my son."

"Would you rather be in prison?" asked Gabe. "How's that going to help him? He'll have a dad he can't visit, sitting in a maximum security prison in Guantanamo Bay or somewhere like it."

"We're not going to be in prison," said Harland. "It's crazy. Gabe, we're not bio-terrorists. Besides, Rita and Nate are the only ones who are even in that industry. I work in the Pentagon for goodness sake. The closest I get to biotechnology is aspirin, or vitamins for my kid."

"Vitamins?"

"Yeah, I'll give Sterling anything I can to keep him stronger, smarter, and healthier, as long as it's legal. I pump all the vitamins and supplements I can into him. When I'm through with him, he's going to be the smartest kid there is, not to mention strong and tall."

Gabe was quiet, somewhat feeling Harland's pain, but also unsure of what to say. He remained quiet for a long period, sailing past Ocean City, and then Assateague. As they passed Assateague, they could see the wild ponies playing in the surf, running wild and free on the beach—a freedom all on the boat felt into the core of their beings.

Harland held his binoculars tight, occasionally looking at the lights along the coast of Virginia, other times just holding his head in despair against his fist.

There was no opportunity or valid reason to change course. Harland knew it, as did everyone else. The risk of being permanently imprisoned—or even imprisoned for years waiting for a trial—labeled as a bio-terrorist was not worth the risk of trying to return home. It was better to head out of the country and to weigh the risks with the aid of an international lawyer, all the while under the protection of political asylum.

GABE BEGAN PULLING DOWN THE SAILS in a quiet and meditative manner. He didn't want to disturb Sandra and Nate as they quietly sunbathed up on the bow. Then the sail fell, more abruptly than he had planned.

"What are you doing?" asked Sandra, her eyes hidden behind sunglasses.

"We're heading to land," answered Gabe, avoiding eye contact as he pulled the sail downward.

"Why are we heading to land?" asked Nate.

"I think we all could use some discreet shore leave," answered Gabe. "Savannah's a nice town. It's law enforcement is more relaxed than the New York to Washington corridor, so I think we can get away with heading to shore."

"Are you out of your mind?" asked Sandra, adjusting her new watch. "Just a couple days ago when we were in South Hampton and you were saying we need to get out of the country as fast as possible. Now you're saying we need to stop in Savannah for a joy trip. . . . You're insane?"

Nate adjusted his new designer shirt. "Hey, I don't believe you're insane. I mean, you and I haven't known each other all that long—"

"Since we met at the Marina Bar," added Gabe.

"That's right," said Nate. "My point is that since we're all on the run—avoiding getting arrested—then why stop in some little port, just because you think we need some shore leave?"

Gabe paused for a moment, finally looking Nate in the eyes. Sandra then raised her sunglasses.

It was a tense moment as Gabe folded the sail, giving him time to delay his response. Pretending not to hear his last statement, he spent extra time folding the sail.

"Did you hear me?" said Sandra.

A sound was heard from the stairs, drawing all of them to see who was coming to the deck.

Suddenly Marti emerged. "I'm sorry, Gabe. I just can't take it anymore."

"What's wrong?" Gabe asked.

"We've been at sea for like five days now," Marti answered. "Can't we just head to shore . . ."

"What!" blurted Sandra.

". . . Can't we head to shore, even if it's just for a couple days?"

Moments later, Harland and Rita climbed the stairs.

Rita wiped some sweat off her brow. "Can't we stop? I'm just not used to all this sailing."

"Me either," added Harland.

Sandra's jaw dropped, turning to Nate and briefly staring into his eyes, though neither said anything to each other.

Nate then turned to Gabe. "Do whatever you want," he said. "What the hell do we have to lose? Our freedom, maybe?"

Sandra was speechless. She looked at everyone, hoping for someone to confirm her fear of stopping in Savannah. She reached for her wrap, and covered her body with it. She slipped into her flip-flops and then headed to the cabin, shaking her head in disbelief.

"We need to put in, 'stop at a marina,'" Gabe continued. "The main sail needs some repair. That storm we passed through last night inflicted some damage on my Mistress."

They all flashed back to the night before. They were down below, trying to sleep. The tossing back and forth was rougher than the usual troubles on the high sea, with the sails consistently whipping in a heavy breeze. Gabe, alone, was on deck. Only he knew how rough and dangerous the sea could really be.

"Definitely," said Marti.

"I agree," said Harland, adjusting his Nike cap. "What does it freaking matter? I hardly feel like living if I can't see my son ever again. Getting arrested is the least of my worries."

Nate followed Sandra down below, grabbing a bottle of wine and two glasses on the way.

SAVANNAH, GEORGIA—Gabe docked the boat in Savannah, a harbor with many docks, overbuilt to accommodate a growth spurt that never occurred in the city. Consequently, Gabe deduced that there would less security along the docks.

Sandra was back sunbathing on the front deck, along with Nate. He was wearing light green swimming trunks, with an aquatic pattern—those knee length ones—revealing his strong upper-body while Sandra was wearing a two-piece with a wrap-around see-through skirt, revealing her size 4 shape. Rita, to everyone's surprise, was relaxing in a thong bikini.

They all pretended to be napping, still not really wanting to talk to each other due to their apparent sharp political differences. Their virtual silence towards each other epitomized a tension that began months ago and continued to the present moment. Although these seemingly ideologically different souls were laying within reach of each other. Ideologically they were worlds apart. Docked in the small town of Savannah, each was as distant as the North Pole from the South Pole.

NERVOUSLY, Gabe leafed through magazines on a newsstand. He went through each stack among maybe 50 magazines in all. His pace quickened as he searched through each shelf.

"May I help you?" asked a clerk with "Bob" on his nametag.

"Oh, I'm just looking for a magazine," said Gabe.

"Which one?" the clerk asked. "We've got about a hundred different ones right in front of you."

Gabe hesitated. "Oh, just any magazine."

The clerk's eyes scanned across all the magazines. "Oh." He turned and headed behind a counter in front of several cases of unsold cigars and cigarettes.

The store was full of memorabilia from the television era, beginning in about 1960 and continuing through the 1980s. Behind him was a poster declaring "Zgob!" with an half-fish, half-man creature gasping for air. An ape man in a Tarzan outfit held a spear in his hands, holding off the creature as hundreds of similar creatures exited the ocean.

Gabe approached the counter, rubbing his hand against his neck. "I guess I could use some help."

"What do you want?" asked Bob.

Gabe whispered. "I see you have Maxim, but what I'm really looking for is the new Playboy."

"It's sold out," said Bob.

"What?" said Gabe, loud enough for others to look his way.

"It's kind of funny," said Bob, snickering and leaning over the counter. "It's sold out apparently because of the article and pictorial about aliens or at least something like aliens. Whoever heard of Playboy selling out because of an article?"

"Yeah," said Gabe, his eyes focusing on the counter.

"I read the whole thing, too," said Bob, snickering. "Those animal-like chicks are so hot! I had forgotten all those types of chicks in pop culture."

Gabe moved his eyes from side to side, making sure a man near the magazine stand did not hear him. "Look, Bob, I really need a copy of that magazine."

"Really?"

"Yeah, really."

"How much would you pay for it?"

"I don't know, say, ah, twenty bucks."

Bob removed a copy of Playboy Magazine from under the counter, holding it in his hands. A scantily-clothed woman was underneath a headline blurting "These Women are Animals!"

"You've got it!" Gabe blared. "I've got to have it!"

"I need a better offer then."

Gabe regained some of his composure. "I need that copy, kid. I'm a collector of that magazine."

Bob glared at Gabe. "A collector? Yeah right!"

Gabe smiled, his eyes big. "I'm going to be honest with you, bud. That woman on the cover is the daughter of my girlfriend."

"I'm just not selling it, dude. Sorry. This magazine means everything to me. I wouldn't take anything to part with it."

"How about for a hundred bucks?" asked Gabe, pulling out his wallet from his back pocket.

"Cash?" asked Bob.

"Cash" answered Gabe.

"It's yours," said Bob, handing Gabe the copy as Gabe handed him the money. Bob looked back under the counter at the remaining stock of Playboy magazines. Taking them off the shelf was one of his best ideas, he thought.

SEVEN COPIES OF PLAYBOY were on the oval table in the Pentagon, each person thumbing through the copy and pretending not to notice the beautiful women—completely naked except for the painted-on designs, like Rebecca Romjim in the X-Men movies. Around the table sat five men, and Jamie Whiteman. No one was smirking, at least not with Jamie there, an advisor who actually ran the Homeland Security Department.

By contrast, only Jamie was grinning, a rare moment for her. It was she who finally broke the silence. "They're bioterrorists," she said, her hands folded on the table.

"We've done our own research," said Harry Sloan, Director of the Federal Bureau of Investigators. "It appears these people are passively involved as bioterrorists. They're not *actively* involved. It's going to be difficult to find them guilty by twelve jurors. We simply don't have enough evidence that they should be classified as bioterrorists."

"Being a bioterrorist isn't something someone aspires to be," said Admiral Owens, sipping a Coke.

"But that doesn't mean they're *not* terrorists," said Zack. "A terrorist can involuntarily be an terrorist."

"Especially bioterrorists," said Jamie, sipping her coffee.

"They're *still* suspects," said Bobby Gilroy, Director of the Central Intelligence Committee. "And if they cross into Canada—or somewhere south—then they're in my territory."

"It doesn't even matter anymore," said Owens. "The whole situation has changed."

"What do you mean?" asked Bobby, leaning forward in his chair.

Admiral Owens shook his head. "Look, I've been watching over this evolution, de-evolution, re-evolution project for the past twenty-some years. Now that the information is available to the international community, it's all going to change. Now there's no point to keep looking for the cure or for these schmucks. We might as well just shut it all down and head for the hills."

"*All* of it down?" asked Jamie, her left eye raising.

Owens turned to Gabe's story in Playboy. "What's the point of employing all these people when most of the secret is going to be out in the media in just a few weeks?"

"He's right," said Harry. "The press is going to be all over those labs, especially the one in Rockville. That laptop of hers has all the information any government needs."

"We already shut them down and cleaned them," said Zack, wondering if anyone read the reports he sent them. "They won't find a thing."

"But they'll think it's about hybrid soldier warriors, not about the cure for de-evolution," said Zack. "But who is going to believe us during all those committee hearings? They'll drag us up to New York to do all the explaining in front of the Security Council but no one will believe our story. And they'll drag us into the Senate and the House."

"That's for sure," said Jamie.

"Do you know how much freakin' money we have invested into this program?" asked Zack, rhetorically. "All those employees now without jobs, too. It's going to be as much of a mess if we shut down the department as it is if we keep it going."

Owens raised his hands into the air. "And why will that matter when we're going to have to design an entirely new military defense within five years?"

"Or even less," said Jamie.

"Exactly my point," said Owens.

"What do we do about Gabe and the rest of them?" asked Harry.

"It all depends on whether or not they get asylum," answered Jamie.

THE SAILS WERE RAISED HIGH as Mistress headed past Fort Lauderdale, Florida. It had been a smooth trip thus far, except for that storm that caused them to make a stop in Savannah. Yet after he returned with the copy of Playboy, it changed the whole picture for them.

They all knew Gabe was a reporter, but seeing his story in a current magazine made everything seem different. It was a comic relief for the group, with Gabe's serious story about scientific technology in Rockville being used to develop hybrid warriors.

A boat in the distance had a blue light spinning on it. It was a cigar style speed boat, white with a blue streak of paint along the side.

"What's that?" asked Nate, looking the boat in the distance through a set of binoculars.

Gabe was at the wheel. "Where?"

"Over there," said Nate, pointing.

"Let me have those," said Gabe, motioning for the binoculars.

Nate handed them to Gabe, as Gabe quickly looked through at the boat. "Oh, crap," Gabe muttered.

"What?"

"It's the coast guard, and there is no way they haven't locked on to us yet."

A HALF HOUR LATER, the coast guard boat was tied up to the Mistress, only a few miles out from Fort Lauderdale. The captain, along with two lieutenants, were standing at ready, each with a hand on a gun and a look of "just try something" on their faces.

The captain spoke into a megaphone. "Everyone in the boat needs to come up on deck. I repeat. Everyone in the boat, on deck now!"

Everyone was already on the deck, even before the coast guard arrived. His beckoning call for them was merely protocol. Everyone knew what was at stake.

"Prepare for us to board the boat," said the captain, again into the megaphone.

Gabe and the others tried not to laugh. The Captain was not more than twenty feet away, but he still felt compelled to speak into a megaphone, amplifying his voice. At that distance even a regular voice would be audible.

Minutes later, the coast guard entered Mistress. They no longer were touching their guns.

"I need to see your registration," said the captain.

Gabe cleared his throat. "I, ah, well, I. . . . I don't have one."

The captain raised his eyebrow. "What?"

Gabe was slow to answer. "I built this boat with my own hands . . . "

"What?"

". . . forty-some years ago. It's an old boat."

"Then why don't you have any registration?" asked the captain.

Gabe scratched his head. "I believe boats built prior to 1970 were unregistered and grandfathered in, in Maryland."

"I need to see your identification, and for all of you."

They pulled their identification papers out, then handed them to the captain. Then the captain handed them to one of the lieutenants.

The lieutenant re-boarded the coast guard vessel and got onto the radio. He then called into South Florida headquarters located down the Keys.

"This is Unit H-431. Copy?"

"Copy, Unit H-431."

"I have ID's for the people on board the boat."

"Okay."

"Vessel is operated by a Gabe Channing. Other crew members include Sandra O'Callahan. Harland Parker. Nate Baschard. Rita Perez. And Marti Svonski." The lieutenant carefully spelled each name.

"Ten-four."

There was a pause as the dispatcher plugged the names into a computer.

"We have a hit on five of those six names. Copy?"

"Copy."

"You may need to arrest them. They're ID'd as terrorists, bio-terrorists. However there is another message from International Intel linked to their names. We'll have to get back to you on what that means."

"Ten-four."

"Give me no more than ten minutes," said the dispatcher.

"Ten-four."

A couple minutes later, the lieutenant reached for his walkie-talkie and boarded Mistress. He then approached the captain, whispering into his ear.

"The Bureau says they probably need to be arrested. Confirmation in no more than ten minutes."

"Okay," said the captain, looking at his watch and instinctively drawing his weapon.

Then the lieutenant's walkie-talkie squelched, drawing everyone's attention. "Yeah."

"Negative on the arrest," said the dispatcher. "Asylum to Argentina granted two days ago."

"Ten-four."

The lieutenant shook his head as the captain stared at him. He then leaned over to his ear. "Asylum granted by Argentina."

The captain nodded. "We just wanted to check on your registration and the safety equipment," said the captain.

"I understand," said Gabe.

The captain stared at Gabe, initially saying nothing. The pause was long and deliberate. "I'm just giving you a warning," said the captain. "You need to get this fixed if you're going to continue to sail. You must leave the U.S. now and not return. You have political asylum granted for Argentina. Luckily, you are about a half mile outside U.S. waters otherwise I would be arresting all of you."

"Okay," said Gabe. "I understand."

"Good luck heading to Argentina in this," the captain snickered.

Gabe raised his eyebrow.

"Your asylum was granted two days ago."

"It was?" said Gabe. "Yeah! Look out Argentina; here we come!"

DEAR DIARY, February 2, 1983—I no longer remember my distant past, as I have only vague memories even of what happened weeks ago. These old journals seem like they were written by a stranger, a completely different person.

I see pictures here in my journal, drawings of people with names like Hugo, Jason, and Amy. And there is a photo of me with Hugo, with the words next to it: "Hugo and me." But it doesn't look like me at all.

Who am I? Or what am I? I don't understand.

This place, where the diaries are?

I think I once lived here. But could I have lived here? Not like this.

The sun bothers me and it's not good for my skin. I would rather swim than sleep in the hut. This is probably my last journal entry. Goodbye diary! Don't worry about me. Don't worry! I survive on my own.

Everyone else is gone. Can't breathe here. Need my ocean.

COVER-UP BEGINS
CHAPTER THIRTEEN

THERE WERE RUMORS that it was the largest effort to destroy data in the history of the United States. The order was to remove the electronic footprint of data that referenced (or implied) the existence of Project M.I.X. It was believed to be the highest classified project in the history of the United States, rivaling the XYZ Affair, prior to the War of 1812 (long before data could be copied).

Because it was so highly classified, technically there was no paper trail that had to be affirmed. In fact, it's existence could be outright denied by senior personnel—without fear of formal penalty. Protocol was to verbally dismiss the existence of top secret information. Hence, there should be no record of it, leading to even politicians being kept out of the loop. Project M.I.X. was no "Area 54." It's classification was higher, so no one could prove it even existed.

Zack McHenry's intra-net search for "Project M.I.X." within the computer records at Homeland Security referenced no information whatsoever—an excellent beginning. A search through its financial records provided similar results. The funding for the various departments—all under Zack's supervision—classified the department as simply "security," a rather broad label for a department within "Homeland *Security*."

Then even Zack's search history of Project M.I.X. was deleted, eliminating even the search of the search of Project M.I.X.

HENDERSON ENTERED ZACK'S OFFICE. There was no need for small talk.

"What did you discover?" asked Zack.

"Nothing," said Henderson. "Just as our agency was planned, it appears that there has been no record of our existence."

"What about payroll?"

"All the employees were subcontractors, which, as you know, gives us broader freedom with information collection and retention."

"What about their names?" asked Zack, his eyes piercing.

"Negative. Every person was paid as if he or she was a number, not actually a person. Then the numbers were scrambled, not allowing direct association with any person's names. We even paid them with checks—not electronically—to minimize banking records. . . . Thus far, it's flawless."

Zack's eyes did not blink. "Every reporter inside the beltway with half a brain will be looking for that data. Plus, the international press and ambassadors from every developed country in the world, are going to scrutinize this department in front of the cameras."

"I understand, sir."

"Do you understand you're going to be on camera?" asked Zack, twirling a pen in his fingers. "Are you *sure* you're ready?"

"I'm ready, sir, but I'll keep trying to find any possible flaws in the search mechanisms."

Zack slammed his pen on the table. "There is no information! There's not even a gap in the information, because it just doesn't exist. Project M.I.X. does not exist—and it never did!"

"Okay, sir."

Zack's face became stern, almost daring Henderson to challenge him. "I'm calling Irvine and Muelleur in the morning. They've proven right on all the important P.R. topics in the past, it's time we trust them again because if this story ever hits the mainstream media, we're dead."

Henderson worriedly chuckled. "No respectable reporter would even dream about touching this story. It's been stripped down to nothing."

NEVER UNDERESTIMATE how many men actually read the articles in Playboy Magazine. Although many people mock its intellectual prowess, Playboy was originally allowed to be printed only if its editorial content was solid—even inscrutable to a congressional inquiry. And with Gabe Channing now being one of the nation's top bio-terrorists, it was Playboy's news content that was driving a massive buzz in the national news media (although behind the scenes, everyone was actually commenting on that brunette chick resurrected from back stories of Buck Rogers).

Playboy's February issue made de-evolution a reality, with several iconic television and movie animal-like creatures gracing its cover and inside stories. An image of Orson Welles' dominated the main page with Gabe Channing's name in larger text. Welles' was wearing a headset beneath the massive headline of "War of the Worlds!" Welles' eyes were somber, the imminent fear of death in them even as he avoided looking into the camera.

With its science fiction flare, the edition spanned a range of topics across several mediums: television, movies, video games, and music. Some aliens were even from international programs. Gabe's story also revealed information about "Project M.I.X.," even calling it by its formal name, thus putting it into the public's awareness for the first time. Being an old Navy hand, he had learned the usefulness of assigning an acronym, one invented from his days as a reporter for the *Annapolis Triangle*, the last newspaper in Maryland to move its information to digital technology.

Gabe's magazine article—which arguably contained more editorial copy than was proper for a veteran journalist—highlighted the development of hybrid warriors by the United States government. The most critically written part was a shocking claim regarding a secret program he had called "Project Mutant," a program identifying the buildings in the Marshall Islands where creatures were kept following the atomic experiments in the 1970s. According to some of his old unpublished articles which he had kept on Mistress to re-read while sailing on the Atlantic, natives were unintentionally exposed to radiation caused by atomic fallout due to the new technology of the time, atomic (and later nuclear) radiation.

With vivid accuracy, Gabe wrote in the Playboy article about the specific buildings where the creatures were kept, all stemming from documents he had observed as an officer reporter with *The Stars and Stripes*, the military's finest newspaper, as well as some details he'd gotten from Harland while talking on the boat. He provided the names of officers (many now deceased) who had written reports about observing sea serpents and mutants decades ago.

Gabe had shaped his new story using his own memory of Marshall Island rumors from his days in the Navy. He used Harland's files to provide quotes from senior officers across various levels of government. He also added that many of the files he was sourcing no longer existed since it was military policy to destroy the files after 20 years, information provided again by Harland.

Openly, Gabe wrote about how the law did not state that all *copies* of the reports had to be destroyed, only the report itself. He then referenced a person who wrote one of the reports: Ensign Sterling Parker, now deceased. Of particular interest was a report by a Major Owens (now an admiral) who wrote about the unethical sequestering of civilians on the Marshall Islands. Gabe, thinly referencing an expired friendship with the admiral, gave several old quotes about the topic, though admitting they used to pound down Jim Beams while the information flowed freely. An editor's note was included asserting that the reliability of the quotes was questionable.

Of particular concern in the article was the fear among officers that the United States government was developing hybrid warriors, and testing the technology on civilians in the Marshall Islands. According to Gabe's article, officer reports classified hybrid soldiers into three categories:

<u>Bird-Hybrid Soldiers</u>: They had the ability to fly in spite of being the size of a humans. Data suggested that the body mass of people had diminished across regenerations of experimentation, allowing people of the same size to become airborne. Further advantages were that they had developed excellent sight, avoiding any need for glasses or surgery, with eyesight comparable to that of an eagle. Flying distances were not recorded, though the height reached was believed to be about that of a hawk. Their feathers were sleek and water resistant and their talons were razor sharp.

<u>Fish-Hybrid Soldiers</u>: Initially, they had the ability to swim underwater for up to ten minutes on a single breath of air. As future regenerations evolved, their gills became more developed and they became capable of remaining underwater for hours at a time. Women could produce thousands of eggs, a miraculous fertility rate. Their bodies were narrow and hairless, making it easier for them to swim. Body hair was replaced with scales. Generally considered near-sighted, they had few redeeming qualities. Although they did appear to be developing a sonar comparable to that of dolphins. However, their birthrates were so extraordinary that one

report questioned its own results, adding that empirical data regarding fertility would make it highly demanded by human fertility clinics.

<u>Land-Hybrid Soldiers</u>: They had strong figures and excellent body definition. They excelled in speed and endurance, giving them high military value. They could live without food or water for periods of time three times the length of most humans. Their hair was thick, colored brown, black, or red. Even bald people developed hair over just a couple of cellular generations. They also had a faster gestation period. There was a concern that they were unruly, not liking conformity or discipline. One report called them "savage and unreasonable, with unparallel strength and speed." They were roughly divided into two categories: cat-like and ape-like.

PRINT MEDIA REACTION to Gabe's story was weak. Journalists were not interested in authenticating Playboy as a source because of its content. Of course, journalists were quick to buy the magazine, though many just paid for Gabe's story online and downloaded it. But to their dismay, the downloaded version did not include any high-quality pictures.

Broadcast media reaction was minimal, with only passing references to the story existing in the commentaries of opinionated journalists. There was no Hardcopy story or Dateline. FOX, CNN, ABC, and CBS did not cover it during primetime, though MSNBC did do a small segment in the middle of the night.

However, internet buzz was extensive. The story received an impressive link on DrudgeReport.com, a media outlet still not accepted by other large media outlets, in spite of its impressive hit numbers. Drudge also used the image of Orson Welles and "War of the Worlds" as a backdrop, insisting the likely rationale of the United States wanting to develop hybrid soldiers was a way to combat declining recruitment rates.

In essence, if the utility of a soldier could be increased by 50-300%, then less soldiers would be needed during war. Naturally, there were immense ethical risks to soldiers being genetically mutated, but the theory was that soldiers would allow their bodies to be slightly modified if their pay rate was increased. In short, money once again was an incentive for bridging ethical gaps.

It would be the first time in modern history when money was invested directly into developing soldiers physically rather than into weapons. Prior to the writing of the M.I.X. report, it was not believed that a soldier's efficiency could be increased. Humans were believed to be a basically fixed variable, with their utility increased primarily by technological advancements through weapons. Yet now it was revealed that the military brass was bringing biogenetics to the forefront of the battle, thus creating a likely international arms race to make soldiers more powerful. The image of a strong and sexy soldier would change. Indeed, tomorrow's soldiers would be as powerful as yesterday's weapons.

The internet, with its wildly creative audience used many pictures to convey tomorrow's soldiers. Mythical creatures were created, following the Playboy theme and even adding a touch of Dungeons and Dragons to it, with characters from mythological times. Men were half-man, half-lion. Others were half-man, half-horse.

Nothing created more buzz than the characterization of the woman mermaid soldier as half-woman, half-fish. *Splash*, the movie, had reentered the cultural internet war with photographs of Daryl Hannah becoming an internet sensation. This was not Jane Fonda in North Korea; it was Daryl Hannah, the soldier of tomorrow—indeed, a sexy fish!

Some internet articles also linked to a new website on biogenetic technology. It contained links to credible information about genes getting switched, with people moving towards full-scale animals. It offered proof that genetics was becoming a simpler science, with the once-cryptic DNA code now being viewed as a rather easy code, similar to a computer's binary base, with DNA research essentially being rooted in zeros and ones.

THE REPORT from the public relations firm of Irvine and Muelleur was sent to Admiral Owens, complete with its standard blue cover. True to form, it contained the names of all key players who could threaten Project M.I.X., including many media personnel, lobbyists, and politicians. Along with each name was also specific contact information along with a history on each person or group.

The report warned of a strong possible threat from the biotech sector, as their stocks would initially dip substantially, then would soar as various international firms would file open-access claims against the United Nations, wanting Rita Perez's laptop information to become public property.

Another issue addressed by the report concerned hybrid warriors plans. The report warned that although the United States government had no hybrid warrior plans in development, other nations would organize around that worry. Promoting the (false) existence of hybrid warrior biotech firms in Rockville and on the Marshall Islands would become a banner issue eventually uniting Third-World nations against the United States, a movement that would likely gain momentum—and ultimately be joined—by Iran, North Korea, and Venezuela.

Further, the report warned that the United Nations would threaten to close the (non-existent) hybrid warrior program with international media depicting the United States (similarly to the denial state of Iran concerning its nuclear program) as hiding multiple secret attempts to invent hybrid warriors. Citing a dire conclusion, the report stated that the capitalization of the biotech sector could move the once-secret Rockville technology into a variety of different directions, including:

1) Vitamin supplements,
2) Memorabilia, and
3) Pop culture.

At the end of the report was a small blocked section:

Continue to deny everything: "*Although the purpose of Project M.I.X. was always to discover a cure for rapid human cell de-evolution—leading to the inevitable conversion of people into sub-human creatures—and never to create sub-human creatures, deny both the desire to discover a cure and the prior existence of hybrid soldiers. Unfortunately, the media will not believe the government's position due to numerous instances of the government lying about other historical situations.*

Businesses will inevitably apply Project M.I.X. research towards their commercialization needs, developing a range of products for the mass market. Inevitably, businesses will over-develop their products leading to a mass creation of de-evolved people, numbering in the billions across the globe. This will lead to a completely destabilized world, as new races of people will develop. Sadly, mankind will exterminate itself by creating a predator, with the new creature being on the top of the food chain.

The only solution to preserve international stability is to delay and baffle businesses from developing (and later profiting) from the now-public information on Rita Perez's laptop. Exposing the truth about the power of these cells will motivate scientists to push the technology. By contrast, baffling people with their power will serve to aide the government to develop a weapon system to battle the hybrid warriors.

Then the report had an attachment, with an ending section in bold:

Opinion: Spanning hundreds of millions of years, mankind has developed into its current life form. Business greed and fearless scientific zealotry has tinkered with limited DNA knowledge to nearly destroy the human race by 2012. Rebuilding efforts will take decades to slowly rebuild the human race to stable numbers. Scientific research has solved many problems, but not until now has it developed

a global problem. Conclusion: Don't tinker with nature unless you're prepared to accept its consequences.

As with most reports written by consultants for government bureaucrats, the authors were paid late and the findings filed in some locked drawer in some secure building in the suburbs of Washington, D.C.

WALL STREET REACTED SWIFTLY to Gabe's story, though only in two leading sectors: biotech and manufacturing related to military components. No other sectors had impacts that could be associated with the new information provided by Playboy.

As an industry, the biotech sector rarely faced ethical scrutiny through mass media, and within hours small groups of protestors began congregating in front of the doors of biotech research companies across the United States. Regardless, initial television coverage of the protestors was avoided, though for reasons that were unclear and unstated.

The biotech sector was vulnerable because its technology was controlled by scientists. Laws against biotechs were lax, too. After all, was it *illegal* for Dolly the Sheep to be cloned. But then why was genetically modified food permissible? Even cattle was no longer bred the "old-fashioned" way. Genetics was completely part of America's food cycle. Only a sliver of Americans resisted the use of G.M.F. (Genetically Modified Foods). Considered outcasts of society, their influence was marginalized.

But why should biogenetics be limited to food technology? Wasn't a stronger military a worthy need for the world's foremost superpower? Did personal liberty issues allow people to put *any* substance into their bodies that they desired? Whether it was cigarettes, drugs, or food, many people believed the government should not (or could not) restrict how people affected their own bodies. Wouldn't biogenetics be similar?

Numerous questions in internet forums led to a negative spike in the sector. It was not an industry accustomed to handling public relations, with many international scientists not even having strong English language skills. Consequently, it's initial reaction was poor, leading to large problems for Congress.

THE SAILBOAT DOCKED at a well-built pier inside a protected cove that was part of the sprawling estate of the Perez family within Patagonia, Argentina. It had been a pleasant 41-day voyage from New York, with little stopping along the way, although the stop in Rio was pretty wild. But just as they say, "whatever happens in Vegas," the same applied in Rio.

As Gabe and Nate tied Mistress to the dock, Ronaldo Perez, carrying binoculars, hobbled down a hill. He had anticipated their arrival spanning a four day period. Yet today was the day, he would finally see his daughter, whom he had not seen in nine months.

A three-piece ensemble joined him, passionately playing Argentinean music. Two played the guitar and the other carried a set of pan flutes. Each wearing a mustache and a sombrero, they symbolized the carefree life of a region far removed from modern civilization. In fact, Patagonia is one of the most remote regions on our planet, with a climate that is often severe.

The cream-colored villa was accented with a circular rotunda and a half-gazebo in the front of the house looking out at the ocean. Twenty tall wooden pillars lined the front, each with a carved image of a Roman god sitting stately on its top, overlooking the bluff. The house was part of a grand design from the brilliance of Ronaldo Perez. It was a completely autonomous estate. It could operate independently despite an unstable government, a fragile electric grid and an unreliable municipal water supply.

The house carried its own power system, fueled by a combination of geothermic, solar, and wind power, backed-up by a full complement of fuel cell generators. A couple of large fresh water basins were built along the Atlantic Ocean, in addition to a wind-powered system that pumped salt water up to shallow pools where solar power was used to separate out the water from the salt and biologicals. Designed by Rita's Perez's now-deceased grandfather, it was a system well ahead of its time in design and economy.

"Where is my beautiful angel?" said Ronaldo, raising his voice to be heard as he neared the dock.

"Sleeping," said Gabe, inspecting the boat's exterior for any previously unnoticed damage. "She had been awake for most of the trip, until she saw the mountains."

Ronaldo respectfully tipped his hat. "You must be Mr. Gabe Channing, and you, Mr. Nick Baschard."

"How do you know that?" asked Nick.

"I'm the one who got all of you your diplomatic immunity. I had to provide photographs for each of you to our embassy."

"But how did you get the photos?" asked Nate.

"Oh, let's just say I have connections in the north," answered Ronaldo, grinning.

"Papa!" shouted Rita, emerging from the cabin. She then clumsily tripped as she hobbled up the stairs, falling to the deck.

"Angel!" said Ronaldo, running—then jumping—onto the boat. Gabe trotted behind. With an exaggerated behavior, Ronaldo scurried to Rita, who was in tears, from the joy of seeing her father after a long absence.

"Papa!" said Rita as she reached for him, rubbing her right knee and returning to the psychological state of a young girl wanting the affection of a parent.

Impulsively, Ronaldo slightly lifted her long skirt and inspected her knee, testing it with his thumb and fingers. "It's not broken," he said, showing extra care, a symbol of his great love for her. "But it appears to be greatly strained. . . . You and you, get me a stretcher!" he said, barking to two of the musicians, all of whom were still playing music.

Obediently, two of the men scurried off towards the villa as the third seamlessly continued to play his guitar and sing. (They were accustomed to this type of exaggerated behavior.)

"Papa, my knee's fine. It doesn't hurt at all."

"I think she's okay," said Harland, removing his baseball cap from his head and glancing into the bright, cloudless sky.

"My angel is injured," said Ronaldo, shrugging off his comment.

Noticing his protection for his daughter, Gabe opened a bench and removed a large emergency kit. "Here," he said, playing to Ronaldo's illogical worries.

"Oh thank you, thank you," said Ronaldo, impulsively opening the box and quickly removing an Ace bandage, and then wrapping it around his daughter's knee with great tenderness.

RACE TO CREATE
HYBRID WARRIORS
CHAPTER FOURTEEN

PURPOSELY SCHEDULED after the November 2012 elections, the hearings were slated for January 2013, a high-profile time for the next congress. It was also a politically expedient time for Senator Bob Dugan from North Dakota to make a name for himself.

When America is angry, it blames politicians. It doesn't even matter if the problem was unforeseen, because few Americans believe their government 100% of the time, or even 50% of the time. It was no longer a country of "America: love it or leave it." Instead, people no longer pressed direct questions, readily allowing the media to shape their opinions on topics of discussion.

Usually apathy worked in the favor of politicians, but on rare occasion, public uproar would unite around a specific topic or agenda. True to other parts of the report by Irvine and Muelleur, it just so happened that the disclosure of de-evolution laboratories in Rockville began a slow but steady media frenzy regarding bio-ethics.

The core of the resistance was in the Pro-Life community, a cultural segment consistent with Rita's value system with its Catholic roots. There were worries among them that a new race of people was being developed. Additional concerns focused on cloning, as bio-genetics was included in that genre of science. Naturalists, people who believed that society (or the environment) should not be dramatically altered, were also lined up against the manipulation of humans for military purposes. Of course, the pacifists were there to protest, using their "bread, not guns" rhetoric to attack the secret spending.

Along largely political lines, Republican senators called for immediate congressional hearings into ethics violations at Rockville GenXY. Since modern laws did not specify a crime, the fury among conservatives was passionate. Was the U.S. government funding the development of a new race of people? Were humans being cloned with animal cells? Did the developing science originate from a desire for the United States to improve every soldier's utility or just certain soldiers? And did the U.S. government understand that it was violating bio-ethics rules with soldiers who had been duped into taking genetic-modifying pills (G.M.P.)?

THIRTY INTERNATIONAL REPORTERS stood within a roped off area in the Capitol building along the side of an elevated platform. Dignitaries and watchdog groups crowded into some of the space typically reserved for the press. The presence of the international press changed the spirit of those gathered, as their interest in United States affairs was normally subdued.

It was the beginning of what was scheduled to be a rare week of discussion with industry experts, scientists and politicians testifying about American genetic research and inter-related military policy. An historic moment, it was the first time the topic had been addressed with such a public platform, making government officials excessively antsy about the topic and anxious to posture themselves most advantageously.

The Wall Street community was also interested in the meetings, a unique combination of seemingly independent groups showing a united interest in a topic that would normally put the public to sleep. Indeed, it was Washington's latest witch hunt. Though because the target of the hunt had not yet been identified, all reporters were eager to see the first sign of blood, and all politicians were eager to see which agency (or person) was going to take the hit.

The first person to testify was Dr. Ernest Bauer, an M.I.T. alumni and the country's most recognized expert on genetic technology. "Junk DNA is predominantly a binary code composed of zeros and ones," he said.

Senator Hilda Glickman scratched her head. "There's not a three, or a four?"

"That's correct. There's not even a 'two.' The genetic code is purely composed of 'yes-es' or 'no-es,' with no existence of a 'maybe.' For purposes of this discussion, we're going to narrow that complex technology into two components. If we simply switch the 'one,' to a 'zero' then we reverse evolution, ah, perhaps a million years," he said.

"I hate it when that happens," said Senator Glickman, spawning a rare chuckle through the Capitol.

The scientist was not amused by her joke. "I want to make myself clear. This science is going to reverse our genetic evolution. This will result in new races of people being created. Our races on earth will consist of the typical races, and whatever each biotech across the entire planet is creating."

Later, watchdog leader Madeline Hastings testified before the committee. "The threat of genetics is that mankind could de-evolve to a pre-homosapien stage when people were not people as we know them to be today."

"What were they then?" asked Senator Glickman, smiling into a television camera.

"They were pre-Neanderthals," said Madeline. "They were creatures with gills and feathers—people, yet not people with substantial animal characteristics.

"I don't think *people* ever had feathers," said Senator Glickman.

Madeline ignored her flip comment. "Genetic science today can reverse a million years of evolution by simply flipping a few switches of binary technology, in essence, turning the dial to use junk DNA. Scientists have discovered the substance in that 96% portion of our DNA, known as "junk DNA."

"I don't understand," said the senator.

Madeline leaned forward in her chair. "Let me use an analogy to describe what's happening with genetics:

At one point in world history, alcohol was created by some caveman (or cavewoman) unwittingly allowing old grapes to ferment on the shelf somewhere for a period of time until someone put those mushy grapes into a glass to drink it. Remarkably, when it was consumed, it provided a nice buzz."

Everyone chuckled at the visual of cave-dwellers sitting around a campfire getting buzzed on homemade wine. "Please continue," said the senator.

Madeline milked the time, enjoying the light laughter. "Soon the process was duplicated, leading to the invention of wine. In short, one person makes the wine and another drinks it. Usually, both people drink the wine at the same time." More chuckles from the listening. "Obviously, it's no fun when only one person is buzzed and not the other. In social interactions, both people usually get buzzed together."

"Please make your point, ma'am, and pass me my glasses," said the senator, looking at her legislative aide.

Madeline continued. "Alcohol has become such a part of the mating process that it's rarely questioned anymore as a problem with ethics. It's the same with genetic research. Just because scientific laboratories across the United States (and the world) are experimenting with the technology doesn't make it right. But unless something is done now, it will become an embedded part of our culture, just as alcohol is."

Senator Dugan cleared his throat. "In 1999, reporter Gabe Channing—whom I understand to be a dear friend of yours—wrote a long story by journalistic standards regarding an extensive interview he did with you the difficult night of a well-publicized fire at the fire station in Annapolis. Is that correct?"

"Yes it is," said Bolton, clearing his throat. "I might add that that was an *award-winning* story, recognized by the Washington Press Club as the best story of the year in 1999."

Dugan exhaled slowly. "I understand that, sir. It was an excessively long interview though; correct?"

"I disagree, with you, senator," said Bolton, clicking a pen he was holding. "You have to understand, Senator, Gabe is the *most-respected* and longest-tenured journalist in the history of Annapolis, the capital of the great State of Maryland. Naturally, I would spend a lot of time with him during a key moment like that. Gabe and I both love Annapolis."

"Are you familiar with a bar owner named Marti Svonski?"

The mayor sipped on his glass of water, creating a moment of extended silence in the room, allowing an opportunity for Senator Tataconni to speak. "I'm sorry, Senator Dugan, but your time is about to expire."

"I'm trying to establish the credibility of the witness," said Senator Dugan.

"And I'm telling you you're only allowed another thirty seconds."

Senator Dugan continued to speak, monopolizing his time behind the microphone. "Okay, please state your position, sir."

"I'm Admiral Nelson Owens, a 31-year veteran of the United States Navy, now assigned to manage ethics concerns addressed by ethics groups across the country."

Dugan adjusted his tie for the camera then paused for the proper media sound bite. "Let me get straight to the point. Are these five suspects considered to be terrorists?

"Absolutely. Yes they are, sir."

"And why are Gabe Channing, Nate Baschard, Harland Parker, Rita Perez, and Sandra O'Callahan terrorists?"

"A previously law-abiding American citizen can unknowingly become a bio-terrorist by sharing information that can terrorize the United States. Something drastically different than with other forms of terrorism, where the guilty parties have to knowingly engage in the process."

Senator Dugan's abruptly raised his hand, stopping the admiral from continuing. "So a person can become a terrorist without even intending to become a terrorist?"

"That's correct, sir, at least with bio-terrorism"

"Then how do you determine the degree of guilt of such a person?"

"It's the pain to national security that is considered, not the presumed innocence of the person."

Dugan scanned his notes, then paused for the cameras to give him the perfect sound bite. "With all due respect to your position, admiral, your terrorism claims are exceedingly too light and undefined."

"I respectfully disagree, senator," said Owens. "The *threat* of bio-terrorism contains the greatest threat to civilization, with the most potential damage being assessed against an innocent public. It's also the most non-ubiquitous form of terrorism. All bio-terrorism requires is the cellular manipulation of one innocent life and mankind across the planet can permanently change.

Dugan was unphased by his answer. "Let me approach the topic differently: From what my sources tell me, all efforts to create a hybrid race of people have been halted by these unknowing bio-terrorists, correct?"

Owens leaned into the microphone. "With all due respect, Senator, your question is impossible to answer with a simple 'yes' or 'no.' Besides, if I were to answer *any* component of that question, I would be violating national security policies and possibly committing treason against our country."

"You're exaggerating, admiral," said the Senator, taunting him further.

"That's false, Senator. Bio-terrorism is quite real, sir, as real as our country is right."

HOURS LATER, David Spelling was at Larry's Steakhouse near the Capitol, in an informal meeting with Jamie Whiteman and Zack McHenry.

David was on his second glass of a highly-priced Boudreaux. "I'm warning you again about Nate Baschard," he said. "He watches these stock prices like few people I have ever seen. He'll do everything he can to increase the value of his stock portfolio. He didn't become a bio-terrorist for nothing, you know? To him, it's all about greed."

"I understand that," said Zack, taking a bite of strip steak. "Yet why would he have orchestrated such a heist of our national security like he did?"

"Like I said, the man is just about as greedy as it gets. He wants to make a name for himself in the biotech field, so he decided to pair up with this reporter chump to do that."

Quietly, Jamie raised her eyebrow, but continued to not speak.

"You do understand what they have, don't you?" asked Zack. "It's not a ride in the park, due to all the classified information they had. Together, it is certainly a threat to our national security, and even to the stability of our country and the entire world."

"He's not to be trusted," said David. "In this case, the man we're talking about knows more than he'll ever admit. He's a swindler. I think he is still up to something."

"A swindler?" asked Jamie, smirking a little at Spelling's exaggeration.

Spelling was so excited, he was spitting as he spoke. "Yeah, all he wants is to ride the biotech sector all the way to the bank. This man is a con artist—a real pro—and probably the worst long-term example of a stock analyst I've ever seen. Dig a little deeper. You may even find something you're not expecting."

THE DINING ROOM TABLE was full of fine foods, more than could ever be eaten in one setting. The twelve (including Ronaldo; Eva the mother; Rita's brother, the program designer; his wife; and their two children) were stuffed to the brim as a servant brought another bottle of wine to the table.

"Is this the bottle you wanted, sir," said the servant as she showed Ronaldo a bottle of 1995 wine.

Ronaldo read the bottle, careful to read each word on the label. "You can never be too careful with these things," he said, subtly making his point clear to everyone at the table, though he looked only at Rita.

"How is the paella?" asked Eva. "I tried to make only your favorite dishes."

"Everything's excellent, just excellent," answered Rita, taking another fork full.

"That's good," said Ronaldo, sipping another glass of wine, his fifth. "I know I've asked this a few times already, but I just don't understand why they chased after all of you in the first place."

"It's a pretty complicated story," said Gabe, sipping his fourth glass of wine. "It all stems back to this retirement story I was writing."

"I thought it was a story about hybrid soldiers for Playboy," said Ronaldo.

"That's how it began," said Gabe. "Then it got kind of carried away, you can say."

"Though they didn't want to buy it right away," said Nate. "We kept pushing them for a higher amount of money, until they finally bit on something."

Marti re-entered the room, smiling. "I'm sorry for the interruption, but I made the final arrangements with the storage company for shipping some of my belongings down here via container. It's going to be the same company I worked with months ago when I had them pack and move everyone's belongings into storage."

"That's great," said Ronaldo. "That means some of you will be staying here for a while. My only question is, why did they chase you all in the first place?"

"*Chase* us? They were trying to *kill* us," said Harland, clanking his fork against his plate. "Their first bullet had my name on it."

"Tell me more about this laptop," said Ronaldo, ignoring Harland. "Why would anyone want to ever spend that much money for a typical laptop?"

Rita was more calm, having developing a higher tolerance to wine by drinking so much over the past few decades. "There's a program Pedro wrote for me on my laptop that helped me analyze DNA. The last simulation I ran showed that the amphibian DNA. I was working on—or at least what I thought was amphibian—might actually have been human DNA."

"Obviously," said Nate. "But what is it?"

"I don't know," said Rita."

"Well, we've gone over this a hundred times already," Sandra began," and we still don't know what it is they wanted."

"What were you doing with those cells you were working on?" asked Eva.

"I don't know, mother," said Rita. "The research was classified as top secret and I only knew a little portion of the complete project."

"The last time we spoke—almost two months ago now—you mentioned something about the U.S. government forcing you to kill human cells."

Rita's eyes sunk in sorrow. "Yeah, the cells were destroyed after their analysis. Of course, replacements were pre-cloned."

"I thought you were working on animal cells," said Eva. "Killing a human life is a mortal sin."

". . . Tell that to the military. . . ." Sandra blurted.

"I know," said Rita, avoiding eye contact with her mother. "I thought they were amphibian, honest I did."

"Well, did you kill *human* cells?"

"Not knowingly," said Rita. "I don't think I did."

Eva's face sunk in shame. "You killed a *person*?"

"No mother, not knowingly."

Eva's head sunk further, dismally ashamed.

"I didn't know they were humans," said Rita. "I thought they were animals, but they—"

"You killed people?" asked Eva, her face quivering, no longer proud of her daughter's work.

"You did?" asked Ronaldo.

Sandra, who was the least drunk in the room, was the first to answer. "Why did you think they were humans?" she asked.

"They were human," said Rita, reiterating herself. "Of course they were human."

Her mother was dismayed. "Why would you do such a thing, to kill human life?"

"I didn't know mother, I swear." said Rita.

"I don't mean to interject," added Nate, "but why do you think you were killing people?"

"Because I was," said Rita. "The experiments I conducted showed the DNA was almost a perfect match with human DNA already in the gene pool. It's out there. What I did has been done."

"On people, though?" asked Sandra. "That's the question we have been debating for weeks now."

Nate was unapologetic, carefree of what he was saying. "Maybe you weren't working on human cells, but animal cells. Maybe it was the animals you were killing, not actual people."

"Why do you think that?" Rita asked."

"Well, there must be some answer to your actions," said Sandra.

"All I did was try to develop those cells," said Rita.

"Human cells or animal?"

"I'm not sure, " said Rita. "It was my understanding that I was working on animal cells, but then when I was working on my research, I discovered I was actually converting them into human cells."

WITH A SPIRIT OF OPENNESS, the United Nations made the information from Rita's laptop available to all nations in the world. Not wanting to discriminate against rogue nations, there were no restrictions on anything related to information.

The policy of Secretary General Duncan Faust was "absolute openness for all," something for which he had heavily lobbied members to support on the platform he ran on when he received his position. His success was attributed to a clever campaign to appeal to under-developed nations. Then, true to his word, he created a policy of making public all new information received into his office within two months, the delay being justified by extensive paperwork due to language barriers.

Duncan was praised by the developing nations of Pakistan, Iran, India, and Cuba because previously acquiring new technology was difficult and expensive. As more technology was made available, more countries developed a liking towards him, though all to the chagrin of leading nations like the United States, Russia, England, China, and France, all leaders on the security council.

Within six months of receiving the data, nations from across the world were developing Rita's technology for military purposes, all the while restricting the technology from commercial avenues and never admitting that they were doing exactly what they were accusing the United States of doing. Wanting to control the development of science under the adage of "information is power," governments across the world were able to begin experimenting with human embryos to insert aspects of the technology into developing human cells. The purpose? It was to develop genetically advanced soldiers capable of evolving militaries with superior soldiers, compensating for discrepancies with military technology. The same thing they had accused the U.S. of doing in the first place.

Similar to the Space Race and the Nuclear Race, the "Hybrid Warrior Race" became a rush by various nations to advance themselves beyond the superior technology of the countries on the security council. Duncan Faust was a major contributor to this advancement, an important player in the histories of countries that would always thank him for sticking with his values, though never directly acknowledging him for his involvement. In short, it was Duncan's world now, a world where information would flow free, and where underdeveloped countries would finally find an outlet for their intellectual freedom. With Duncan, all the world could do as it pleased!

And, indeed, it did! Half the countries in the world were developing human cells into hybrid warriors, and not a one of them gave a damn about the malleable ethics behind their work. All the while, nations all around the world prepared a defense against the United States' latest tactic, rooted in superior genetic technology.

THE MEETING HAD COLLAPSED into the core of its shell. No one was interested in talking anymore, and the popcorn was stale, at its worst moment for any government meeting.

Zack was aghast, his coffee no longer comforting him. "They're converting her technology into advanced soldiers. Nothing could be worse for us. All these second-rate countries are converting her technology into soldiers, seriously, into soldiers. Don't they realize the entire world is going to fall into disarray?"

"It's hopeless," said Jamie, a rare moment of openness. "We're going to finally be outwitted. It's over for us. They won."

"Not yet," said Erin. "There are still options, you know, albeit desperate options, but options."

Jamie said, "Compile a list of our options, Erin, and let's meet back here in 24 hours."

THE DECISION WAS MADE IN COMMITTEE, far removed from the hustle and bustle of life in New York. Not wanting to harm his excellent world image, Duncan Faust had initially refused to make an announcement in front of the cameras. Instead, he issued a press release regarding the laptop purchase and how the U.N. would continue to act in the best interests of the world. Then as media tension escalated, he spoke through Ingrid

Johansson, Assistant Secretary General, and the weakest member of the council. Ultimately, though, he was out of options and had to face the cameras.

"After a thorough review by member nations, we have determined the United Nations we will no longer tolerate the use of genetic research for military purposes."

"Why is there a sudden change in policy?" asked a reporter.

"It's not a change in policy," Duncan began, "only a reconfirmation of existing present beliefs within the United Nations. It's in our interest to pursue policy within our means."

His dialogue was consistent with U.N. babble, hypocrisy typical for people unsure of how to respond to a flood of media attention. As for the U.N., they were no longer going to allow any nation to participate in the hybrid warrior race, instead they would make their technology available to all participating nations, ignoring all the while the complications of protocol, as long as the technology was used only for peaceful purposes.

"We determined it was morally wrong and globally destabilizing," said Duncan. "In short, we conclude that hybrid cell technology used incorrectly towards the purposes of war is unethical and immoral, similar to nuclear weapons and chemical weapons."

"What will you do with the existing technology?" asked a reporter.

"We will make all information we have gathered available to all countries of our great world, to aide responsible world leaders in developing superior techniques to develop healthier capabilities for our bodies. The General Assembly has voted that the genetic technology is safest if it is developed for commercial purposes, where consumers will determine its value and longer utility. I will take one last question. . . ."

"Why did you spend six million dollars on a laptop?" asked a reporter.

Duncan smiled. "It's not just the laptop, it's the information on it we spent all the money on, probably the most advanced design program ever developed, and a program that literally contains tens of thousands of variations of hybrid cells, technology never seen by any commercial scientist in the history of the world."

IN 1983, Sterling Parker lay dying on the deck, mortally bitten by a shark-like creature that had miraculously scrambled onto the deck from the sea. In spite of the boat traveling at twenty knots, somehow it had swum and overtaken the boat. After it had jumped aboard, it seemed to utter angry gibberish that terrified the eight-man crew far more than its large scales, the same color of human flesh, and then proceeded to gnaw on Ensign Parker. It then returned again to the sea, after half-running like a human, half-scrambling like a fish out of water.

The order came from Major Nelson Owens: "Hit it!"

Within seconds, a harpoon was fired which was a direct hit on the creature. The first mate adjusted the harpoon's coil mechanism, drawing the fish nearer to the boat as it floated in the water.

A lackey called out, "It's a mermaid! We hit a damn mermaid! A real mermaid!"

On the deck now laid Sterling Parker and the mermaid, creating an uncomfortable silence that lasted longer than anyone wanted it to. It was a moment when man and beast bond, like when a horse dies, or an elephant falls forever to the ground. Side by side was a dying man and a dying beast.

"Kill it and then get that damn beast on ice right away," shouted Owens, waving his hands and pointing his finger at a man. "You, captain, form a search party and get over to that island. Bring back—dead or alive—anything that's the slightest bit unusual."

"Yes, sir," said the captain, saluting. He then turned to another man. "Ensign, prepare the landing craft and bring two marksmen. . . . Now!"

"Sir, yes, sir," said the ensign. "We're going hunting, boys."

DEVELOPMENT & COMMERCIALIZATION
CHAPTER FIFTEEN

RITA'S LAPTOP contained a beta version of a product developed by her brother, Pedro Perez. A mechanical engineer, Pedro had created a program whereby a blueprint could be reduced to its most basic components, streamlining the process for change-orders for mechanical designs. For instance, if the designer of an automobile decided he wanted to shift the steering column one inch to the left, several car parts would have to be redesigned to government specs. With Pedro's design, all the designer had to do was scan the final completed working blueprint into a computer and mark the part which needed to be changed and the program would automatically redesign the rest of the car.

The program was effective for a wide range of design which made it unique. Another example was if the architect of a finished skyscraper would upload his completed blueprints into the computer, then his program could easily change the entire blueprint to each floor being eight feet, instead of seven feet. Further, it calculated the costs associated with the change, along with addressing many potential previously unforeseen factors.

Rita had received the program from her brother on her last visit back to her father's estate in 2007. She then uploaded it to her laptop. However, she did not install a mechanical blueprint, but the blueprint of the DNA helix, she was working on, the most complicated blueprint known to man.

She then began manipulating the DNA helix through playing with her $1000 laptop, experiments she could do at any place—any time—without anyone suspecting her of reconfiguring nature. It was her way of tinkering with genetics without actually using live cells. Her goal was to manipulate the DNA of computer-generated cells on her computer—or the cyber version of real cells—by using a program more similar to Tetris. Consequently, she nicknamed it "REvolution."

Every time she played REvolution (a combination of Re and evolution) the changed results of the DNA helix would automatically be saved into the program, allowing for future changes to those changes. Playing the game daily for a couple of years, she literally had developed tens of thousands of variations of the hybrid cells she was experimenting with, always believing she was tinkering with data, never anything real. In her lab, the cells were real; on the laptop they were just data.

In her spare time, she would change one characteristic of the billions of characteristics on the DNA helix, then see what creature it would evolve (or de-evolve) into. Since most organisms were composed of about 95% junk DNA, usually the changes created differences that were not statistically different from before the change. For instance, maybe after rearranging two of the parts of the helix, the only difference showing on her laptop would be a pinky finger on the left hand that grew an extra quarter inch.

Playing with her computer was an ethical way for her to advance her scientific research without ever conflicting with her Roman Catholic ideology. Effortlessly, she would de-evolve (or evolve) her complex cells into life forms that could have existed thousands of millenniums earlier or might yet come about. However, usually the cells would die after they changed because of their weakened genetic code.

When the United Nations released all of its paperwork to the national press and to all the countries in the world, at the core of its finding was Rita's beta technology with literally tens of thousands of saved combinations of de-evolved human cells, sub-human, or advanced.

Rita never stole any cells from GenXY, she merely copied the DNA helix of the cells on which she was working. It was not a crime in the least bit either, as who owns one's DNA code? Alas, the rules of genetics were *severely* underdeveloped and untested.

FROM YOUR DNA's point of view, aging isn't really a normal process at all. DNA may change slightly, but only due to the environment. DNA can change its replication but that is due to environmental changes within the cell, not changes in the DNA. Thus, replication can go wrong. Aging, itself, does not alter DNA. The aging process is influenced by choices people make with their lifestyles. Another choice is to tell the cells to grow—to build a strong, vibrant body and mind.

Everyone's body is literally composed of trillions of cells. Some of those cells live for a few weeks or a few months, and then get replaced by new cells, day after day, month after month, and year after year. Taste buds, for example, live only a few hours, while white blood cells live 10 days, and muscle cells live about three months. This is why it takes a few months of exercising to notice muscular change. Even bones dissolve and are replaced, over and over again. Key stem cells in each area are responsible for becoming the right replacement cells. Change the stem cells and the future of those cells is changed. Almost all of your other cells are in a constant state of renewal.

On average, people replace about 1% of their cells every day. Consider the body to be an old car that requires routine maintenance. In time, replacement parts are needed—often purchased at reduced rates. However, if the mechanic knows that the part is highly utilized, then a durable, replacement part is needed. It's similar to how the body regenerates. In those terms, people walk around in a rejuvenated body every year or so—new lungs, new liver, new muscles, and even new skin.

The replacement cycle evolved over billions of years out in nature, where all animals face two great cellular challenges. The first is to grow strong, fast and fit in the spring, when food abounds and calories fuel hungry muscles, bones and brains. The second is to minimize as fast as possible in the winter, when calories disappear and surviving starvation is the key to life. Ironically, activity originally controlled the body and the signals to changes, not food.

Though mankind now lives indoors, their bodies still think we're living out on the savannah, struggling to stay alive each day. Thus, evolutionary change has not kept pace with manmade changes to the environment. There are no microwave ovens or supermarkets in the wild. Out there—in nature—when people ate they had to hunt or forage each day. That movement is a signal to the cells that it's time to grow. So, when people exercise, their muscles release specific substances that travel throughout the bloodstream, telling cells to grow. Sedentary muscles, on the other hand, let out a steady trickle of chemicals that whisper to every cell to decay, day after day after day.

THE SPIRIT IN THE ROOM WAS HOPEFUL, but not cheerful. Several identical massive files of information from the United Nations concerning Rita's laptop were on the table, with towering stacks made for each of the seven people in the room.

Zack McHenry avoided eye contact with Henderson Duvall. "You weren't involved with the laptop; Rita was," said Zack. "It's her brilliance that got us into the mess we're in today."

"I was the one who trained her," said Henderson, his neck stiffening. "She was a good worker at GenXY until she stole that technology and become a terrorist."

Brad rolled his eyes, trying to hide the reality of what happened. "You *know* she's not a terrorist. And it was her laptop, personally paid for by her, and it was a program written by her brother. All we wanted to do was arrest all of them to stop the spread of the information they had, not to convict them."

"It was a sincere bluff and the media played right into it," said Erin. "Of course, none of us knew she was a genius." (It was actually Rita's brother who was the genius, but H.S.A. did not know that yet.)

Henderson's mouth dropped. "I told you she was a genius months ago. Most of the people who work under me are geniuses."

"The blind leading the blind," said Zack, smirking, causing Henderson to stand up and tense all his muscles.

"Go to hell," said Henderson. "She's a terrorist now, which is out of my control. Now am I going to get this contract or not?"

Jamie swirled what remained of her coffee then looked at him, unphased by his anger, which she considered to be more acting than sincerity. "Can you pass me the coffee?" she said to Admiral Owens, ignoring Henderson.

"Sure," answered Owens. "Cream, too?"

"Yeah," said Jamie.

The intensity lowered as Owens walked the cream over to Jamie, then poured it for her, as a gentlemen would. When there was enough cream added, Jamie signaled with her hand to stop.

Jamie controlled the room as she fumbled with opening the sugar packets. "The way I see it is that we have six months until some biotech develops its pills, then another six months to a year until it is manufactured and distributed. Then according to the diary, we have three months until the de-evolution takes affect, then another three months until it turns violent."

"That's up to two years," said Henderson. "I can beat that by at least six months."

Jamie cleared her throat. "You both can leave now," she said, staring coldly at Henderson and Senator Glickman. "We're going to begin the executive portion of our meeting now."

"I haven't had a chance to talk yet," said Senator Glickman.

"That's for the best," said Zack, also avoiding eye contact with Glickman.

A few minutes later, they left the room. Admiral Owens then stood, his face somber.

"I'm the only person on this planet still living whose seen one of these creatures alive," said Owen. "They're not friendly humans we're talking about. And all I encountered was a fish woman: a mermaid, if you will. The rest were just carcasses, but from what I saw of them, they just devoured the hell out of each other and anything else they could find. There was blood everywhere. One even had its intestines sliced by the talons of another."

"I know," said Bobby Gilroy with the CIA. "I'm the one who conducted the investigation." He reached into the towering stack and removed a file labeled "Project M.I.X.—Enewetak Island, original photographs." Then Gilroy opened the file and looked at the photos, a nauseous look growing on his face."

Jamie stared at her coffee. "Let's plan on two years until we have to have a new weapon system developed. Right?"

"Yeah, two years," said Owens.

"I agree," said Gilroy.

"Me, too," said Zack.

Erin and Brad just nodded.

Jamie kept staring at her coffee. "That Rita was working on a cure, but instead she outfoxed everyone, including herself. Take her off the terrorist list, all of them. Then contract with her and even maybe her brother to rebuild a lab and recreate what she was doing before. The hell with protocol. We're all going to be dead unless we think faster than them."

"Where do you want the lab to be?" asked Zack.

"I don't care, just as long as it is secure, isolated and acceptable to Rita," said Jamie, hating the power it seemed Rita was gaining.

"Alright, let see what we can do," said Owens.

Jamie grimaced. "I know the report from the consultants sounds bogus with its outlandish claims, but if what they said is even half correct, then life is going to become, well, rather complicated for the military. Zack, I want you to personally oversee this lab. We can't afford any mistakes or any delays."

Owens nodded. "I agree."

"Okay," said Zack, smiling as he flipped over to the file on Rita. "I'm on it 24/7."

REGRESSIVE HUMAN VARIANCE, or R.H.V., was the new term given for the process of scientific de-evolution when the body would select a regressive DNA structure and transform itself into it. The selection of what DNA blueprint it would adapt was R.H.V. Being a new science, no one understood what DNA blueprint would be selected during R.H.V. Why did the body pick the DNA it picked as it de-evolved? Scientists would have to try to understand R.H.V.

The initial United Nations research spawned by Rita's original research showed that the cells she was studying were easier to reprogram their R.H.V. The problem was that she was unable to isolate the R.H.V. to pick a specific DNA blueprint. R.H.V. was the source for changing the binary formula of DNA, the formula for life. And since every human DNA helix contained many sections of pre-human DNA structures, if the R.H.V. was applied improperly, then people could regress into animals.

Obviously, it was not the intention of biotech companies to de-evolve people into animals, thus, biotech companies across the world worked on stopping the de-evolution to only the positive characteristics of animals or previous human traits. For instance, by adding some of the characteristics of fish DNA, man could swim underwater longer with gills and faster with fins. If mankind did evolve from the sea—and as some believed actually had gills while a fetus—then turning those switches back on would lead to the growth of gills.

With the characteristics of birds, man could fly if he could develop feathers and a lighter body mass. He would also survive with a much different diet.

With the characteristics of a owl, man would develop greater night vision and greater patience. Other unknown factors could also exist.

The original concern among biotech companies was a worry rooted in a drug called Thalidomide, a product popular in the late fifties and early sixties that created thousands of severely deformed babies in the United States, leading to many lawsuits. Because of its great potential benefits, there was a fear among drug companies that the hybrid cell drug would be branded as a wonder drug, like Thalidomide.

Hence, the drug companies began their sales approach foremost from a marketing perspective, wanting to position the drugs as creating only a slight benefit for its recipients. Underperforming any demand was a crucial element in drug company strategy. And avoiding being labeled as a drug was key to getting to market fast.

CONSISTENT WITH Jamie's prediction, within six months there was a claim by Shermine Industries, a small Canadian biotech company that they had successfully isolated the R.H.V. genetic component to limit the degree to how much of the DNA binary code would be switched. It had also tested it in its laboratory with successful results, meaning that the de-evolution would not continue beyond one level of development, allowing the gene sequences within any particular animal's DNA to be isolated and controlled.

Another month later, a biotech company out of New Zealand had also isolated an R.H.V. component, followed by a biotech in Boston, Massachusetts. Indeed, the biotech sector was soaring once again, with huge profits ahead being predicted by Wall Street all across the industry.

There was then a rush for the different companies to take their products to market, with all biotechs rushing the development and commercialization of their specific drug, or "natural enhancers," along with refining what human characteristics could be enhanced. Ultimately, there were many firms across several countries claiming scientific breakthroughs had been made.

IT WAS A BEAUTIFUL SUNRISE that greeted Nate as he walked out of his room and headed for the dining room in the main house. He planned today to head into the hills and see a secluded waterfall area Rita had recently mentioned.

"Good morning," said Nate, fidgeting.

"Good morning," said Sandra as she sat on the back porch drinking Brazilian coffee from freshly roasted beans. "Shade grown, fair trade," she added, pointing to the coffee.

Nate continued to fidget. "How about if the two of us relax and head up to that waterfall area Rita's always talking about. We could pack a lunch and head out on one of the ATV's.

Sandra smiled. "I like the idea, except I want to make one change."

"What's that?"

"Let's take horses instead. It's less destructive and certainly more peaceful." She wanted to say something more romantic, but her environmentalist nature spilled out of her mouth, instead.

"You're on," said Nate. "I'll take care of the lunch stuff, and you find the horses."

Okay," said Sandra. "Let's meet at the barn in an hour. Remember, no meat."

THE HORSE RIDE to the falls was an adventure along a lightly treaded dirt path past ferns, wild flowers, and caverns. In time, they climbed the hill until they made it to the top. They dismounted, found some flat rocks to sit back on, giving them a fairy-tale view of the Argentinean countryside. The pool below the falls was crystal clear. They could see the bottom—an estimated twenty foot depth. In the pool, brightly colored koi could be seen swimming lazily. Overhead, Nate and Sandra caught sight of a majestic condor flying westward.

On the other side of the stream was an excellent place where a blanket could be spread for a picnic. They remounted after a brief spell and headed across the stream. When they arrived at their picnic area, Sandra untied a homemade rope made of horsehair, connecting the picnic basket to the leather saddle while Nate spread out the blanket.

They both settled down on the blanket as Nate reached for a bottle of wine nestled in the basket near fresh fruit, cheeses, and homemade bread—all produced on the estate. Nate opened the wine, and poured it into crystal glasses. Soon they drank a little, ate a little, and then drank a little more until the warmth of the sun and the gentle sounds of the waterfall made them both grow sleepy, tired from the long journey.

After a long nap, Nate finally opened his eyes and saw Sandra lying next to him, her head on his shoulder. Sandra sat up and then reached for an apple from out of a satchel. She was about to take a bite out of it, but then offered it to Nate first. "Would you like to take a bit out of my apple?" she asked holding the apple in the air.

Nate grinned. "Sure." With Sandra still holding the apple, he took a bite out of it. Then she bit the apple in the spot right next to it.

Something inside Nate's heart told him he needed to lean over and kiss her. As he moved his lips close to hers, he whispered, "May I kiss you?"

"Yes."

After a soft, gentle kiss, they looked at each other, eye-to-eye and simultaneously said, "Thank you." Then they gently laughed.

"Let's go swimming," said Nate.

"Okay, let's go," said Sandra, who then began to strip off her clothes. Within seconds, she dove into the water.

Nate cocked his head, stunned by her instantaneous compliance. Then he stripped off his clothes and dove into the water, joining her.

The water was cool, refreshing, and invigorating. They played in the crystal clear pool for almost an hour, until deciding to return to the blanket, and open a second bottle of wine. Nate felt incredibly different, with the city noises and pollution thousands of miles away.

He poured another glass of wine for himself and Sandra's ash-colored eyes stared into his. He hoped Sandra would stay on the estate, instead of returning to the U.S. Why not stay where everything was so peaceful?

FOUR PACKAGES ARRIVED on the day before Harland and Sandra were scheduled to return to the United States. Inside the packages—all of which looked identical on the outside—were packets with different types of cellular enhancers.

For Harland, the package contained pills meant to give him superior intelligence, excellent eyesight, and a killer instinct for survival on the battlefield. For Rita, the pills would spawn the beginning of her laboratory, which would analyze the exact way these were altering a user's genetic make-up. For Nate, the pills were merely a trophy which symbolized the great wealth he was assembling by his ability to forecast the trends in biotechs, in addition to representing his vindication over David Spelling, who tried to ruin his career. For Gabe, the pills symbolized his first encounter with now-Admiral Nelson Owens, a riddle of a story he had encountered during his days as a Navy reporter—the first story his gut had made him question, leading to the wealthy life he now enjoyed and a woman, Marti, whom he had loved, but was previously too shy to tell.

Now in the evening with the propellers humming on the small twin engine plane that was waiting to take Harland and Sandra to Rio where they would get their connection flight to the United States, everyone gathered along the edge of a landing strip carefully built in the middle of a pristine vineyard.

Harland twisted the cap on the pill bottle. "If it wasn't for being without my son, this would have been one of the greatest days of my life. I wanted to take my first pills with everyone to watch. It's a great day in my life, a day I will finally return to my son. Plus, I so miss the life I once had. Finally, I can get rid of these damn glasses and regenerate my eyes to normal 20/20 eyesight. For my entire life I've had bad eyesight."

"Oh stop it with the speeches," said Ronaldo, who then looked at Sandra. "We're going to miss you."

Harland then ascended the stairs to the passenger compartment of the airplane, waving to Gabe and Marti as he got to the top.

Sandra frowned. "I really appreciated the opportunity to stay with you and your wife here on your estate, sharing meals and experiencing hospitality like I've never seen before. I hate the idea of leaving, but I've really want to get back."

"You're welcome to return whenever you want, for as long as you want," said Ronaldo.

"Why don't you stay, then?" asked Nate, showing more kindness towards her. Have you ever been anywhere more beautiful? This place is as much of a paradise as any you will find on this planet."

Sandra smirked. "For me, all I need is a beer in my favorite Irish pub in Dupont Circle and I'll be just fine. There aren't any pubs down here."

"Come on," Nate began, "with the money you have, you can set up your own pub here."

"I'm just getting my stuff out of storage and buying myself a little condo in Dupont, then I'll be happy to settle down for the rest of my life."

"What about a boyfriend?" asked Nate, his eyes looking at the ground. "Aren't you ever going to want someone special to enjoy life with?"

Sandra hesitated when she answered. "I don't need a man. . . ."

Nate's eyes remained fixed on the ground.

". . . But I wouldn't mind giving one a try someday." Then she gave everyone a hug and a kiss. She turned, rolling the new suitcase she had purchased in San Julian, Argentina toward the plane. She then ascended the stairs onto the small airplane and turned at the top, smiling to Nate. Then she turned again and walked inside the plane. Within seconds, the door closed, the engines began revving and the pilot started the plane down the runway. Harland and Sandra were disappearing into the clouds as everyone standing there was looking a little misty-eyed themselves.

ENTERTAINERS had long learned that bold actions in their personal lives paid large dividends for marketing their careers, rarely with any penalty. Jane Fonda visited North Vietnam, making her name recognized in most households in America. Madonna frequently mocked the Catholic Church with devilish antics, always leading to headline placement in entertainment news. Mike Tyson placed a tattoo across his face, drawing the continued interest of boxing fans worldwide.

Combining *weak* genetic knowledge with *proven* marketing knowledge was a bold step for biotech firms. Similar to marketing in other industries, consumers trusted known personalities when they promoted products, especially risky products.

The most similar marketing strategy was using the trusted weathered face of Senator Bob Dole to promote Viagra. Shortly after Dole was associated with Viagra—a former presidential candidate even—men had faith in placing a previously unknown medical product into their bodies, giving rise to skyrocketing worldwide sales.

Regardless of the country or the reach of the media within it, the testimonial templates were similar, using popular actors, athletes, and politicians to promote life-enhancing hybrid pills. The noblest qualities of animals were now to be safely added to the superior structure of human DNA, "creating people with superior minds, bodies, and souls." Another popular slogan was: "Your health is our life's work." Each slogan was tailored to give people peace of mind and comfort as they popped the pills into their bodies once a day for up to three months, until the first visual results would start to appear.

Why have a breast augmentation when you could grow bigger breasts by taking pills? Why go to a dermatologist, when you could shed off the old skin and grow beautiful new skin? Why fly in an airplane when you could develop your own wings? Why use a snorkel to swim under water when you could swim for hours under water without cumbersome manmade technology? Didn't we all have gills while in the womb? Why worry about getting pregnant when you could develop hundreds of eggs, then have science pick the one for a superior child?

BECAUSE THE PILLS WERE SUPPLEMENTS, no F.D.A. approval was necessary. They did not claim to be medicinal in nature, nor did they contain any substances known to be harmful. Regardless, initially worldwide drug sales were low until a marketing campaign began using Sebastian Elestar, an Indonesian child known throughout much of the world for surviving the tsunami.

Sebastian was the sole surviving child from the Elestar family and was saved by a scrambling up a tree. Sebastian was being taken by a plane from Germany to meet U.N. Secretary Duncan Faust in New York when his plane was rerouted to Miami due to extreme weather surrounding the NYC region. After a layover in Miami, the plane took off, only to be hijacked to Cuba, an incident which led Sebastian to lose a front tooth due to his poor eyesight. Embraced later by the brother of Fidel Castro, the freedom of Sebastian was celebrated across the world. The series of unfortunate events generated international sympathy for him.

Posing with a golden tooth given to him by Castro's brother, Sebastian was declared "the most famous child in the world," a title repeated about him by numerous media outlets all around the world. He was the first child to achieve such a status, making him a natural proponent for an international advertising campaign for a hybrid drug.

During the marketing campaign, Sebastian meekly discussed how he wanted to be "smarter, faster, stronger, and taller, with perfect eyesight and hearing. Soon children across the world started mimicking his cute accent and his desire to be a better person. Millions of parents bought the pills for their children and often for themselves in China, India, and Brazil. In China alone, it was estimated that 200 million people were taking "enhancers." The only consistent exceptions were people set in their ways, or people against it for naturalistic or religious reasons. Over a few months, a range of bio-genetic hybrid pills—marketed by only a handful of companies—were being consumed by a billion people across the world. Indeed, one in every six people on earth had hybrid cells growing in their bodies.

RONALDO PEREZ TOLD HIS SERVANTS to open another bottle of wine. He was both happy for his daughter—sad for himself because he was afraid he was going to lose her again to another job in the United States. The past six months he had spent with her had been one of the happiest times of his life.

Rita had spent the last few months improving the wine technology through working out the kinks in the fermentation process used on the estate. She had made another scientific development in that time, creating a more efficient use of the skin of the grapes, making the process another six days more efficient and slightly improving the quality of the wine, producing a drier—but fuller—taste. Needless to say, Ronaldo was elated at her short-term work, wishing she could continue doing it.

In Rockville, her work had been laborious, causing her to be unable to travel to Argentina during important holidays like Easter and Christmas. Her visits had become sporadic, causing her to only head south about once a year. This visit—albeit with Gabe, Marti, Nate,

Sandra, and Harland—was a joyous time, especially for Ronaldo, because it was the most time he had been with Rita since before she had left to attend a university in the United States.

"What you've done to this wine is excellent, a true first for any completely organic winery," said Ronaldo, taking a hearty sip of wine. "You are more than a perfect daughter, you are also a wonderful scientist."

Rita was blushing. "Thank you, Papa."

Ronaldo looked across everyone at the table, each enjoying a festive dinner. "Your friends, are our friends."

Gabe nodded. "None of us thought we'd be here more than a month, two months at most. Hell, we could have sailed all the way to the Marshall Islands and back a couple times, just to find one of those carcasses and start the whole adventure all over again."

"I hope I never hear about the Marshall Islands again," said Rita, cutting her swordfish with her fork. "I just never knew that all along I was working to create an antidote for stopping the development of hybrid cells. Here I thought I was working on a way to isolate junk DNA in a rare but natural species. I thought I was researching animal cells, not sub-human cells, I swear."

Eva smiled. "Don't worry. From what Gabe said a couple weeks ago, it looks like all those carcasses weren't even human when they found them, so don't worry about it, dear."

Ronaldo swallowed. "Well, are you going to take that job?"

Rita avoided eye contact. "I think so, Papa."

Nate stormed into the room, holding printouts from an outdated continuous-feed printer. "I was right. After the U.N. announcement, every one of those biotechs tanked, some dropping to all-time lows. Then after they used that Sebastian kid to do their marketing for them, the whole industry skyrocketed. No one anywhere predicted this type of growth, except me. Spelling was completely wrong." Nate approached Gabe, showing him a line graph which spanned three years and clearly showed substantial growth in the sector over the past few months.

"That's amazing," said Gabe. "How are my stocks doing?"

"A little better than Harland's," said Nate.

"You're making a small fortune managing our stocks, then, huh?" Gabe asked.

MAJOR OWENS ARRIVED IN ANNAPOLIS in 1984 and was greeted by Gabe Channing, senior reporter with the *Annapolis Triangle*. Dressed in a frumpy beige sport coat with brown padded elbows and navy blue pants, Gabe was the first to engage him as he exited the boat and activated his tape recorder.

"How was your trip around the world?" asked Gabe.

"Excellent," said Owens.

Gabe cleared his throat. "According to wire reports, your ship contains a valuable cargo discovered in the Marshall Islands. Can you explain what's in that cargo?"

Owens smiled, his demeanor comforting the only reporter to greet him. "We found some valuable diaries on Enewetak Island, the result of a shipwreck from a six-man yacht originating in New Zealand.

"Were there any survivors when you arrived?"

"Negative," said Owens. "When we arrived on Enewetak Island, none of the six were alive and all were seemingly devoured by animals."

"So, what is so valuable about these diaries?" Gabe asked.

"Um, well, mostly navigational stuff," said Owens, hedging.

"Can I see the diary?"

"Sorry," replied Owens as he scratched his head. "Right now the diary is considered classified, so I can't even open it myself."

"Thank you for your time," said Gabe, wondering to himself why a diary from a civilian boat of New Zealand ended up being classified.

Gabe scratched his head, as something didn't make sense to him. How did Owens know it was navigational stuff if he couldn't open it?

ADVERSE CONSEQUENCES
CHAPTER SIXTEEN

A MONTH LATER, Gabe and Marti prepared to head out to sea for a trip to nowhere on the Mistress. It would be the beginning of the rest of their lives, a grand adventure.

"Why would you ever want to leave?" Nate asked, wearing a new hat from a trip into San Julian. Nate was starting to really settle in.

"This place is great," agreed Gabe. "We just want to see the world spend some time alone, just the two of us. You understand? Aside from Vietnam and a brief stopover in Guam, I haven't been anywhere except for Annapolis. I haven't had the time or the stomach to do anything else. Now all that has changed." He then put his arm around Marti and kissed her forehead. "I assume you're staying then?" he asked Nate.

"I'll be here for as long as Ronaldo lets me stay or until I build my own villa," said Nate. "This estate is the most beautiful place I have ever seen, and certainly the most relaxing place. I feel like a totally new person. It sure beats a Manhattan apartment, some little space, so small everything is in the same little room. I can't believe I ever called that little place a home. Look at the space out here! It's wonderful!"

"The world's even bigger when you're out to sea," said Gabe. "I don't even know where we're going."

"Maybe some island hopping," said Marti. "I'm just glad I'm not running the bar anymore."

"Don't remind me about that bar," said Gabe. "I miss my stool. And it is my stool. I bought that stool!"

Marti rolled her eyes. "And I helped you upgrade your boat this past couple months. That sucker's as good as it will ever get: a new engine, new sails, state-of-the-art electronics and all shined and ready to head to sea. Besides," she added, teasing Gabe, "I already told Holly she could remove your plaque." Gabe's face reddened, indicating he didn't like her comment. Then she added," just kidding!"

"I'm just glad I bought that new communication link. No more three mile limitation anymore. We can go anywhere the Mistress will take us without being out of touch. We can now ship-to-shore from anywhere." Gabe and Marti were now ready to sail away on the newly rechristened boat, "The Marti."

THE THIN REPORT on Stewart Polanski's desk contained a light green cover, drawing his immediate attention. As he slowly removed his wool jacket and instinctively activated his computer, he ignored the red beeping light on his phone, savoring the last couple seconds of peace before he opened the cover and read what was inside the report.

Being the CEO of what had only recently become Canada's largest biotech company, Shermine Laboratories, Stewart held a responsibility that most CEOs never faced. With each orphan drug that was initially produced there was massive pressure from investors to rush it to market, minimize any potential risks associated with it, and maximize the profit. Stewart's job was relatively easy, with the corporate perks and lengthy vacations being offset only by the secrets beneath a rare light green cover. It's the responsibility part that was the real stress of the job.

The report contained condensed information, all written in a passive language with nothing stated as factual, all hypothesized to purposely minimize the usefulness to lawyers representing consumers looking to maximize their lawsuits based on adverse consequences of the products of Shermine Laboratories. In this case, a thin report was to the advantage of the defendant, who could attest to the truth of the facts within the report without ever having to reveal its underlying context.

It was unfortunate that biotech/pharmaceutical firms in the United States found themselves constantly being sued. The litigious nature of the United States had become so excessive, firms like Shermine Laboratories were leaving the U.S. in record numbers, relocating to Canada and Mexico, where multi million dollar awards due to spilled coffee were not possible.

Stewart glanced through the early pages of the report that showed record profits for Shermine Laboratories, profits never conceived possible by the most bullish predictions of the most ambitious analysts on Wall Street. It was the "Railroad Age" (or "Internet Age") of biotechs, with a sudden growth spike catapulting the relatively unknown firm into the ranks of the most profitable companies in Canada. Under Stewart's leadership, his firm in Kitchener, Canada had quickly become one of the most profitable companies not only in his own country but also worldwide. Consequently, Stewart had just returned from a trip to London, England, where he had been knighted by the queen, who was personally taking the Queen Bee variety of his company's hybrid pills, exceeding his most lofty college dreams.

People across the world were ordering any one of 31 new brands being produced by his company, all following the recent scientific breakthrough of the R.H.V. process, the recently discovered selection process for every living organism's DNA blueprint. The marketing feedback from each person taking the pill, had thus far been nothing but accolades. Reporting "significant but reasonable" improvements in memory, strength, fertility, and whatever attribute the designer pills were meant to enhance.

After thoroughly reading the report, Stewart's ego collapsed further and further. Remarkably, the report he was reading was similar to other internal reports from all seven biotech companies across the world who were producing similar hybrid pills isolating DNA through the R.H.V. process. The conclusion of the report was that unplanned gene switches were occurring. With a worldwide saturation level of the seven biotech firms amounting to an estimated 900,000,000 people. One in seven people on earth were developing their own hybrid cells.

IN SPITE OF SLIGHT PHYSICAL CHANGES, people taking the hybrid pills were not angry. It was an unusual reaction which stunned the biotechs, and particularly the media. Did the consumers believe the improvements in their targeted area—whether it be strength, or, as in Harland's case, eyesight—were worth slight changes to other aspects of their bodies? Or were people less angry at the biotechs because they were taking the pills by their own free will? Considering the vast numbers of people with the hybrid in their system, it would seem that someone would sue. But not a single suit had been filed anywhere.

Along with the expected benefits, people did notice side effects such as slight webbing if they bought the swimming enhancer, or small feathers if they wanted the eyesight of an eagle. Initially, people kept the physical changes to themselves due to the embarrassment of the situation.

Soon news media outlets were covering the story, though with tempered involvement, due to the free will nature of the pills and the lack of complaints of people whose bodies were changing, not to mention most of the media personnel were also taking one form or another.

IT WAS A PERFECT LANDING for the agency plane bringing Zack McHenry, a pilot, and six U.S. soldiers to the Argentinean villa of Ronaldo and Eva Perez. Ronaldo scurried down the hill with his three-man band to greet them, a happy day for the him, as Zack's appearance meant Rita could stay at his villa indefinitely. After greeting each other, Zack's eyes hardened and he handed Ronaldo a large envelope, which he immediately opened.

Ronaldo's eyes widened as he looked at the check, paper clipped to a set of basic blueprints of four structures surrounded by several cameras and complex sensors. "This is triple what we agreed."

"It's going to require more security detail than we anticipated because all the communication links need to be secure. That price will fairly cover the additional structural requirements, with the same percentage of profit built-in as we agreed. So, is it all still a go? Does she still want to do it all from here?"

"She's already started," answered Ronaldo, continuing to look through the blueprints. "And what's this about a cabin for you? I just assumed it was going to be someone other than you staying here. A bedroom, private bath, office . . . "

"They wanted a senior level person, and I was nominated," said Zack, scratching his head. "Let's just say that I've been monitoring Rita for quite some time and feel personally interested in her safety and her success. Plus, after reading some reports, I'm not so confident in the future of the U.S. anymore. I'm upset by our leadership at H.S.A. My whole life has been poured into this agency and now we're subcontracting with people who were once classified as terrorists."

"That was absurd. She was *never* a terrorist."

"I understand your perspective," said Zack, frowning. "On behalf of H.S.A., I sincerely apologize for how badly H.S.A. treated your daughter. But, despite asylum and the presidential pardon, I probably wouldn't go back to the U.S. if I was her, either."

SANDRA, HARLAND, AND HARLAND'S SON were scheduled to meet at the Santa Maria Restaurant in Annapolis. Ever since returning to the U.S., Harland refused to go anywhere without his son. Also joining them would be Carley, Holly, and her daughters. Four months after returning to the U.S., it was the first time all of them had reunited. Harland and his son were already seated at the table when Sandra arrived.

"Sorry I'm late," said Sandra, adjusting her blouse and her scarf. "We've just been getting so many calls at the Watchdog Group that my workload is overwhelming these days."

Jasmine was still there sitting at the piano, softly playing a tune. The webbing between her fingers was just beginning to affect her ability to play.

"Why did you want to meet with me?" asked Harland, twisting his watch and revealing a set of feathers on his forearm.

"Can I ask you a personal question?" asked Sandra.

"Sure."

"Are you bothered by the those feathers on your arm?"

"Not really."

"Why not?"

"My eyesight is excellent now," said Harland, purposely blinking his eyes. "I won't ever need to use glasses again. It's been the best change in my entire life, and I didn't even have to have surgery to improve my eyes. It's those pills that have made all the difference."

"What other changes to your body have you had?"

"My whole body is developing features, and my nails need to be clipped almost once a day. I've lost a lot of weight, too, but that's perfect for me. Overall, I've never been in this good shape."

Sandra shook her head. "That's what I can't understand. With everyone undergoing unanticipated changes—and I mean millions and millions of people in the U.S. alone, only the family members complain. Never—and I mean never—is it the person who takes the pills. It's like they've all been brainwashed."

Harland delayed his response. "I see."

"You've been taking those hybrid pills since the first day they were introduced on the market. Remember? I was there when Nate ordered them directly from Shermine Industries. You don't mind at all?"

Harland shook his head.

"For God's sake, you have freakin' feathers growing all over your body and you don't mind? Why don't you mind?"

"Even my boy is happy with all the changes with his body. We're both happy. These pills are making us into new people and my body has never felt better."

Sandra looked over at Harland's son, who was just sitting there, quietly nodding his head.

A waitress stopped at the table. "May I help you?"

"Yeah, I'll have a shot of Tequila," said Sandra. "Better yet, make it a double."

"And for you, sir?"

"I'll have a glass of water," said Harland.

"Water?" blurted Sandra. "You're a heavy drinker. When did you give up drinking"

"Anything else?" asked the waitress.

"Yeah," said Sandra. "Bring me a Corona Light, too."

"Okay," said the waitress, who then turned and walked towards the bar.

"I'm sorry," said Sandra, clearing her throat. "When did you give up on the booze?"

"I didn't even know I had," said Harland.

"I just don't get it. It's the same story with everyone on those pills, and I mean with millions upon millions of people. Nate was right. This biotech bubble where I put all my money is *never* going to burst. They're all living nutritious lifestyles, but their bodies . . . are turning into animals."

Just then, Carley, Holly, and her daughters arrived. Sandra got up to greet them. As they hugged, she realized that both Holly and her daughters were developing feathers also.

With Carley, she didn't notice any change, but perhaps with her, the changes had not yet started. For the first time in her life, Sandra started to believe that it might just be too late to fix things. This was a lot bigger problem than a lumber company cutting down 2000-year-old trees.

SANDRA ARRIVED at her office and immediately turned on her computer. After researching the sales of these pills—through a worldwide search—and finding no litigation pending, Sandra decided to flee the country. She then logged onto a travel website and booked a one-way flight to Argentina. They she typed a short letter to Madeline Hastings on her computer.

"Effective immediately, I resign. Science has finally gone too far. Not only has mankind been irreversibly destroying the environment, now they are destroying the human race directly with these hybrid pills.

"My advice is: don't take them. If you have them, get rid of them. Don't mess with nature, because Mother Nature does not like these genetic tricks. Natural adaptation through natural processes is what works. If we want mankind to not become merely a footnote in the history of our planet then we all need to head to the hills and the caves and to the isolated islands for our safety."

After booking her flight and writing her resignation letter, Sandra emailed Nate and Rita. To Nate, she wrote that the pills were ruining people and that he should immediately sell all her biotech holdings. Then she added that she had purchased a one-way ticket, she missed him, and would be arriving in two days. She also wrote that, in her opinion, everyone should sell those stocks. Further, she told Nate that she was certain that a worldwide disaster was imminent and that everyone should be warned against taking the enhancers. To Rita, she simply wrote that she would arrive in two days, in addition to requesting that she not serve any veal when she arrived.

ADMIRAL OWENS' REPORT was one of the longest reports in the history of the Department of Defense. At exactly 4,000 pages, it was a complete overhaul of the weapons systems of the United States of America, with the most aggressive effort ever to increase civilian containment. Fearing a surge of civilian discord through a massive evolution of people, the report advocated an immediate surge in small weaponry, and a huge build-up of secure holding facilities within the U.S., the first such movement in the history of the U.S.

At the end of the report was a simple paragraph: "The United States military must develop and *be ready to implement* civilian containment to counter a present and immediate threat to national security. Further, an order must be made for all military personnel and non-military personnel engage in national security, to cease taking any form of hybrid pills, immediately."

SANDRA'S TWIN ENGINE CESSNA touched down on the runway at 4 p.m., though Nate arrived at the runway at 2:30 p.m., anxious to see her. As Sandra started to descend the stairs, Nate moved to the bottom of the stairs to greet her. As soon as she got both feet on the ground, Nate gently took both of her hands in his and wanted to say how much he had missed her. But before he could get a word out, Sandra moved his arms into a hug and leaned in to give him a kiss.

Nate shifted immediately from trying to get a word out to try to make Sandra understand how much he missed her. It was a time when a man's body language was more effective than his words.

As the two kissed, they forgot about everyone else standing there until Ronaldo should, "Musica!"

The band started playing and Nate and Sandra blushed while still holding hands, tears filling their eyes.

"Welcome back," Eva shouted. "Let's go eat and share some wine. Sandra is home!"

Sandra and Nate looked at each other and said, "home."

Then they both laughed, just like they did at the waterfall.

THE FOUR were gathered around an oval table in the Pentagon. Admiral Owens; Harry Sloan, Director of the F.B.I.; Jamie Whiteman, Deputy Director of Homeland Security; and Zack McHenry who was temporarily back in Washington. The tone was somber.

Owens was frustrated. "Back in 2000, the Marshall Islands Nuclear Claims Tribunal spent over $300 million for that nuclear cleanup mess."

Jamie rolled her eyes. "Plus we paid another $6 million a year to them for what we still claim to be education and health programs."

"You know what happened when we shipped those bodies back to our facility in Nevada to be analyzed," said Owens. "Everyone thought they were aliens."

"Let's get to the *real* point of this meeting," said Sloan. "Are these pills *definitely* a threat to national security? These pills?" he repeated. Pointing to a group of pills in his hand.

"It's the ability to undermine moral and discipline that threatens national security," said Owens, sitting tall in his padded chair. "I've seen what that one creature did to Harland's father. And I saw what they did to each other. If the science to create those creatures is now embedded into our society, civilization as we know it will completely change. Estimates state that over one billion people worldwide are now concerning hybrid-enhancers."

Zack raised his eyes. "All we've done so far is try to create a cure for de-evolution. Now, what I am hearing is that you think that we should have a targeted kill against the son of the man who died from the same process, as well as another billion or so people?"

Owens was somber. "We can't take any risks here. Killing one or 1,000 could save billions. Isn't that the whole logic behind war and sacrifice? Some loss early will result in avoiding greater losses in the future."

"I've read the report, too," said Sloan. "I'll put my best men to create a plan. Meanwhile, keep giving those speeches on ethics to keep those nutty watchdog groups at bay. Regardless, what the hell are we going to do with one billion of them is the real issue."

A MONTH LATER, there was a growing gathering of tens of thousands of hybrid people at international monuments. Not one of them was protesting anything, or even holding a sign in anger. An eerily peaceful gathering, they all had characteristics of animals, though their dominant physical appearances were still human.

It was quite a sight for photographers throughout the world, with hybrid people standing around or perched on the Eiffel Tower, on the Great Wall of China, spanning across the Golden Gate Bridge, the Leaning Tower of Pisa, the ruins of the Coliseum in Rome, the St. Louis Arch, the memorials of the National Mall in Washington, D.C., and swimming around or perched on the Statute of Liberty, to name just a few.

Reports from the news agencies around the world showing footage and offering quotes from these "hybrids" were being played on every television and radio station, as well as throughout the internet and the print outlets.

All gathered in virtual solitude, and none spoke an inflammatory word to scores of reporters who all sought an incendiary lead line for what they hoped would be the greatest story of the new century. Regardless, it was an anonymous twelve-year-old boy in Washington, D.C. whose remark captured newspaper headlines across the world the next day: "All of them are there because they can be there!"

HARLAND PARKER SAT ON AN EXAM TABLE without his shirt on in a small medical office in a windowless room in the Pentagon. He was sent there by his superiors who were alarmed by his unusual behavior.

Over the past couple months, Harland no longer had feelings of ambition, love, happiness, or curiosity. A shell of his previous self, Harland's work in the Pentagon had slowed to a crawl. He would sit at his computer for days on end and would exclusively surf internet images of rodents, vermin, kittens, and raptors. Salivating to the point where drool would almost stream from his mouth, when viewing the rodents and feeling kinship when viewing the raptors, Harland's behavior made even his most loyal friends uncomfortable.

Two nurses walked into the room, Joann, a manager in her late 20s who watched the examination from a distance, and Clare, a nurse with long curly hair and a graceful neck.

"What seems to be the problem, Major?"

"Huh? What? Sure, sure," said Harland, mumbling as his eyelids drooped.

"I'm sorry, sir, what did you say?"

"I'm hungry," he said, swallowing and focusing on Clare's neck.

The nurses exchanged glances, then stared at him. His chest was completely covered in oily feathers. At the end of his fingers were long nails, like talons. According to his examination report, his weight was half that of only two years ago, when he last reported to the exam room, bothered by flu-like symptoms.

"You're hungry?" asked Clare.

Harland's saliva dripped from his mouth, his eyes still drooping. "Yeah, hungry."

Joann poured water into a glass from a faucet and handed it to Clare, who then held it in front of Harland.

"Would you like some water?" asked Clare, her arm extended in front of him.

Harland refused to take the glass.

"It's like he's not human," whispered Clare.

Uncomfortable, Joann nodded.

Clare shook the glass, urging Harland to take it. "Would you like some water, Major Parker?"

Harland did not answer. His eyes now closed completely.

"His symptoms are so odd," said Clare. "Look at that saliva just dripping from his mouth. He hardly even knows we're in the room."

Again, Joann nodded.

Harland began twitching. His neck jerked from left to right. Then he sat at a ninety-degree angle, though his head faced Clare. He swallowed his saliva with a sucking sound that reverberated in the room with its tiled floor, marble counters, and wooden cabinets.

Clare moved in closer even as Joann backed away, moving closer to the door.

Clare cleared her throat, pushing the glass closer to Harland and tapping it lightly against his hand. "I said, Major Parker, are you thirsty?

He did not respond.

"It's like he's sub-human," said Clare, her hand now shaking.

Joann looked at Clare, then at Harland, and motioned to Clare that the two of them needed to leave the room immediately. Joann nodded.

Clare slowly turned toward the door, her back now to Harland.

Suddenly, Harland reached out his hand and grabbed her neck, his eyes still half-closed as his sharp hands squeezed tightly and his sharp nails dug deeply in until blood began to emerge.

Clare choked for air. She tried to break free, but his grip was strong as his hand tightened. She grabbed his arm with both her hands, but was powerless against his grip. Harland said nothing. Within seconds, her neck was broken and she fell to the floor.

Terrified, Joann fled the room, screaming. "Oh my God, oh my God, he killed her. He killed her. That damn mutant killed her!"

The MP's came running as fast as they could, guns drawn.

As Harland fled, he somehow knew that he was not alone. Somehow he knew that all around the world sat thousands upon thousands of people—hybrid people and mutants. And they were all salivating, waiting to prey on humans—now an inferior race.

About the Author

Roger W. Marshall was born in 1954 in New York State. He attended Harpur College at S.U.N.Y. where he studied Economics, receiving his B.A. in 1975, and his M.A. in 1976. Roger has worked in and around the financial industry since 1977, including time spent at the American Stock Exchange, Smith Barney, Riggs Bank, and the U.S. Securities and Exchange Commission.

Currently residing near Baltimore, Maryland, Roger is focusing his efforts toward Green and humane living. Specifically, he believes that we—as the only species capable of changing the planet—must make sure we do not harm the planet, either for ourselves, future generations, or for co-inhabitants. As a vegetarian, Roger believes people should not eat animals, unless it is a matter of life or death. He believes if most people had to kill their own food, they would chose not to kill. He can be contacted at roger.marshall2007@gmail.com (Please write "TERROR WITHIN" in the subject line.)